THE DRAGON STONE

The "Stone Collection" Book 4

NICK HAWKES

Hawkesflight Media

Titles in The Stone Collection:

The Dragon Stone

First edition published in 2019 *(v.1.3)*
by Hawkesflight Media

ISBN 978-0-6481103-9-2

www.author-nick.com

Cover Design by Karri Klawiter

For Jackie

The Dragon Stone

A novel

by
Nick Hawkes

Chapter 1

The Dragon Head was sixty-two years old and looked every bit his age.

Although this man was his father, Kai never related to him as such. He wouldn't dare. No one related to a Dragon Head with anything other than formality. Operationally his father held the rank of First Route Marshal in the 14K triad society. The symbol of that rank was a dragon's head. Of course, most people didn't know that and simply referred to him as Mr. K, but those who knew him even slightly were careful to show respect.

Kai stopped six paces from his father's desk, bowed, and waited.

The window shutters were closed, and the room was dark. It was always dark. A pungent, spicy smell filled the air. Joss sticks were burning in the household shrine recessed into the wall. It was lit by a dull red light.

His father looked at him, saying nothing.

It was an old game: one designed to put Kai in his place.

Wooden screens stood to the right of his father's mahogany desk. Two armed guards would be behind them, watching through the fretwork. Kai wondered which guards would be on duty today.

Probably Ah Fung and Ah Keung. Ah Fung would have a shotgun. Ah Keung didn't need one.

His father spoke in Cantonese. "I am displeased."

Kai lowered his head. It was the right way to signal mortification. "I am sorry sir."

The Dragon Head slapped the desk. "Do not interrupt." His father's blackened teeth snapped shut. Ten years of smoking opium had rotted them. He'd quit the habit many years ago through sheer willpower, but he'd never had his teeth seen to. He hated dentists.

Kai stood stiffly to attention.

The old man pointed to him. "You are *Goko*, a 438, and more is expected of you. Money from your section has plateaued. You have not grown business for nine months. Why is that?"

Kai kept his silence. He was in charge of *Hak Nam*, the 'City of Darkness,' and was therefore responsible for the income it generated for the 14K.

"Are other societies taking our business?" His father's querulous voice whipped at him again.

"No sir. Our enemy, the *Sun Yee On*, have given up trying to infiltrate – at least for now."

"What about the *Ging Yi*?"

"We have had a *gong-sou*, a peace talk, with the *Ging Yi*. It is now agreed where their boundary in the City ends. We can work alongside them."

His father slapped the desktop again. "See that the boundary is policed. I don't want any other triad society encroaching on our territory."

Kai nodded. "The real problem is that the City of Darkness is filled to capacity. The Building Ordinance Office are enforcing the only building code they insist on, that no building can be more than seventeen stories high." Kai shrugged. "The wheels of the planes flying into Kai Tak airport nearly touch them as it is."

"Is that an excuse?"

"No sir, that is reality. Only so many drug dens and brothels fit on six acres of land."

The old man sneered. "There is always room for more, particularly among the squatters along the edge of the city."

Kai wondered whether the gods in the household shrine were listening to their conversation, and what they were thinking. He glanced at the shrine on the wall. Food offerings had been placed next to the joss sticks to placate the spirits of his ancestors and to ensure good luck. Kai approved. It was important to venerate the household gods, as they had more influence on the day-to-day affairs of life than the big gods. Any favors that could be cajoled from the big gods of Taoism, Confucianism, and Buddhism were simply a bonus.

"Pay attention," his father snapped. "Where does your mind go?"

"I was thinking about our gods, sir."

His father grunted and leaned back in his chair.

Nothing was said for a while. But the silence was relative. Kai could hear a cacophony of street noises coming from Nathan Road just outside. It was one of the busiest streets in Kowloon.

His father broke the silence. "I thought I would have to pay a drug addict for his son, so he could become my son and pray for my spirit when I'm dead. But then you were born." He sniffed. "Just be sure you fulfill your duty."

"Yes sir."

His father looked at him balefully and pointed a finger. "I want you to diversify into high end extortion and kidnapping. This is 1972…and there is more money in Hong Kong and more rich people now than there have ever been. They need to know of our reputation and fear us to such an extent that even a phone call with a threat will cause them to pay."

Kai wondered idly what the gods of the rich people would think about that.

His father shouted. "Do you understand?"

"Yes sir."

"You must show an iron fist." His father jabbed a finger at him again. "You particularly must work hard at this because you look like an American. That makes it harder for Chinese people to respect you."

Kai knew he didn't have an ounce of American blood in him, but he didn't press the point.

Kai could just see enough through the window slats to make out the top of a red and white double-decker bus burrowing its way along Nathan Road. Everyone seemed to be going somewhere. Kai, on the other hand, had no idea where he was going.

"You may go," barked his father, waving him away as if he were a bothersome insect.

Kai bowed and left.

He collected his own two bodyguards from the foyer and headed outside into the maze of narrow streets, shopping stalls, bars and nightlife that made up the district of Mong Kok. The 14K were active in this area, particularly in the brothels. However, he was not responsible for this region. As such, he did not know which areas were in dispute between the competing triad societies. He was away from his own area and was therefore vulnerable. The *Sun Yee On* often waited for occasions such as this to spring an ambush. Kai grimaced. The curse of it was that he, with his European features, was easily recognizable.

He glanced up at the ugly high rises surrounding him. They had caged steel balconies perched on their side. Bamboo poles, holding people's washing, poked out from them. However, at the base of these buildings was another world. Market stalls spilled out from under untidy awnings along the laneways. Stalls with boxes of vegetables cluttered the alleys barely leaving enough room for pedestrians to walk. It was a sea of color. Scrappy billboards and posters were stuck on almost every vertical surface. Some of these were advertising Bruce Lee's latest film, *Fist of Fury*. The film star was very popular. Every triad fighter aspired to be like him.

The business of Mong Kok was in full swing all around them. There was the hiss of cooking from the noodle stalls; steaming woks; and the clack of tiles being turned by the Mahjong players sitting at tables.

The 'devil beaters' were also busy. If you paid them money, they would use a shoe to whack an image of your enemy drawn on a piece of paper. That enemy could either be a person or an evil spirit.

Kai understood this to be serious business. Good fortune, particularly as it pertained to money and good health, was everyone's obsession in Hong Kong. Rich and poor alike consulted mediums and fortune-tellers when they needed to make a decision.

They passed an alley leading to a brothel he knew was controlled by 14K. Squatting on the ground near its entrance was a small boy. Kai recognized that he must be the *tin man toi*, the 'weather man.' His job was to report on those who entered the alleyway, either to bring danger, or business. What attracted Kai's attention was the boy's pitiful state. He was emaciated and filthy – barely an animated skeleton.

Kai stopped beside him and nudged him with his foot.

The young boy looked up in terror. It was a look that stayed on his face when he noticed the signal Kai was making with his hand.

The urchin now knew that Kai was part of his own society, 14K.

Kai spoke curtly. "What's your name?"

"Sai Di," the boy mumbled.

"You are *sai lo*; a little brother?"

"Yes."

"Who is your *dai lo*, your big brother, the one who is meant to be looking after you?"

The boy pointed across the laneway to a group of three young men who were eating at a noodle stall.

Kai turned and stepped across to the three young men.

The men immediately got to their feet and braced themselves for a fight. Fear was plainly written on their faces. Kai could understand it. He was large by Chinese standards. And his two bodyguards Ah Tsoi and Ah Ming were just as big. Eventually their gaze fell on the hand signal Kai had made, and they relaxed slightly.

"Who is big brother to Sai Di?" Kai demanded, pointing to the urchin across the laneway.

"I am," replied one of the men.

Kai noticed that the man who spoke was well built and had plenty of flesh.

Anger began to boil up within him.

"Do you know what your duty is as a *dai lo*, as a big brother?"

The man said nothing.

Kai waved a hand at Ah Ming, one of his bodyguards. "Ah Ming is a 'red pole.' Do you know what that means?"

The eyes of the man in front of him widened, and then he nodded. It meant that Ah Ming was responsible for organizing the strategy and weapons needed to carry out 14K's fights and ambushes. He was a fighter.

Kai turned to his bodyguard. "Ah Ming, tell him what it means to be a *dai lo*."

The man cowered back as Ah Ming stepped forward. Without a word, the bodyguard took Kai's right forearm and lifted it for everyone to see.

The ugly scar that crossed the top of Kai's forearm was clearly visible.

Ah Ming said in a low voice, "I am *sai lo* to Mr. Kai. He is *Goko*, 'my big brother.' One night, I was ambushed by five *Sun Yee On*. They had meat cleavers and steel pipes. I would have died if Mr. Kai hadn't come to my aid." Ah Ming glared at the man. "We were outnumbered, and he was badly wounded in the fight, but we drove them off." He let go of Kai's arm. "That's what it means to be a *dai lo*."

The man in front of him dropped his head.

Kai barked, "Look at me."

The man jerked his head up.

"You are duty bound to share what you have with your *sai lo*. That is basic to our code. Do you understand?"

The man nodded.

Nothing was said for a while.

Kai allowed the silence. Then he picked up the man's noodle bowl, and took it across the laneway to the boy.

"Eat it," he commanded.

The boy did not move.

"Go on," Kai urged.

Tentatively, the boy reached out, took the bowl, and began to eat, at first hesitantly, and then with feverish haste.

When he'd finished, Kai took the bowl back to the noodle stall and banged it down on the table.

The men jumped back in alarm.

Kai pointed to his other bodyguard. "This man is Ah Tsoi. He is also a red pole." He glared at the men.

"We will be watching you."

Chapter 2

The pike rose slowly to the surface of the water, and stayed there, as if wanting to be seen. Emma held her breath. It was at least two feet long. A pike, the hunter, the apex predator of the River Cherwell. In all the years Emma had been at Oxford, she'd never seen one until now. Its olive brown back moved languidly, keeping it on station against the flow of the current.

Emma lifted her gaze and glanced across the river. The Cherwell was flowing peacefully between the beech trees edging Christ Church Meadow Walk. No one else was on the footpath to share the sight.

When she looked back, the pike was gone.

She shivered. Evidently, today was going to be a day of 'firsts', and she was not sure she was ready for any of them. Emma glanced at her watch for the umpteenth time, willing time to stop, wanting to retreat to the safety of the past.

The second hand of the watch ticked on remorselessly.

It was time to go.

Taking a deep breath, Emma made her way back to St. Hilda's College and her interview with Professor Harrington.

Forty-five minutes later, her worst fears were realized. Professor Harrington sat in front of her beaming. "You've passed, Emma." Your PhD has been accepted. They don't even want an edit, let alone a re-write." He leaned forward to shake her hand. "I must say, you've done extraordinarily well."

She shook his hand mechanically, then leaned her elbows on the professor's desk and put her head in her hands.

No, no, no!

The professor, all solicitous, walked around the desk and laid a hand on her shoulder. "I know it's a bit much to take in, Emma, but you've finally finished." He paused before adding, "It must be rather a lot to take in right now. Showing emotion is quite understandable."

But you don't understand. Her stomach churned and twisted.

The professor continued on, blithely. "How long have you been a student with us in Oxford?"

Emma swallowed and spoke between her fingers. "Um…seven years. Three for my Bachelor's degree, and four for the doctorate."

"Hmm, that's a long time in anyone's life." He gave her shoulder a squeeze. "Now off you go and celebrate."

She suppressed a sob, stumbled to her feet, and found the door.

Professor Harrington called after her. "Oh, Emma, I nearly forgot. Someone wants to meet with you. He's in town on business and staying at the Randolf Hotel. Evidently, he wants to talk with you about doing some post-doctoral work into the socio-political changes taking place in China. It's very much your area of expertise." The professor picked up a folded piece of paper from the desk and held it out to her. "He's hoping you might be able to meet him at 5pm today at the Randolf. Is that possible?"

Emma took the piece of paper, nodded dumbly, and stumbled out the door.

A minute later, she was leaning on one of the pillars supporting the two archways of St Hilda's entrance porch. She held a fist against her stomach, bent over, and felt sick. After seven years, it was over. She would have to leave Oxford, the safe womb that had held her, and protected her against the indifference of her parents...

What on earth would she do now? She glanced up at the brick and stone grandeur of South Building with its crenulated bay windows and views across the river to the spires of Oxford.

St Hilda's was one of only two Oxford colleges that admitted women, and it was the nearest thing she'd ever had to a home. Moves were afoot to have women admitted to some of the men's colleges, but she suspected that change was still a few years off. Even though it was 1972 and the country was heaving with social revolution, nothing moved quickly at Oxford. It was one of the reasons she loved it. Its colleges gave her a sense of history...and safety.

Get a grip on yourself, girl. She sniffed, then began searching for a handkerchief – an act that reminded her that she was holding the piece of paper given to her by the professor. Emma unfolded it and scanned the contents.

There wasn't much to read. It was a short note scribbled on some stationery paper from the Randolf Hotel.

Dear Miss Templeton,

My name is John Egerton. I work for a department answerable to the Home Secretary. I would like the opportunity to talk with you about your thesis and perhaps explore the possibility of some post-doctoral work.

I am in town at the Randolf until tomorrow. Can we meet at the Acanthus Restaurant at 5pm?

John Egerton.

Emma glanced at her watch. It was four o'clock already. If she were going to meet with John Egerton, she would have to get moving straight away.

Was she dressed smartly enough?

Probably not. She was wearing jeans, a white shirt, and a waisted jacket. It would have to do.

As she walked up Cowley Place to the High Street, Emma gave herself a stern talking-to. The result of this was that she resolved to at least try to celebrate her achievement. She'd phone some of her girlfriends from OICCU and invite them round to her place tonight for some wine and nibbles.[1] It wouldn't be much, but it was all she had the emotional energy for. She was pretty confident the girls would cheer her up. They generally did. The team at the Inter-Collegiate Christian Union had become her family, the family she'd never had. They'd been generous in their love and, over the years, had given meaning and hope to a shy introvert, desperately trying to please the world.

Emma turned into High Street and walked over Magdalen Bridge. She paused to watch people poling their punts along the river beside the water meadows. It was an idyllic May day. Her route into town was one she'd walked hundreds of times, but today, she looked at the features along High Street as if for the first time.

There was the austere face of Magdalen College; the extravagant Baroque arches of Queen's College and University College that claimed links to King Alfred. A little further on was St. Mary's church, the place where bishops Latimer and Ridley were tried for heresy. They were found guilty and burned at the stake because of their desire to return the church to a more biblical foundation.

Emma looked at the soaring spire and wondered for the umpteenth time how such a beautiful place could be used for such evil. But then again, nothing good ever seemed to come from institutionalizing the church.

Eventually, she came to Sainsbury's on the corner of Corn-market Street. She loved this store. It had decorative tiles on the wall, beautiful mosaic floors, long marble counters, and men in aprons waiting to serve you. She bought some Stilton cheese and liver pâté, paying for them with the new decimal currency that Britain had so recently adopted.

She liked the new currency. It was tidier. Emma loved tidiness and order; they helped her feel safe.

The Randolf Hotel was just a little way up the road, opposite the Ashmolean Museum. It was a grand Victorian affair, built in the Gothic style, presumably to make it fit in with the character of the ancient colleges that surrounded it.

She paused in the front entrance to gather herself together, then walked inside.

The entrance foyer featured a marble staircase with an intricate iron-wrought balustrade that curled round the reception desk. The young man behind the desk pointed the way to the Acanthus Restaurant. It was a room filled with gilded portraits and mirrors. High above, heraldic crests of the different Oxford colleges decorated the eaves.

It was not yet dinnertime, so she was not surprised to be the only one there.

She took the opportunity to inspect herself in one of the mirrors.

A depressingly ordinary-looking girl stared back at her. Her face was pretty enough, but she had brown hair. Brown! So ordinary! It was currently pulled back into a loose bun. She reflected ruefully that so much about her was average: average height, average figure – there was nothing about her that was special.

Emma chose a table near the door and began straightening the napkins as she waited.

In the event, she did not have long to wait. A slim man with a pencil mustache entered the room and walked toward her. Although middle aged, his hair was jet black and brushed backward over his scalp. He was dressed in a gray suit and was in every way unremarkable. The only arresting feature about him, was his eyes. They had an intensity about them that warned her not to underestimate him.

"Emma Templeton, I presume."

"Yes."

"Ah, good. I'm John Egerton."

She stood up and shook his hand. It was a firm, no-nonsense handshake.

Egerton ran his eyes over her, conjured a smile, and said, "Let me order some tea, or whatever else you'd like. But do forgive me, I need to slip up to my room, dump the briefcase, and freshen up. I'll rejoin you in a moment. What will you have?"

"Tea is fine."

"And scones?"

"No thanks."

He glanced at his watch. "Aah, the sun's over the yardarm. I think I'll have a brandy. It's been a long day."

A waiter approached. Egerton placed the order, then added, "And may I also have a glass of water?"

The waiter nodded. "Of course," and turned away.

Her host took a copy of The Times from under his arm and dropped it in front of her. "Just started the crossword, and I'm already stuck. Help me out and have a go at it while I'm gone."

He left, moving lightly on his feet.

Two things bothered Emma. The first was the man's manner. The second was the fact that she'd managed to see Egerton come down the stairs to the foyer of the dining room because of a large fortuitously placed mirror. He'd not just come in from outside the hotel at all.

She picked up the paper and turned to the crossword. He'd filled in seven words. One of them was wrong.

Emma managed to complete well over half the puzzle before Egerton returned. The man glanced briefly at the paper, smiled, and put it down beside his chair.

Both the tea and the brandy had arrived, but Egerton did not touch his drink. Instead, he leaned forward and lit the candle in the table's centerpiece with a lighter. "Let's have some ambience." His mercurial mind changed tack again. "I understand you have just been told that your thesis has been accepted. Congratulations."

"Thank you."

"What will you do now? Will you head home to your parents?"

Emma managed to suppress a shudder, or she thought she had. But Egerton had seen something change in her demeanor for he said, "I take it that doesn't appeal. Why's that?"

His question was way too personal, being only just on the right side of rudeness. She glanced up at him, and saw by the set of his jaw that he was not a man to fob off with a polite rebuff.

"I…I, er, don't really know my parents. And they have made it clear that they don't want to have much to do with me. When I was

five years old, they put me into boarding school here in Oxford –
the Dragon School. You may have heard of it."

Egerton said nothing.

Emma continued. "The thing was, they only lived ten minutes
away." She shrugged. "I was their only child and viewed as an
inconvenient complication to their social life."

"How did that affect you?"

Emma laughed, but without mirth. "How do you expect? I
displayed all the symptoms of an emotionally abandoned child.
First, I tried misbehaving to get their attention. Then I tried to be
good at everything to try and win their approval. But I never could."

"You must have been lonely."

"Very. The only saving grace was that they provided me with a
nanny. She was Chinese and wonderful. My parents even employed
her to care for me when I came back from boarding school on holiday. That's why I developed a fascination with China."

"Do you speak Chinese?"

"I'm moderately good at Cantonese and have a smattering of
Mandarin."

Egerton nodded. "Go on."

Emma shrugged. "There's not much else to say. My parents
divorced. Father is now on his third marriage and has sired five
more children. He lives in London and trades in stocks and shares.
Mother is caught in an unhappy second marriage to a lawyer in
Exeter."

"So yours was not a happy childhood."

"It wasn't great…but neither was it all bad. Trying to please my
parents turned me into a good student and gave me a love of
learning."

"What's your relationship with your parents now?"

"Cordial but distant. I think they feel a degree of guilt about me
– at least, my father does. He's given me a generous allowance all
the time I've studied here in Oxford." She shrugged. "I suspect it is
conscience money."

Egerton drummed his fingers on the edge of the table. "So you
have no ties and are free to go anywhere?"

"I suppose so."

Emma felt it was high time the inquisition into her personal life ended. She elected to take the initiative. "Why are you talking with me, Mr. Egerton? How did you even know of my existence?"

"I learned of you through Mary Bennett."

Emma furrowed her brow. "What? The principal of St Hilda's College? Why would she speak to you?"

"Well, she, like you, is a historian. But what you may not know is that she worked for the British Ministry of Information during the Second World War."

Emma shook her head in bewilderment. "Just who did you say you worked for, Mr. Egerton? What organization are you with, exactly?"

"Oh, didn't I say?"

"No, you didn't."

"I work for MI5."

The hair on the back of her head began to prickle. "Why on earth is MI5 wanting to speak with me?"

"Because you have an understanding of recent Sino-European history."

Emma took a sip of her tea to steady her nerves. Egerton, she noted, had yet to drink his brandy. "And why would that interest you?"

Egerton sucked on his lips. "It's a delicate time in politics at the moment. Northern Ireland is a mess. Political terrorism is on the rise, and the Soviets have stepped up their activities." He grunted. "We've just broken up a large spy ring of theirs."

Emma kept her face composed and waited for more.

"America is withdrawing its troops from Vietnam. Nixon is trying to extricate himself from Watergate, but he's at least managed to score a coup by being the first president to travel to China to visit the Chairman of the People's Republic." He glanced up at Emma. "As you probably know, China was admitted to the UN last year and is gradually opening up to the West. We need to be ready for it."

"And how does that affect me?"

Egerton tapped the table with his forefinger. "What, in your opinion, is Britain's relationship with China like?"

Emma replied without hesitation. "Not great. England hasn't acquitted herself well in China's history, and that may come back to bite us. China is an emerging power with huge political ambitions and a massive workforce."

"Are we so much on the nose with the Chinese?"

Emma laughed. "We sent warships to China last century to batter the ships and cities of the Qing Dynasty. Do you know the reason we did this, Mr. Egerton?"

"Opium."

"Yes. We wanted to rectify our trade imbalance with China, so we forced them to legalize and then buy the opium we shipped to them from India. When they refused to comply, we rained hell upon them with our gunboats. The Chinese were compelled to open their ports and cede Hong Kong to the British Empire."

Mr. Egerton tilted his head back and sniffed. "That was some time ago."

Emma folded her hands in her lap. "The indignities inflicted on China did not stop there. Did you know that there are forty grave-yards in northern France and Belgium holding ten thousand Chinese men?"

Egerton said nothing.

Emma continued. "They were part of the Chinese Labor Corps, some 140,000 men who were paid a pittance to repair roads and work in armament factories so that British and French men could be released to fight on the Western front. The contribution of these Chinese men has never been acknowledged. China foolishly hoped that their city of Tsingtao on China's Yellow Sea coast might be returned to them as it had been under German control." She shook her head. "But it never happened."

"Politics is a dirty, pragmatic business."

"But it should never be a morally vacuous one."

"How important is morality to you, Miss Templeton?"

Emma was now not at all sure she wanted to win Egerton's favor. She let her usual reserve drop. "You better know now, Mr.

Egerton, that my faith is sacred to me, and it informs everything I do."

The man steepled his fingers. "How highly unfashionable."

She met his gaze. "It is not a question of fashion, Mr. Egerton; it is a question of what is true. I assure you, I am no irrational neurotic who is unable to accept my mortality. I have good reasons for my faith – and that faith informs my morality. If that bothers you, then our conversation finishes here."

"So, 'rightness' matters to you?"

"Yes, but it must be a rightness that is properly applied. Truth without grace can be harsh."

Nothing was said for a while.

Egerton smiled. "Would you like more tea?"

His question was ridiculous. However, as the man had yet to reveal his hand, she chose to give him a little more time.

"Yes."

He turned toward the kitchen door looking for a waiter. As he did, his elbow knocked over his tumbler of brandy. He jerked out a hand to try and save it but succeeded only in knocking the glass into the candle on the table. The candle fell out from its stand and immediately set the brandy alight. Seconds later, the center of the tablecloth was in flames.

Egerton appeared stunned by what was happening. He didn't move.

Emma placed her cup and saucer on the ground, picked up two corners of the tablecloth and folded it over the flames. Then, she reached for Egerton's glass of water and tipped it over the top.

The flames died out.

Waiters rushed to her aid and eventually, order was restored.

Egerton was apologetic.

"So sorry. So terribly sorry."

The smell of burning hung in the air.

A fresh tablecloth was laid, and a new centerpiece put into position. The waiters did not light its candle.

It didn't take long for Egerton to regain his momentum.

"Hong Kong is a place where East meets West. It stands at the confluence of two cultures in a theater of the world that is changing rapidly. Some of the Chinese culture developing there is now being exported here. And not all of it is good, so we want to know about it."

"What do you want to know about, specifically?"

"We want to know about an area you touched on in your research – the Chinese triad societies. It seems as if some of their activities are now starting to take root in the UK." He shrugged. "We want to know what we're dealing with."

Emma blinked, trying to get a sense of where the conversation was going. "You want to know about the triad societies of Hong Kong?"

"Yes. What can you tell me?"

Emma again straightened the napkin sitting in front of her and began marshaling her thoughts.

"Triad societies are secretive, mafia-like gangs. At least forty of them are thought to exist in Hong Kong. It's difficult to know the real number as affiliates and subgroups exist within them."

"When did these, er…societies begin to appear?"

"They are thought to have come into existence some time in the 17th century. Originally, they were a subversive force dedicated to the overthrow of the Manchurian Ching Dynasty. They wanted to restore the Ming Dynasty." She sighed. "But today, the triads have degenerated into gangsterism. Many new recruits to Hong Kong's triads have come from Mao Zedong's Red Guards."

Egerton raised an eyebrow.

"It's true," said Emma. "Mao turned on his Communist student movement when they began to threaten his power base. Some fled to Hong Kong. There's some irony in this as refugees from Chiang Kai-shek's nationalist army had also fled to Hong Kong a few decades earlier." She sighed. "But, in the typical Chinese way, the opposing ideologies dissolved in the face of the need to get on and make a living. Some allowed their convictions to dissolve to the extent they felt able to join a triad society. It made survival more likely."

"Where does the name 'triad' come from?"

"It comes from their symbol." Emma drew with her finger on the tablecloth. "It is the Chinese character 'hung,' which is a reference to Hung Wu, the founder of the Ming Dynasty. It's enclosed in a triangle representing the threefold union of heaven, earth, and humankind." She shrugged. "When the English saw the triangular symbol they coined the term *triad*."

"Hmm."

Emma straightened the teaspoon in her saucer. She had to do something to mask her growing irritation. "Mr. Egerton, where is this conversation going?"

The man in front of her placed both hands on the table. "Miss Templeton, would you be interested in going to Hong Kong?"

"What?"

"It will be your first assignment if you agree to come and work with us."

Thoughts whirled in her mind in a giddying swirl. None of what she heard made sense.

"Don't you have people in Hong Kong already who are able to interview police and political leaders?"

"We do. But we need fresh eyes." He paused. "The truth is, many Chinese detective superintendents have amassed incredible wealth from their dealings with the triads, and it's not easy for us to know who to trust. British officers are not entirely clean in their dealings with them either. So we need someone who can fly under the radar and tell us what is really happening on the ground."

"You want me to work for MI5?"

"Yes."

Emma shook her head. "But you hardly know me. I haven't been through any interview process, or anything."

Egerton leaned back with every appearance of self-satisfaction. "Oh yes you have, Miss Templeton. You have just passed an exacting interview."

Emma frowned.

Egerton continued. "You are punctual." He picked up the newspaper beside him, placed it on the table, and stabbed the crossword with his finger. "You are clever, and you check your facts. You know

yourself and are well grounded. You have a strong moral compass."
He pointed to the candle in the center of the table. "I do apologize
for that little pantomime. But I needed it to show me whether you
are able to keep your head in a crisis." He smiled. "And on top of
that, you know your subject."

"Oh," she said, weakly.

"When can you let me know your answer? I'm afraid I need one
fairly quickly."

"How quickly?"

"Now would be good."

"Where… she choked slightly. "Where would I live?"

"We want you to come to London for a month or so before you
go. Your accommodation will be organized."

Emma forced herself to think. It was totally absurd. Just
moments earlier, she'd been sick at the idea of leaving everything
she was familiar with in Oxford – her friends, her study – everything
that defined her. Now, someone was asking her to leave England. It
was ridiculous. And yet…and yet… Something was playing gently
in her heart, something that floated above her sense of fear.
Strangely, it was a sense of peace. She pinched the top of her nose
and resolved to delay her answer for long enough to check whether
that peace was significant. She needed to know if the peace had
substance and if she could trust it.

"Will you be at your London office tomorrow?"

"Yes."

"Then I'll call you tomorrow afternoon with my answer."

"Do you want me to give you my number?"

"No, I want to find it myself. I'll phone your department and ask
to be put through to you."

"So you can check I really work for MI5?"

She nodded.

He nodded approvingly. "Very wise."

Chapter 3

The cottage was stripped bare. There were no pictures on the wall; no arm chairs, bookshelves or beds. All that remained after the furniture van left was a kitchen chair, a Formica-topped table, and a mattress.

Elliot walked from room to room in a daze trying to overcome his sense of violation. Only the dust motes remained. They drifted in the shafts of sunlight, too scandalized to settle.

But at least he'd managed to rescue his childhood home, and that was everything. He loved the cottage. It was one of the most charming in Hamble; and that was the problem. The house was valued at twelve-thousand pounds by Revenue and Customs – an exorbitant sum that reflected the price people were prepared to pay for a seaside house in the south of England. Elliot was required to pay estate duty equivalent to twenty-five percent of its value.

He reflected again on the scandal of England's inheritance tax. It left him with the choice of having to either sell the house, or of selling every stick of furniture in it, together with his father's art collection, to pay it. He'd chosen to do the latter. There was, in fact, no alternative. Elliot was never going to be able to pay the debt on the modest income he earned as a part-time sailing instructor. He was just twenty-three and had yet to establish himself in his main profession – that of being a yacht designer.

"Yohoo, Elliot! Are you there?"

He recognized the voice of Nettie Leasman.

"I'm up here, Nettie."

The stairs creaked as Nettie made her way up. He could hear her tut-tutting and exclaiming as she went.

"My, my. Oh my. Oh goodness."

She made her way along the landing at the top and poked her head around the doorway of his bedroom.

Elliot was sitting against the wall with his head in his hands. He was too emotionally drained to get up, but he managed a weary smile. "Welcome to my hacienda."

"Oh Elliot," she cried, "the lovely Chesterfields, your father's desk – everything's gone."

"Yeah."

She came into the room. Her portly frame was, as usual, squeezed into an old fashioned floral dress. Nettie was famous for her aversion to all things stylish. She noticed the real estate flier at Elliot's feet. It had been torn in two.

"I take it that you are over the idea of engaging an estate agent."

"Parasitic bastards. I don't even know how they found out I would probably be forced to sell." He picked up the two pieces of flier and grinned. "I was going to use this as toilet paper, but it's too shiny."

She looked at him and tapped a finger against her lips. "Hmm. I don't suppose you'd know anything about a 'For Sale' sign from the same real estate company that went missing last night?"

Elliot said nothing.

Nettie continued. "It was taken from a house not too far from here and re-erected in front of St. Andrew's church." She continued to tap her finger. "Fancy that: someone putting God's house up for sale."

He kept a straight face and nodded. "Diabolical."

Nettie grunted. "It certainly is. Don't do it again." She used her foot to poke at the dust marks on the carpet where the furniture had been. "I'll bring the vacuum cleaner round tomorrow and give the whole place a clean."

Elliot got to his feet and kissed her on the cheek. "Thanks, Nettie. Do you want a cup of tea?"

"What with?" she retorted. "There's no kettle in the kitchen."

"It's at the second-hand shop. But I've got a heating element you can put in a mug. I keep it for traveling."

Nellie blew out her cheeks. "That's the trouble with you young ones: never stopping still." She pointed at him. "You particularly; you're always off on some boat or another."

"But I always come home, Nettie. I can't bear to be apart from you for long."

Nettie rolled her eyes. "Oh spare me."

She tossed back a strand of iron-gray hair. "I've brought some scones. They're downstairs. I thought you might need them."

The pair made their way down the narrow stairs to the kitchen.

Nettie unpacked her tray and put scones, plates, and napkins on the table. Elliot found two tin mugs and heated the water in them one at a time.

"Ow! It's hot," complained Nettie. She put her mug down quickly on the table and blew on her fingers.

Elliot's hands were hard and calloused from pulling ropes on boats. The heat hadn't bothered him at all. "Sorry, Nettie." He pulled his ponytail out of the way and slid down the wall until he was sitting on the floor.

Nettie sat herself down on the only chair and sniffed. "Why don't you get that ridiculous ponytail cut off? You've had it way too long."

"Then you'd have nothing to complain about, Nettie."

"Seriously, Elliot. Why do you have it?"

He could have said it was because he was living in an age of revolution and free expression. But Elliot knew the truth was very different.

"Why?" Nettie insisted.

He sighed. "If you must know, it is my protest at life."

"What do you mean?"

"Look at me, Nettie, I've got high cheek bones and look a bit Asian."

"You look pretty good to me, boy. You're strong, fit, and have a face that's turned a few heads, I can tell you." She wagged a finger at him. "I've spoken to plenty of the mothers of young girls in the village, and I know."

Elliot said nothing.

The only sound came from a light aircraft flying overhead. The plane came from the airfield operated by the flying school nearby. From the sound of its engine, it was probably a Chipmunk. Elliot tried to make his mind think on these trivial things, but the emotional toll of the day caused him to fixate on Nettie's question – and relive the angst behind its answer.

"You know how much I hated school, Nettie."

"Yes, but I never understood why. You were good at it."

He grunted. "I was teased for being a wog."

"A what?"

"A wog."[1]

Nettie's eyes filled with concern. "Oh you poor dear."

Her compassion encouraged him to continue. "Even one of my class teachers seemed to take delight in humiliating me."

"What on earth happened?"

Elliot wasn't sure he wanted to say more, but felt obliged to at least give some sort of answer.

"The teacher once saw I had dirty hands from playing down by the river. She scraped some of the dirt off and made everyone look at it through a microscope. Then she encouraged the kids to make their feelings known about what they saw." He shrugged. "They were pretty free in expressing their revulsion, and it all got unpleasant."

Nettie put a hand to her cheek. "Good grief! What did you do?"

"I ran home, went up to my room, and cried." He paused, then continued. "Mum came in and put an arm around me. She didn't say a thing. I...I think she understood because she was part Chinese."

"Oh Elliot, I'm so sorry. People can be cruel."

Elliot gave a dismissive wave, embarrassed at himself. "Nah, I'm over it now. It's just that on that day, I resolved to look as much like an Asian as possible and grow a ponytail." He grinned. "It was my protest. I stopped trying to get them to include me in their games and went down to the river instead. That's when I learned to sail."

Nettie grunted. "Well, there's no shortage of misfits down there to entertain you, that's for sure, including my Horace."

"He was one of those who taught me." He paused. "Where is he, by the way?"

"He's with his other woman."

"Ah." Elliot smiled. That meant Horace was down with his boat, *Windsong*.

"Is he sailing her today?"

"No, he's got her leaning against the careening piles. He's hoping to have her bottom scraped and the new antifouling painted on before the tide refloats her. I saw him in the distance when I came up here." She wrinkled her nose. "He'd only just started painting the second side."

Elliot got to his feet and consulted the tide table pinned on the back of the door. He chewed his lip as he did a mental calculation using the yachtsman's 'rule of twelfths' for tides. The result told him Horace hadn't a chance of painting half a hull before the tide overtook him.

"I'll get my boots on and give him a hand. Can you let yourself out Nettie?"

"Take some scones with you. I'll wrap them in a napkin."

Elliot stepped out onto the cobbles of The Quay and walked past the 'The Bugle' pub to the hard[2] on the river's foreshore. He could see *Windsong* offshore, sitting on the mud, leaning against two careening posts. She was a twenty-five foot, sloop-rigged Folkboat, and was looking pretty in the late afternoon sun.

He splodged across the mud toward her.

Horace was bent over under the bilges applying antifouling to the bottom of the rudder – his shaggy white head was highlighted against the red paint. The man stood up as Elliot approached.

Elliot nodded to him. "Thought you could use a hand. Have you got another brush?"

"Bless you boy, but ain't you a good sight." The old man stretched his back. "I'm fair knackered, I can tell you. Ain't as young as I used to be." He pointed his paintbrush at the ladder leaning against the boat. "You'll find one in the cockpit locker."

Elliot unwrapped Nettie's napkin and showed him the scones.

Horace waved them away. "Later, boy. We ain't got no time to waste."

Elliot rewrapped them and climbed up into Windsong's cockpit. Before long, he was working alongside Horace slapping on paint.

Neither of them spoke for a while. Each had learned to be content and let the magic of the estuary sing its own song. The shadows were lengthening, and the Hamble River was still. Boats sat above their reflections at their moorings, and the river birds were beginning to fly in to their evening roosts. Elliot loved the place.

Horace caught him in mid-reverie. "Get on with it boy!" he growled.

Elliot applied himself to the task with fresh vigor.

These days, there were a lot more boats on the Hamble. Most of the new ones were modern designs made of fiberglass. They reflected their owners: tidy, expensive, and too time pressured to cope with the maintenance of a wooden boat.

The 'misfits' who had taught Elliot to sail belonged to an alto-gether different class of people. They were old men mostly, who had a wealth of maritime experience between them. Almost all of them had a distrust of modern technology and a scorn for everything to do with life on land.

Horace again interrupted his musings. "Have you entered for the Round the Island Race?"

"No. I haven't got a boat, and there's also a chance I'll be overseas."

The old man grunted. "Boy, you could stand on a floating log and still win the bloody race. There will be plenty of people glad enough to have a chance of winning if you're not in it." He paused. "What's this business overseas?"

"The Royal Yachting Association has asked if I'd be interested in accrediting sailing instructors in Hong Kong."

Water was lapping around their boots by the time they'd finished painting. Horace and Elliot climbed up into the boat's cockpit and waited for the tide to bear *Windsong* afloat.

"I'll make you some tea," said Horace. "You break out them scones."

Twilight gradually drew a curtain on the day as the tide stole into the estuary. Elliot nursed his thoughts as he gazed across the water. It had been a long and emotional day, but it was finishing well. He was on the river. Elliot thought fondly of his mother. She had passed away two months ago. Her death meant that he'd lost his greatest champion and the one who made life at home special. She'd laughed when hearing stories of his latest adventures, and encouraged him to press through the dark times. Her irrepressible nature had even survived the death of Elliot's father seven years ago.

Elliot missed them both. Memories floated like clouds across his consciousness – delicate, always changing, and infinitely sad.

"Right boy. We've been afloat for fifteen minutes. We can go. You cast off from them posts while I start the engine." Horace made his way down the companionway.

Ten minutes later *Windsong* had moved across the estuary and was secured to her mooring. Elliot was now rowing the two of them back to the hard in the dinghy.

"You'll have a pint with me, boy, in 'The Bugle.'" It was a statement.

"I think Nettie will be expecting you home for dinner. It's already late."

"Blast boy, you've earned it. We'll have a pint."

Elliot didn't argue.

The cottage was in darkness when he returned home. There were no lights in the window to greet him.

It was a poignant reminder.

The heating in the house had, however, come on two hours earlier, and the hot water radiators were warm.

Elliot went upstairs and swapped his paint-splattered overalls for a canvas smock top, now well faded by the sun. He kept his clothes in an army kitbag. The bag contained almost all of his worldly possessions. The only other things he owned were books and photograph albums. These were currently sitting in several cardboard boxes against the dining room wall.

Elliot went back downstairs and looked again into the bare rooms. So much that represented his former life was now gone. But the house that had been his bastion against life, within which he'd enjoyed the love and encouragement of his parents, was now his.

It was a relief.

In truth, he'd never put a great deal of store in owning things. So parting with the accoutrements and clutter of life had not been as traumatic for him as he had feared. His mother had sometimes teased him about his frugal lifestyle and called him a minimalist. He'd countered by claiming that all sailors had learned to keep their dunnage to a minimum. He couldn't see the point of owning much when there was a world outside that could be enjoyed for free.

The house, however, was sacred to him.

He gave a deep sigh. There was now a little ceremony to perform. It was one that he'd promised he would do once he knew he'd managed to secure ownership of the house.

He walked into the sitting room and squatted down before the fireplace. His fingers explored the bottom of the right hand pillar of the mantelpiece. He was searching for a little piece of wood on its side, one with a protruding screw. When he found it, he gave it a pull.

The secret drawer he had made when he was twelve slid out. It wasn't a very sophisticated affair. All he'd done was screw a tin pencil box onto the back of the piece of wood. But the secret drawer had a special place in Elliot's heart. His mother had hidden notes of encouragement in it during his traumatic years at school. It was their secret place.

Many years had passed since Elliot had last opened the drawer but he'd promised himself that he would fold up a photo of the title deeds to the house, and put it in the pencil case once he knew the house would remain his home. He wanted to make a statement, one that he knew his mother would've appreciated.

When Elliot prized off the rusting lid of the pencil box, he was surprised to find that it wasn't empty. Inside, was a pendant and a piece of paper.

Elliot picked up the ornament and turned it over in his hand. It looked to be made of jade. The pendant was round and had a raised margin. Its middle had been carved away to leave a silhouette of some strange creature. The whole thing was beautifully made.

He picked up the piece of paper. His heart skipped a beat when he realized it was a letter from his mother.

My Dear Elliot,

The wretched cancer means that I may not be with you for long.

I just want to tell you that you have been a beautiful son, all that a mother could hope for. Your father and I have known you to be a gift to us, all the more so given the death of your sister, who died before you were born. So, whatever else you might find out in life, never doubt our love for you.

I want to give you this jade pendant. You may not recognize what it represents. It is a dragon, and its story is very much tied up with you. As such, the pendant has been sacred to me.

And now it is yours.

I will love you always.

Mum

Chapter 4

The cloying heat of the tropics assaulted her the moment she stepped out of her room. Someone had turned off the air-conditioner in the communal living area. *Ridiculous!* It might only be 8am, but Hong Kong's summer heat was already intense.

Emma looked for the culprit, and saw him. She could only see his shape in silhouette because of the harsh topical light. Broad shoulders; narrow waist. The man's feet were on the railings of the patio balcony, and he was balancing himself on the back two legs of a chair.

She turned her attention to breakfast. The rooms she was staying in were on the twelfth floor of a high-rise block of flats that stood behind the beautiful beach of Repulse Bay. The unit had been converted into three bedsits, each with their own en suite. All the rooms opened into a communal kitchen and living area. She'd been told that they had been designed to accommodate unaccompanied people staying in Hong Kong on government business.

Well, she mused, she was certainly on government business – and was certainly unaccompanied.

Emma plucked her shirt from where it had stuck to her chest and stepped into the kitchen. She was already beginning to sweat uncomfortably. An unwashed collection of cups and plates had been left beside the sink. Causing even more affront was the sight of the remains of her pawpaw and pineapple – her breakfast. The stranger, who had obviously arrived some time during the night, had made himself free with her provisions.

She sighed. It was disappointing to have to share the unit with someone else. For the last two weeks, she'd had it all to herself.

Emma walked to the sliding glass doors that led out to the balcony. They were open, allowing the heat of the morning to flood in. She cleared her throat. "Hello; my name is Emma Templeton. I'm in room three."

The man presented a disturbing sight. He was naked to the waist, tanned, and sported a long ponytail. Some sort of pendant hung around his neck. He seemed completely untroubled by the heat despite his body being covered by a sheen of sweat. The shorts he was wearing were frayed.

He turned his head and ran his eyes over her. They took in her gray business skirt, lingered briefly on her white shirt, and then made contact with her eyes. He was doing a poor job of suppressing a smile. "Hi. I'm Elliot Gleeson. I came in late last night. Hope I didn't disturb you."

"No, I wasn't disturbed until I stepped out into the heat just now. The air conditioning had been turned off."

But the wretched man refused to receive her rebuke. "Well Emma, you look scarily institutional, so you have to be someone important."

Emma was at a loss as to what to say. "I...er, I work for a department of the Home Secretary, and I'm important enough not to enjoy people making free with my breakfast provisions."

He waved a hand, dismissively. "There's plenty left for you. I'll buy some more this morning." He looked at her and smiled. "I knew you'd have to be a civil servant, getting up so late. Would you like me to make you a soda and lime drink? I noticed some in the fridge."

She shook her head in disbelief, not trusting herself to say anything. Instead, she stalked to the balcony rail and tried to calm herself by looking at the view. It was wonderful. The splendor of the Pacific spread out in front of her; its blue surface dotted here and there with islands. She'd learned that the largest one was Lamma Island. Its steep sides rose up from the sea like a green Chinese coolie hat.

She allowed the rich sounds and smells of Asia to wash over her. Car horns, arguments, and laughter could clearly be heard, even from the twelfth floor. She looked longingly at the long, curving beach below her. It was already dotted with people. Some had swum out to the floating pontoon anchored just offshore. It all looked so idyllic and inviting.

She was startled from her reverie by Elliot returning from the kitchen. He'd not only brought her a lime soda, but had prepared a bowl containing chunks of pineapple and mango. Slightly mollified, she uttered her thanks and sat down to eat it.

Elliot leaned over the veranda rails. "What's that big, white, two-storied building with the orange tiled roof – the one at the end of the beach?" he asked.

She swallowed a piece of mango, coughed, cleared her throat, and said huskily, "That's Repulse Bay Hotel. Apparently, the English and Japanese soldiers bowled hand-grenades down its hallways at each other during the Second World War."

"Wow, you know a bit about history, then."

"A bit."

He pointed to the beach. "The beach looks good. What's the water like?"

She didn't answer.

He turned to her and raised an inquiring eyebrow.

Emma waved a dismissive hand. "I've never been."

Elliot's mouth dropped open. "You've never been! How long have you lived here?"

Emma dropped her head. "Two weeks." She tried to think of something else to say that wouldn't make her look quite so pathetic and unadventurous. "I've been very busy."

Elliot stroked his chin. He had strong features: a straight

aquiline nose, high cheeks, and dark brown eyes. It was a slightly exotic look.

"When do you have to be at work?" he asked.

"I have a meeting after lunch. I'd planned to write up some notes this morning. Why?"

He grinned. "Let's go for a swim. I'm not teaching until after lunch."

She shook her head. "No."

"Come on. Why not? It's a great morning."

Emma didn't answer.

He persisted. "Have you got a swimming costume?"

"Ye-yes…but I haven't actually…"

Elliot clapped his hands. "Brilliant. Come on, let's go." He grinned. "You know you want to."

She was not at all sure he was right. But the sheer force of his positivity resulted in her walking back to her bedsit before she realized it. She shut the door behind her, leaned against it, and remonstrated with herself. *What on earth am I doing?* The trouble was, she couldn't pull out now without looking ridiculous.

With a sigh, she opened the chest of drawers and pulled out her swimming costume. Feeling incredibly self-conscious, she put it on. It was the first time she'd ever worn it. Emma threw a loose flowing caftan over the top as much to hide her bare flesh from herself as anyone else, and slipped her feet into a pair of sandals.

When she came out of her room, Elliot was waiting for her. His only concession to getting ready for a swim had been to throw a towel over his shoulders. He was still in bare feet.

They went down in the lift and out into the sunshine.

Emma's sense of disquiet grew as Elliot towed her across the busy road running along the foreshore, and onto the beach. She would have to take off her caftan in front of him – in front of everyone. Emma was not sure she had the courage. She remembered how he'd first looked at her – completely without shame.

She stood on the beach with a thousand uncertainties screaming at her.

Elliot dropped the towel on the beach, looked at the water, and breathed in the sea air.

Emma snatched the opportunity to shed the caftan whilst he wasn't looking. Then she stood on the sand with her arms folded, cupping her elbows with her hands.

Elliot turned back to her and raised an eyebrow when he saw her. "Hmm, excellent. You are no longer a government bureaucrat."

She wanted to kill him. She was standing in front of him in a navy one-piece swimsuit feeling very vulnerable.

"Come on, let's get into the water."

Emma didn't move.

"Come on. What's the matter?"

"I, I…have a problem."

"What's that?"

"I can't swim."

Elliot's eyes opened wide. "Really?"

She shrugged. "I never learned."

"Doesn't matter," he said. "Just wade in the water and splash about. That's all most people do." He looked round. "Ah," he said. "That's what we need."

"What?"

He ignored her, fished in his pocket, and unwrapped a water-proof money pouch. "I'll be back in a moment."

Emma watched him lope off toward a little beach shop just above the sand. It was advertising everything from ice creams to beach balls. She turned away so as not to give Elliot any sense that she was watching him, and began to twist her feet into the sand. It was a delicious feeling. She couldn't remember the last time she'd felt sand between her toes.

Elliot was back in just a few minutes. He was carrying a plastic kick board that had handles on the side and the front. "Here," he said. "I thought this would be a bit more dignified than blow up arm bands."

The water was surprisingly cool, but it didn't take long to become accustomed to it. She gradually gained enough confidence to head into deeper water, prompted by a desire to allow the water to hide as much of her as possible.

"Just go steady. Get used to kicking your feet to go forward. Keep your legs as straight as possible." Elliot swam around her like a seal. "Hang onto the board and float if you get tired."

He may not have intended to sound patronizing, but Emma felt he came dangerously close to it. His words irritated her enough to ask, "Do you think I could kick out to the diving pontoon?"

Elliot rolled onto his back, squirting out a mouth of seawater like a fountain. "I don't advise it. It's a long way."

Wretched man, she thought. Emma swung the kick board around and began to kick toward the pontoon. *Keep your legs straight. Show him.*

Elliot swam beside her, sometimes doing a lazy crawl stroke, and sometimes sculling himself along on his back with a sardonic grin on his face.

It didn't take very long for Emma to realize she couldn't make it. The swimming pontoon stubbornly refused to get any closer despite kicking her legs in the prescribed manner. As weariness and lactic acid began burning in her muscles, her kicking became slower and less tidy.

She was relieved when Elliot surfaced just in front of her and blocked the way. "Rest for a while," he commanded. There was an edge to his voice that brooked no argument. It surprised her. She'd not heard it before. Emma hung onto the kick board and let herself dangle in the water.

"How are you feeling?" he asked.

"I…I'm not sure this was such a good idea."

He smiled. "I've been watching you forcing yourself to keep going. I'm pretty amazed you've got this far. But it's time to head back."

Emma gave a nod of acquiescence. She had sought to put Elliot in his place, but it had all come badly unstuck. The thought of having to kick all the way back to the beach appalled her. Anxiety began to insert its icy fingers into her heart, and she began to breathe rapidly.

"Steady on, girl. Breathe slow and deep. Only start kicking when you're ready. You've got all the time you need, so don't be afraid to take a rest."

After five minutes, she was ready to kick toward the shore. However, when she tried to move her legs, they didn't move. Her abused muscles had cooled to a point that they simply refused to function.

Panic again rose up within her. "I can't move my legs. They... they won't work," she squeaked.

"Then just hang on to the board, and I'll tow you back." Elliot's voice was calming, and he appeared completely unfazed.

Moments later she had the sensation of being towed through the water. It was actually very pleasant. She could feel the powerful thrusts of water from his swimming eddy around her.

An eternity later, Elliot stopped swimming, stood up in chest high water, and towed her into the shallows. Emma began to rehearse what she would say to him, but she discarded each speech. Finally, she let go of the kick board and knelt on the sand on all fours, allowing the waves to buffet her as they rushed past to the shore. Summoning her remaining strength, she clambered to her feet.

But her legs wouldn't hold her. She fell.

Elliot caught her against his chest and, for a moment, he held her there.

The effect was disastrous. Her body responded physiologically in a way that was beyond her control.

It betrayed her.

Chapter 5

Elliot could hear the student screaming. She was in the water under the mainsail. The Bosun sailing dinghy had capsized, and the army major whom Elliot was assessing was making a complete mess of talking his student through the process of righting it.

The major yelled, "Get to the stern, woman. Get to the stern."

A muffled frightened voice replied, "What's a stern? Help! I'm trapped under here. I can't get out. Help!"

Elliot was just ten yards away in the rescue boat. A moment later he was in the water swimming to the boat. He duck-dived under the mainsail and bobbed up beside a girl who was punching at the sail lying on top of her head.

"Woah, girl! Settle down," he said soothingly. "Nothing bad is going to happen to you under here. You've got a life vest on and you're quite safe." Elliot had an impression of blond hair – lots of it – and a stricken face – a very beautiful face. He held the girl by the shoulders to settle her. Then, forcing a smile, added, "Let's get out from under here. Follow me."

Elliot towed her out from under the sail and swam with her to the rescue boat. His two assistants in the boat lifted them both inboard. The young woman sat shivering on one of the thwarts. She had long tanned legs, he noticed.

Elliot smiled at her. "Catch your breath. You did well. Now, excuse me while I sort something out."

Elliot turned his attention back to the dinghy. The major had levered the boat back upright and was now bailing out the water. Elliot called out to him. "Mate, that was a balls-up."

The major was not in a good mood. "The stupid woman didn't do as she was told," he barked.

Something in the man's tone triggered memories of the hectoring voices Elliot had been forced to endure as a child. He felt his jaw tighten. "Mate, shut up and listen to me. You didn't talk your student through what to expect, and you didn't go to her aid. All you did was spook her."

The man said under his breath, but loud enough for Elliot to hear. "Bloody long-haired lout."

Elliot stepped over to the driving console of the rescue boat and edged the boat alongside the dinghy. His heart pounded and his muscles were tense as he leaned across to speak to the man.

"I'm going to say just two things to you before I write 'fail' on your application to be an instructor. First: if you don't foster a love of sailing in your students, you don't deserve to be an instructor."

The major glowered at him.

Elliot reached over, uncoupled the rudder from the back of the dinghy and pulled it into the rescue boat. "Secondly," he said. "If you're such a good sailor, let's see you sail this boat back to the yacht club without a rudder. It's a skill all instructors should have."

"Don't be ridiculous," the man expostulated. "It can't be done."

"I'd shut up and listen if I were you." Elliot was in no mood to brook any opposition. "If you lean the boat over, you will increase the boat's wetted surface on one side. This will cause the boat to turn in that direction. If you do this as well as work the sails so the boat acts like a wind vane, you'll get home." He gave the major a wave and gunned the engine leaving the man shouting obscenities in his wake.

Elliot glanced at the young woman on the seat beside him. She now had a towel draped across her shoulders, but she was still shivering, probably from shock as much as anything. If ever there was a girl who was never going to get into another boat, it was her, unless he did something.

He headed the rescue boat across the harbor to where a pair of Flying Fifteen keelboats was practicing racing tactics by having a tacking duel. They were also being supervised by Elliot. He called out to one of them. "Hove-to, guys, and call it a day. Hop into the rescue boat, and I'll sail your boat back for you."

The boat's crew agreed readily enough, and Elliot stepped across into their vessel. He held out a hand to help the young woman to join him.

She held back.

"Come on," urged Elliot. "This boat has got a thumping great lump of metal as a keel and can't capsize. And I won't ask you to do anything other than to enjoy the sail."

Looking anything other than confidant, the woman stepped into the sailing boat.

Elliot waved the rescue boat away. "Have a beer waiting for me," he yelled after them.

He turned his attention to his crew mate. "What's your name?"

"Kendal Shiffer."

"Well Kendal, sit on the side deck next to the shrouds and make yourself comfortable." He pointed to the wire stays that held up the mast. "Hang on to them if you need to." He smiled. "All you need to do is to sit in that position on the high side of the boat and enjoy yourself. Okay?"

She nodded.

Elliot freed the jib so that it was no longer backed against the mainsail and sheeted it home on the other side of the boat. The Flying Fifteen heeled in the wind, dipped her bow through a wave, and began to cream through the water. Elliot settled the boat on a beam reach and let the magic of the boat's movement begin to calm the fears of the woman sitting beside him. He stole a look at her. *Fantastic legs*, he noticed. Her hair was beginning to dry and strands of it were now blowing in the wind, sometimes whipping against his face. It was a fabulous sensation.

Elliot shifted his gaze to the scene around him. He'd been so preoccupied with teaching that he'd not really had time to take in the fact that he was sailing in Victoria Harbor, in the waters between Hong Kong Island and Kowloon City on the mainland. It was one of the busiest waterways in the world and arguably the most exotic.

"Are you a permanent resident here in Hong Kong, Kendal?"

"Yes, I've lived here since I was three."

Blue eyes, very blue...and a classically beautiful face. An odd feeling stole over him – something between shyness and awe, not a feeling that he'd ever been bothered with before in his adult life. So he repressed it. He cleared his throat. "I only arrived here last night. It's my first time here."

"Oh," she said, and paused. She pointed to the peak soaring above them behind the skyscrapers of Hong Kong city. "That's Victoria Peak. A special hill tram will take you up there. It's worth going. It's a marvel of engineering, and the view's very good."

"I hadn't expected everything to be so mountainous. What's the peak over there, the one behind Kowloon?"

"That's Lion Rock."

Elliot was keeping half an eye open for other traffic on the harbor. Green and white ferries from the Star Ferry terminal were everywhere. Most were plying their way back and forth between Hong Kong and Kowloon, but some headed down the harbor, presumably going to the islands that were dotted about. There were cargo ships, bluff-nosed local wooden trading boats and, amazingly, an actual authentic Chinese sailing junk. Elliot was delighted to see it. He'd studied their design in books, but here was the real thing. It was carrying three tanned, slatted sails and was sailing well in the afternoon breeze. The boat looked incongruous against the backdrop of Hong Kong's towering skyscrapers.

Elliot sailed toward it to have a closer look. As he did, he saw something glint in the water – and recognized it straight away.

"Stand by to go about," he said. "Just duck under the boom

when we turn and sit on the other side of the boat. I'm going to try and pick something out of the water."

"What?" asked Kendal.

"I'm pretty sure it's a glass fishing float."

"Wow," she said. "Where is it?"

Elliot pointed. "Twenty yards away, over there. If I sail back to it, can you try and pick it up?"

She seemed to be caught up in the excitement of the challenge. "Sure. I'll have a go." Her eyes were shining.

Elliot was relieved. Her previous fears and apprehension seemed to have gone.

Moments later, Kendal was lying over the side on her stomach, her legs stretched out across the cockpit. Elliot swallowed, and began spilling wind from the sails causing the boat to bob and rock as it slowed to an easy walking pace.

"Got it!" she yelled as she scooped it out of the water with two hands. She wiggled herself backward into the boat.

Elliot swallowed again, and said huskily, "Keep it as a memento of your first day of sailing."

She put the glass fishing float into the plastic bucket under the foredeck and resumed her place next to him on the side deck. "Yes," she said, continuing his conversation. "It has certainly been a day of extremes."

"How are you feeling now?"

"Terrific. I'm loving this." She paused. "Thanks, by the way, for rescuing me…" she paused, "back there."

"It was…a pleasure."

She looked at him.

Blue eyes.

"You don't look like a sailing examiner. I take it that's your job."

He grinned. "Something like that, at least for some of the time. What do you do?"

Kendal looked at him for a moment, saying nothing. It was as if she was weighing him up. Her breasts lifted as she drew in a breath. "I manage my father's investment firm."

"You what?"

"I manage my father's investment firm." She lowered her eyes. "He died last year, so now I manage it…along with my uncle."

Elliot looked at the gorgeous woman in front of him and was lost for words. "But…but you're so…"

"…young?" she finished.

He gulped, and thought feverishly how he might rescue the situation. "I was going to say that you're too beautiful," he grinned, "but I suppose that's just as crass."

She inspected his face. "It could be. It depends on why it was said."

Elliot had the uncomfortable feeling that he was getting out of his depth. "How's business going?" he asked lamely.

"Hong Kong is currently going through an investment boom. Land prices are soaring and people are falling over themselves to invest in Hong Kong's building bonanza."

Elliot nodded. "Yeah. I've noticed buildings going up everywhere." He grinned. "Skyscrapers being built with bamboo scaffolding. Crazy."

"Not so crazy. They bend in the wind when typhoons come." Kendal paused. "Seriously, if you have any money, Hong Kong's the place to invest."

Elliot pictured his home in Hamble, stripped bare of everything through lack of money, and smiled.

She mistook his smile for lack of conviction for she continued. "Honestly. Since the passing of the Banking Ordinance of 1964, our banks have become a safe bet. New stocks are coming on sale every day and our brokerage houses are mushrooming. People are even quitting their jobs in order to become full-time investors. It's been estimated that there are half a million of them in Hong Kong."

"Wow."

She smiled. "It's even led to an urban disease that doctors are calling 'stock illness.'"

Nothing was said for quite a while. Elliot headed the boat west. He'd now managed to persuade Kendal to take charge of the jib sheet. "Just ease the sheet out until the front edge of the sail begins to shake. Then pull it in a bit until it's full and round. Then you'll have a perfectly trimmed sail."

She was doing well.

Elliot noticed the wreck of a huge ship away in the distance. Although it was lying on its side, he could still see its two funnels. He pointed to it. "What's that up ahead?"

Kendal turned. "Ahh. That's the wreck of the *Queen Elizabeth*. It caught fire and sank in January. There's a bit of mystery surrounding it all."

"Why's that?"

"Some are suggesting it was an insurance fraud. The ship was costing a lot of money."

"Do you think there's any truth in it?"

She sighed. "This is Hong Kong. Everything here is to do with money."

Forty minutes later, they arrived back at Kellett Island yacht club and handed the Flying Fifteen over to the boat attendants who worked there.

Kendal retrieved her fishing float and weighed it in her hands. "I think these things are actually Japanese fishing floats." She smiled. "Amazing really that they can survive intact in a stormy sea."

Elliot nodded. "Perhaps it's a parable for life."

"Perhaps indeed." She glanced around her. "Did you know that the name, 'Hong Kong' literally means 'fragrant harbor'?"

"No."

"Well, whatever else it is, it is a place of opportunity for those seeking to invest."

Elliot ferreted in his pocket for his money pouch. He took out five Hong Kong dollars and gave it to her. "This is dangerously close to all the money I have."

She looked at him in disbelief, then laughed as she reached out and took it. "I'll invest it carefully for you." Kendal became serious. "Thank you for a wonderful afternoon. I…I think you've persuaded me to become a member of the yacht club – but perhaps just as volunteer crew in someone's Flying Fifteen."

He grinned. "You've just made my day." He paused. "And you'd make it even more special if you'd let me buy you dinner here at the yacht club tonight."

She raised an eyebrow. "And who would pay?"

"The yacht club," he confessed. "They've sponsored me to come out here."

She smiled. "Unfortunately, I'm booked tonight." She paused. "Where are you staying?"

"In a block of high-rise units at Repulse Bay." He told her the address and phone number.

"Hmm, very nice." She paused. "Why don't you let me give you a meal to say 'thank you' for a lovely afternoon. I could send my car around to pick you up at, say 7pm, and take you to the Tai Pak floating restaurant."

"Really? Wow. Where's that?"

"It's in Aberdeen, in the south-west corner of the island."

"That would be great…I think. But I'd be on my own?"

"Yes."

She gave him an enigmatic smile, turned, and walked up the pontoon to the clubhouse.

Chapter 6

The chauffeur opened the back door of the Mercedes for him, but Elliot chose to sit in the front seat. The Chinese driver was not to be thwarted a second time, however. When the car came to a halt, he raced around the car and opened the door before Elliot did it for himself.

Elliot gazed around him at the harbor scene. It was deliciously oriental. Blunt-nosed bumboats with car tires hanging along their sides plied the waters between the mainland and Aberdeen Island two-hundred yards offshore. A tangle of fishing boats could be seen crowded together at one end of the harbor. It looked like a floating village.

His driver saw him looking at it. "Tanka people live there," he said.

"What! All the time?"

"Yes. They live on their boats."

"Wow." Elliot could see how the island just offshore would provide good protection for the boats from the typhoons that periodically lashed the islands.

The driver closed his door. "I wait for you here. You go to pier

45

and catch ferry to Tai Pak." He smiled. "Sad you can't go to the really big floating restaurant. It was very grand."

Elliot raised a questioning eyebrow.

"The Jumbo Restaurant. It was big. It caught fire before it was opened. Very sad. Many people died. They repair it now, but it not ready yet." The driver smiled. "But Tai Pak also very good. Missy Kendal like it very much."

Elliot nodded his thanks and walked down to the pier.

Minutes later, a bumboat was threading its way through the harbor toward an incongruous-looking floating building. It was two decks high and built in the style of a richly ornate pagoda.

He stepped out of the boat and walked into the entrance. Two staff members greeted the handful of passengers who had arrived. When one looked up and saw Elliot, his eyes opened wide in surprise. He instantly stopped talking to the customer in front of him, walked over to Elliot, and bowed. The man stood up again and spoke to him in Chinese.

Elliot was bewildered. "Er, I'm here to have a meal. I think you'll find I'm booked under the name of…"

He got no further. His host beckoned impatiently to an attractive Chinese girl standing behind the counter. She came scurrying out and also bowed to Elliot. The woman was dressed in a figure-hugging silk dress with a dangerously high slit in it. Her boss rattled something off to her in rapid Chinese. She nodded and motioned for Elliot to follow her.

Wow, thought Elliot, Kendal Shiffer must be a woman of some clout to warrant this degree of attention.

He was led though the main dining area to a small private dining room. It was richly decorated with gilt carvings and had a magnificent view across the harbor. As soon as he was seated, his Chinese hostess surprised him by standing behind him and massaging his shoulders. It was a delicious feeling. He was weary after his long flight to Hong Kong and an afternoon of sailing.

She moved to his neck, kneading it skillfully.

"Aah," he groaned.

Slowly, she moved across his shoulders and began to work the muscles in his upper arm. Elliot rested his forearms onto the table to assist her.

The woman suddenly paused what she was doing, gave an involuntary squeal, and ran from the room.

Elliot didn't know what to think. Had he upset her? He couldn't think how. All he'd done was sit down.

A short time later, a male waiter came in, left Elliot with a menu, and waited by his side until he'd made his choice.

The food came, and it was delicious. In the typical Chinese style, the different courses arriving at intervals. The only surprise was how long it took for the courses to arrive. Elliot had worked his way through two pots of jasmine tea before his dessert arrived. Eating was obviously a leisurely affair in Hong Kong.

He dearly wished Kendal was with him to share the experience. He was conscious of something visceral moving within him when he thought of her. What a woman! She was smart, sophisticated, and golden, like honey drizzling from a spoon.

His reverie was disturbed by the arrival of two men who stood in the doorway. They were large and had grim expressions. Neither of them looked like restaurant staff. The men stared at him for a moment, then came forward and stood either side of his chair. A moment later, Elliot was hauled to his feet, and patted down to check for concealed weapons.

"Oi! Hands off." yelled Elliot.

Without ceremony, he was pushed back down into his seat. Hands on his shoulders imprisoned him in his seat.

Nothing was said.

Elliot was in shock, and wondered briefly if he'd woken up in someone's nightmare.

Still nothing was said.

Then, another figure stepped into the doorway.

Elliot's mouth dropped open, his sense of reality whirled and swirled like a bird unable to land.

There standing in the doorway, was himself.

The figure stared at him, but it was as if Elliot was staring into a mirror. The man had the same build as his own, the same face, and a similar ponytail. It was surreal. They were even dressed in the same colors: white shirt and tan trousers. The only difference was that Elliot wore shorts.

His mirror image said nothing. He stayed stock still twirling something around on his forefinger – first one way, and then the next. It looked like a bead on a thin piece of chain. Back and forth, back and forth, it went.

At last, the man spoke. "*Hai bin do ah?*"

Elliot shook his head. "What?"

"Where are you from?" the man added impatiently.

He even had the same voice. It was uncanny. Elliot was at a loss as to what to say. Should he say Repulse Bay, or Kellett Island Yacht Club, or England?

The man spoke again. "*M'Gong.* Not talking eh." He nodded to the two men either side of him.

They hauled him to his feet. He'd barely got his balance when one of them slapped him across the face. Then he was pushed back into his seat.

The sheer speed and viciousness of the attack shocked him. Shock stopped him feeling the full pain. "Woah!" he yelled.

Everything was quiet for a moment.

His interrogator continued to swing the bead clockwise, then anticlockwise. He lifted his chin disdainfully. "Who are you and where are you from?"

"My name is Elliot Gleeson." Elliot looked at the man standing before him. "And just who the hell are you?"

The two men either side of Elliot grabbed him by the collar and began hauling him to his feet again. His shirt pulled open. Suddenly, the two men froze – then dropped him in his seat.

A terse conversation in Chinese followed.

The man who was his mirror image pocketed his swinging bead, then stepped forward and pulled open Elliot's shirt. The dragon pendant sat high on his chest, hanging from a piece of cod line.

His tormentor reached forward and examined it, turning it slowly this way and that, taking his time.

Eventually, the man stepped back and stared at him. Then, without a word, he undid his own shirt to reveal an ivory pendant.

Elliot could make no sense of what was happening.

The man took the pendant off from around his neck and used a fingernail to move a clip on its side. The pendant revealed itself to be a locket.

It opened.

There, nested inside its ivory case, was a jade dragon's head.

The man tipped it out and held it between finger and thumb. He reached out and took hold of Elliot's pendant. Then he slid his dragon head over Elliot's piece of jade.

There was a faint click.

The two pieces fitted together perfectly.

The significance of the two pieces fitting together seemed to shock both men in equal measure. Elliot's double lifted his chin at the two men standing either side of Elliot.

They took their hands off Elliot's shoulders.

The man sat down on the edge of the table in front of him.

Elliot slowly reached forward and laid his hand on top of the man's hand, and pulled it forward to reveal the ugly scar on his forearm. He realized then what his hostess had seen that had so distressed her. Elliot had no scar.

Elliot tried to speak, but something caught in his throat. He tried again. "What is your name?"

"My name is Kai."

Whatever else was the case, one thing was certain. Elliot knew he was looking into the eyes of his brother – doubtless, his twin.

His brother had obviously come to the same conclusion, for he let Elliot run his finger over his scar.

A familial warmth, an identity, seemed to flow through his finger – so alien, and yet so known – sharing its hurt.

Kai pulled his arm away. "Are you 14K?"

Elliot frowned. "What is 14K?"

Kai said nothing.

"And what is all this?" demanded Elliot. "I didn't know I had a brother. How is this possible? Tell me."

Kai shrugged. "I don't know."

"Who would know? Who are your family?"

Kai said nothing, then nodded. "Perhaps my auntie will know."

"I want to meet her, then."

"No!" barked Kai, slapping the table. "You see no one until I say."

"Don't you bully me," retorted Elliot. I have a right to know." He suddenly realized that the two of them sounded like squabbling brothers. In any other situation, it would have been humorous.

"Where do you come from?" asked Kai in a softer voice.

"I come from England, from a place called Hamble. I'm visiting here for a month to teach sailing."

"And where are you staying?"

Elliot told him his address and telephone number at Repulse Bay.

Kai nodded. "I will be in touch." He nodded to his two men, and all three of them left.

Elliot sat in stunned silence, unable to finish his dessert.

Chapter 7

E mma heard the noise again. It sounded like a hoarse bark. She glanced at her travel clock. It was 2am. What had woken her?

The sound came again.

She wondered if she was hearing the sound of a barking deer that reportedly lived on the steep hillside behind the tower blocks. Consciousness battled with her unwillingness to let go of the mists of sleep.

The noise came a third time, and she came fully awake. Someone was in trouble. It was the noise of a person coughing and retching.

Emma got out of bed, wrapped a cotton dressing gown around her, and opened her door. Light was coming from the crack under the door into Elliot's room.

She listened for a moment to the sounds of his obvious distress.

"Are you all right?" she called.

There was no reply.

She called again and tapped on the door.

Tentatively, she turned the handle.

The door opened, and instantly she could smell the vomit. Elliot was on the floor of the en suite hanging on to the toilet bowl. He tried to mumble, but retched again. Filth spilled over the floor. Elliot didn't seem to have the strength to pull himself up. The stench not only came from the vomit, but from diarrhea. She glanced over to the bed and could see that the sheet had been soiled.

Elliot was now lying on the floor, dressed only in pajama shorts. He was covered in sweat.

Emma stepped across to him and laid a hand on his forehead. It was burning hot. Careless of the filth on the floor, Emma rolled him into the recovery position. She reasoned that the cool of the floor tiles would be of more benefit than a bed. It was important to bring Elliot's temperature down and get some fluids into him as quickly as possible.

Emma turned up the air conditioning, dampened some flannels, and laid them on him. Elliot's head lolled on his arm. He was trying to speak, but he was semi-delirious.

"Sorry. Sorry." A pause, then: "Brother. I have a brother. Aargh!" He vomited again.

Emma went to the phone and called the emergency number on a list hanging beside it. A medical orderly at Fort Stanley answered. She explained the situation, and was told that a doctor should be with her within twenty minutes.

By the time the doctor arrived, Emma had rinsed the soiled sheets and put them in the washing machine. She'd also cleaned the floor and toilet, while periodically checking Elliot's breathing and pulse. His breathing was shallow and his pulse was racing.

The doctor assessed the situation with brusque efficiency and gave Elliot an injection.

Emma put new sheets on Elliot's bed, while the doctor dressed him in a clean pair of shorts. When the bed was ready, she helped the doctor carry Elliot to it. Emma stood up and looked at him. Mercifully, Elliot appeared to be more peaceful.

The doctor nodded his approval. "It's probably some form of food poisoning. Keep him hydrated. I'll leave you some sachets of drink mix for him and some bendable straws. He may need help to drink." He glanced at Emma. "Can you manage?"

"Yes."

"Good. Call me if you are concerned."

After seeing the doctor to the door, she returned to Elliot's room and wondered what to do next. She checked his breathing. It was regular and more settled but still shallow. As she watched his chest rise and fall, her attention was drawn to the pendant hanging around his neck. She'd been close to it before – way too close, but she'd never had a serious look at it. She bent over and inspected it.

A second later, a frisson of alarm swept over her. She looked again. There was no doubt about what she was seeing. A thousand questions immediately clamored for attention. Emma looked at Elliot speculatively. Whatever else was the case, one thing was important, and that was to make sure Elliot did not choke in the night. With a sigh, Emma dragged a cane chair beside his bed, switched the table lamp off and made herself comfortable.

———

She woke with a start. Her neck and shoulders were stiff. Emma sat herself upright and stretched extravagantly. It was then that she discovered Elliot's eyes were open and that he was watching her. It was not an entirely comfortable realization. She'd been awake for much of the night. There would be bags under her eyes, and her hair would be a mess.

"How are you feeling?" she asked.

"As if I've been hit by a truck."

"The doctor thinks you've had food poisoning."

Elliot grunted. "Have you been here all night?"

"Pretty much." She paused. "How much of last night do you remember?"

"Some. Most of it not nice."

"Hmm."

Neither of them said anything for a while.

Emma lifted the beaker of fluid up to him. He took it with a shaky hand and sipped from the straw. Then he flopped back down on the bed.

Emma reached out and put a hand on his forehead. The

temperature still felt slightly warm. A sheen of sweat could still be seen under his curling chest hairs.

"You've tidied my room."

Emma wasn't sure whether it was an observation or a complaint.

"Things got pretty messy last night." She could not, however, repress a small pang of guilt. She'd certainly needed to clean the place, but she'd also tidied the bundle of clothes he'd thrown onto a chair. She'd folded them and placed them in a row on top of the dresser.

Emma changed the subject. "There's no way you'll be able to go to work today. Do I have to call someone to let them know?"

"Yes please."

She furrowed her brow. "What exactly do you do?"

"I'm an examiner."

"An examiner of what?"

"I've been asked by The Royal Hong Kong Yacht Club at Kellett Island and the British Army to accredit their sailing instructors. They want to bring everything into line with the new RYA National Coaching Scheme."

"The RYA?"

"The Royal Yachting Association. I'm what's technically known as a Coach Examiner."

Emma looked at him doubtfully. None of what she was hearing made sense of the pendant hanging round his neck. She pressed further. "You look too young to be an examiner."

Elliot gave her a wan smile. "I think I am too."

She probed again. "What do you need to do to be a Coach Examiner?"

Elliot put a hand on his forehead and closed his eyes. He was the picture of weariness. Emma scolded herself for testing him with questions when he was so tired.

Elliot surprised her by answering. "I was appointed by the RYA Training Divisional Committee on the recommendation of a bunch of National Coaches."

"Wow. How long have you been sailing, then?"

"Since I was twelve. I've been an RYA Coach for four years." He sighed. "And now, quite irresponsibly, they've appointed me Coach Examiner."

"So, you studied sailing?"

"I wouldn't say 'studied.' It just sort of happened. I actually studied marine engineering at Southampton Technical College."

"Oh." She still had no answers.

Emma got to her feet. "I've worn you out with my questions. So sorry. I should let you sleep."

He reached out a hand to restrain her. "No. Don't go."

She blinked in surprise. "But I need to get dressed, have breakfast, and begin typing up my notes."

"Later." Elliot closed his eyes again. "Tell me what you do. Why have they banished you to this fetid, culturally bereft, colony?"

Emma was now well practiced with her story, and launched into it without demur. "The Home Secretary is concerned with the level of recidivism in Hong Kong's prisons. My job is to unearth some of the reasons for it and report back."

"So what do you have to actually do?"

"I interview people – particularly prisoners, as well as police chiefs and some of the Governor's staff."

He smiled. "You look too young."

Emma glanced again at the pendant around Elliot's neck. She'd not managed to learn anything that might explain it. And it was too late now. Elliot's breathing had become slow and even. The man had fallen asleep.

Emma made phone calls, showered, and then set about typing up her notes. Sadly, there wasn't much to type. The real problem was that she was unable to interview anyone of serious rank in any of the triad organizations. As such, she was unable to discover how the top echelons were organized and what their ambitions were for exporting their activities to other countries.

What she did learn was that Hong Kong was in turmoil. There had been Communist-fueled riots in recent years, and the new Governor, Murray MacLehose, was bringing in sweeping reforms to improve infrastructure, environmental management, welfare, education and housing. Of particular significance was the Governor's program to root out corruption from the police. Emma was appalled to learn how endemic it had become. She couldn't help but feel it would have contributed greatly to the flourishing of Hong Kong's triad societies.

From time to time, she looked in on Elliot, mainly to check he was drinking enough. She was relieved to discover at lunch-time that his temperature had returned to normal. He'd shaken his head at her suggestion she make him some chicken broth, but at least he was well hydrated.

Emma ate her breakfast for lunch and then walked out onto the balcony.

Darkening clouds glowered from a leaden sky. She wasn't at all surprised when it started to rain. It did so with tropical intensity. Stinging rain lanced in underneath the balcony roof forcing her to retreat a few steps. The view out to sea became veiled and opaque. Middle Island was just eighty yards offshore from the bluff at the western end of the beach, and she could hardly see it. The streets below were running with water and cars were sending sheets of water over the footpaths and those unlucky enough to be on them.

She sat in a cane chair and ate her bowl of fruit.

By the time she'd finished, the sun had come out again, bringing its optimism. Only the oppressive humidity remained to remind her of the tropical downpour.

She went back inside and wandered about in a desultory fashion tidying things up and straightening things that she'd already straightened. The truth was, she was trying to resist going in to see Elliot again. In the end, she gave up, went to his door, and knocked gently.

"Yep."

The man was awake.

She pushed open the door.

He had a derisory smile. "Ah, the Lady with the Lamp."

"I doubt Florence Nightingale was as ignorant of medical things as me. How are you feeling?"

"Stronger. I might get up for a bit."

She nodded. "Do you want a cup of tea?"

He nodded.

Ten minutes later, they were both sitting on the balcony.

Elliot was running a finger around the top rim of his mug. "Emma, can I share with you something really weird – " he paused, "amazing, actually – that happened to me last night?" He shook his head. "I'm struggling to find the words…and I need a bit of help… to process it."

Emma found it hard to believe Elliot was ever lost for words, but she kept her thoughts to herself. "Certainly," she said.

Elliot leaned back in his cane chair and began to tell the story of all that happened to him the day before.

It was an extraordinary tale, almost ridiculous. Emma would not have believed it had it not been for Elliot's pale, stricken face.

For a long while, she said nothing.

"Wow!" she said eventually. "Amazing."

Elliot nodded. "Crazy."

They were silent for a while.

"Tell me about your parents." she said. "What do you know about them?"

"Well that's just it. They were just ordinary people. Dad was your archetypal English civil servant with a love of fine art and fly-tying. And mum…" he smiled, "well, she was terrific. She was half Chinese. Dad met her in Malaya."

"So she has no family here in Hong Kong."

"No."

They were both silent for a while. However, Emma's mind was racing. Eventually, she couldn't contain herself any longer.

"Who gave you your jade pendant?"

"Mum did. She left it for me after she died – just recently."

"Oh! I'm so sorry. How long ago was that?"

"About ten weeks."

She nodded and said softly, "So her death is still pretty raw?"

Elliot nodded, and dropped his head.

Something of his pain reached her, and it took a while before she could speak. She placed a hand over his. "Elliot, I'm going to say something that might shock you. I do so only in the hope that it might help you make sense of things."

Elliot turned to her.

"I actually know what is symbolized by your carved pendant."

He waited for her to say more.

Emma took a deep breath. "A dragon head enclosed in a circle is a symbol of the triad society. Only senior triad operatives would dare to wear it, and they would do so secretly."

Elliot snorted a laugh. It was harsh. "So you are accusing me of being a triad gang leader?"

Emma said nothing.

"Hmph. The only gang activity I've heard of in Hong Kong is the cartel of boatmen who look after the boats on Kellett Island. Evidently, you cross them at your peril."

She smiled. "I'm not accusing you of anything, Elliot. I'm just telling you what your pendant signifies."

"And my, er...brother, had the piece of jade that was cut out from the middle..."

"Which means..."

"That he is probably a senior operative in a triad society." Elliot rubbed the sides of his temple. "Good grief!"

"Do you remember anything else about what he said? Did he give any clues at all?"

"He...he said something which didn't make sense."

"What was that?"

"When he saw my pendant, he asked me something."

"What?"

"He asked if I were 14K."

Chapter 8

K ai got out of the taxi and began to walk down the crowded
street toward the temple of Tin Hau. It was an odd feeling
to be without his bodyguards. He couldn't decide whether he felt
liberated or vulnerable. It didn't matter. His real concern was
meeting his brother, and trying to get some sort of explanation for
his existence from his father.

As he walked down Temple Street, shouldering his way through
the crowds, he swung the bead around his forefinger. Clockwise for
entreaty; anti-clockwise for power and wrath.

It wasn't long before he saw Elliot. He was waiting where Kai
had told him to wait, beside one of the pillars of the temple's gate-
way. The pillar was topped with the same green glazed tiles as the
temple building behind it. He paused to look at it. Waiting at a
temple must help with luck, surely. The goddess Tin Hau, so revered
by Hong Kong's fishing community, would approve – wouldn't she?

Kai noted that Elliot had made an effort to dress differently
from him, as instructed. He was wearing some sort of canvas top.
Kai sniffed. It looked scruffy and would be hot. He ran his eyes over
his twin brother, then said curtly, "Follow me."

"And good morning to you too." Elliot levered himself from the pillar and followed him as he walked back up Temple Street. "Where are we going?" his brother asked.

Kai replied in Cantonese. *"Daih paih dong."*

"What?"

"To a street stall." He pointed to one just in front of him. "The pineapple buns here are good. You sit here while I make a phone call."

"Yes sir," said Elliot, giving him a mock salute.

Kai walked fifty yards further up the street and into a café. Its owner was standing behind a tray of glazed ducks, ladling bean curd into bowls. Kai pointed to the phone, and the owner nodded assent. He flipped the bead on his finger into his hand and began dialing.

The phone was eventually answered, and he asked to speak to his father.

There was a long wait – there always was. It was part of their ritual.

Two minutes later, he heard the voice of the Dragonhead. "Yes?"

"Sir, Kai here." He paused. What on earth should he say? He wanted to rail against the man and curse him for his secrets and deception. Kai wanted to demand answers. Conflicting emotions boiled within him, tangling with each other. Just who was this man who was so obviously his twin? Why hadn't he been told about him? But he knew better than to betray any emotion to his father. Repeated thrashings as a child had taught him that.

He swallowed. "Sir, I have seen a man who looks exactly like me on Hong Kong Island. He is called Elliot Gleeson, and is visiting from England." Kai paused. "Sir, how can this be? Who is this man who is so obviously my brother?"

His question was met by silence. It took some time before his father's reedy voice came through. "He is no one you need to worry about. He will be gone soon. Leave him alone."

Kai knew he was gripping the phone too hard. His tendons were standing out, and his heart was pounding. *You can't casually dismiss the fact that I have a twin brother. It is ridiculous. I have every right to know. Who is he… and who am I?*

He spat out his politeness through clenched teeth.

"Sir, he has a connection with us."

"How so?"

"He wears a pendant, a round piece of jade from which my own dragon's head was carved."

There was a pause. "Ah yes."

'Ah yes.' Is that all you have to say Father? Damn you! Tell me what's going on! He breathed in deeply. "I take it this does not surprise you."

"Not entirely. Does he know what it signifies?"

"I don't think so. He knows nothing of 14K."

"See that it stays that way." His father hung up.

Kai stood there for a moment, his head bowed, pressed against the end of the phone. "Aaargh." He banged the phone against the wall, and then replaced it in its cradle. Kai had not even been given the chance to say that he and Elliot were just two-hundred yards away and wanted to visit him.

He stepped out onto the bustling street and began walking back to the street stall, where he'd left Elliot. For a few fleeting moments, he could see him between the people on the street. Elliot was craning his neck, obviously looking for him.

Kai noted the group of six young men lounging in chairs at a noodle bar a short distance from Elliot.

There was going to be drama.

Kai breathed in deeply. *Let it begin.*

The men launched themselves at Kai when he drew level with them.

He yelled, but someone put a hand over his mouth, and he was summarily bundled through the doorway into a small warehouse.

Once inside, he could see that it was half filled with boxes of food and bags of rice.

The men released him. One of them was Ah Ming, his bodyguard.

Kai nodded to him and straightened his shirt.

Three of the men braced themselves against the little side door into the warehouse to prevent anyone from pushing it open. Then Ah Ming and the other men began to shout and bang their fists against the wall.

Kai sat down on a bag of rice and began flicking the bead around his finger.

Moments later, he heard the voice of Elliot calling from outside. "Kai. Are you all right? Yell something. Let me know."

Kai said nothing.

"Kai, if you don't yell out, I'll be coming in."

The men at door braced themselves.

Seconds passed.

What happened next seemed to occur in slow motion.

The little wooden door came off its hinges and flew across the air with three men underneath it. Elliot had not just tried to push the door open. He'd hit it at a very fast run. Elliot landed on top of the door and spun round at a crouch, looking for those who had kidnapped Kai, ready to fight.

It took a moment for Elliot to see him sitting calmly on a rice sack.

A puzzled look crossed Elliot's face. "What the…?"

The men under and beside the door picked themselves off the floor and circled round to stand next to Kai.

Then they clapped.

Elliot glanced round at them. Realization dawned. "This was all a set-up, then?"

Kai ignored him, turned to one of his men, Ah Pui, and gave him a nod.

At that point, an Indian man ran into the warehouse and began to shout his outrage at having his door broken. Kai beckoned to him, and handed over a wad of money that would more than cover the cost of repairs. The man had the good sense to accept it, and went off grumbling, presumably to find a toolbox.

Ah Pui walked up to Elliot and prodded him in the chest. "You want to fight? I give you a fight."

Elliot held up his hand in a placating gesture. "No, no, I don't want to fight."

Despite his small stature, Ah Pui was an excellent street fighter. He was very fast, which was the reason Kai had chosen him.

Ah Pui persisted. "Then we have a play fight, eh?" He spun on his feet and kicked Elliot in the thigh.

Elliot rubbed his leg ruefully. "I don't want to, but if I must." He lifted his hands to ward off another attack and bent to a crouch.

What followed was an embarrassment. Ah Pui was lightning fast and obviously enjoying the chance to show off in front of the others. Elliot was made to look like a lumbering, incompetent Westerner. Kai scowled. It was embarrassing to think that Elliot could be his brother.

He was about to put a stop to it all, when Ah Pui spun round the back of Elliot and gave him a bear hug, barely half a second.

It was a mistake.

Elliot suddenly jack-knifed down and grabbed Ah Pui's ankles from between his legs. He moved with amazing speed.

Poor Ah Pui could do nothing. He was caught and could not move.

Elliot allowed himself to fall backward and crash on top of his tormentor.

Kai nodded in appreciation. His brother's apparent slowness and clumsiness had been a ruse.

Ah Pui was badly winded. It took a while for the little street fighter to pick himself up and slink to a corner of the warehouse to recover both his breath and his dignity.

Elliot stood in front of Kai with his hands on his hips. He was not looking pleased. "Have you quite finished?"

Kai slipped the chain and bead into his pocket. "Yes, I have."

His brother continued to scowl. "Why all this crap?"

"You've earned the right to see my auntie."

It was an odd feeling pushing through the throng of people on Temple Street walking beside a twin brother. An invisible bond linked them. It didn't have to be acknowledged; it simply was. And it changed everything. There were, however, many things that Elliot very definitely did want to explore with Kai.

"Let's stop and have a talk," he said.

Kai nodded, as if he'd been expecting Elliot's request. He pointed to a café. "In there. They have a phone." As the two of them sat down, Kai spoke to the café owner in Chinese. A short time later, a pot of Jasmine tea arrived together with a plate of egg tarts.

Elliot picked one of them up. "Kai, you and I are twins. That is obvious."

His brother said nothing.

Elliot chose his words carefully. "Who do you think…who do you believe…your mother and father to be?"

His brother tensed and clenched one hand into a fist. "Who do you think they are?" he fired back.

"I was born here in Hong Kong. My father was a mid-level bureaucrat working in the Governor's Office. And my mother was half European, half Chinese. They'd met in Malaya." Elliot leaned back in his chair. "What have you been told about your parents?"

"My father is…er, a Chinese business man."

"What? Here in Hong Kong?"

"Possibly."

Elliot leaned forward. "What do you mean possibly?"

Kai ignored him. "And my mother was English. She died in childbirth."

"Tell me about your father."

Kai took out his bead and chain, slipped his finger through the ivory ring at the end of the chain and began spinning the bead around his forefinger.

"I never really knew him."

Elliot had the impression that he wasn't being told the whole truth, but decided that he'd pushed hard enough. "What is that thing you spin around on your finger?"

"It is a Tibetan prayer wheel. The ring has prayer engraved on it. Every time it spins, the prayer is meant to go to the gods." He laughed. "So I swing it around in case it helps." He shrugged. "I'm still alive, so it must work."

It was a bleak comment, but again, Elliot chose not to pursue it. He changed the subject. "When shall we visit your auntie?"

"When are you available? Are you free in the evenings?"

"Mornings would be better. I sometimes have to lecture in the evenings."

"Mornings are not possible. Auntie works with an English missionary teaching kids in the Walled City. She's a Christian, so she's a little bit crazy."

Elliot dusted crumbs from his canvas smock top. "I suppose your auntie is my auntie too."

Kai glanced at him. "I suppose she is."

"Tell me about her."

"Auntie is my *Kai ma*, my godmother. She's really the only mother I have ever had. Auntie is the daughter of my father's Number One Wife, and she has raised me since she was eighteen years old."

"Is that why you speak English so well?"

"Yes. She made me go to school and gave me extra lessons at home." Kai screwed up his nose. "It wasn't easy because I also had jobs in the Walled City."

"The Walled City?"

Kai waved his hand dismissively. "It's a place in Kowloon."

"Some of your words have an American accent."

"I watch American films."

Elliot shook his head. Sitting with his brother was a surreal experience. "Let's organize a meeting with your auntie, then."

Kai got to his feet. "I'll call her." He stepped over to the telephone on the wall of the café.

Elliot lifted his teacup to his lips, but the action was actually used to disguise the fact that he was watching the numbers Kai was dialing.

After his brother had dialed, he stepped close to the phone and began to speak secretively, in low tones. Elliot could barely hear it, and what he could hear was in Chinese. He took out a ballpoint pen from his pocket and wrote the number Kai had dialed on a paper napkin. Then he folded it over.

It was quite a while before Kai rejoined him. When he did, Kai pointed to the pen and the napkin on the table. "What is that?" he demanded.

"That's to remind me to get your telephone number so I can get hold of you if I need to."

"Oh." His brother seemed to consider it for a moment, and then said "Okay. If you call this number, the message will get to me and I will phone you back." He gave Elliot the number. Kai then pointed to the remaining egg tart. "Have you eaten enough?"

"Yeah. I'm going a bit steady with food at the moment. I got food poisoning four days ago."

Kai raised an eyebrow.

Elliot continued. "Yeah. After the meal you interrupted last time we met."

"Are you blaming me for it?"

"No. I'm saying that I've had a bit of an uncomfortable time, recently."

Kai nodded. "But you were still prepared to fight?"

Elliot said nothing.

His brother got to his feet. "I will pick you up at 6pm tomorrow. I'll be in a taxi."

Chapter 9

The colonel handed Emma her drink and sat himself opposite her in an armchair.

"What do you think of our new Cross-Harbor Tunnel?"

Emma took a sip of her lemonade and bitters. "Very impressive. How long has it been open?"

"Just a few weeks."

She leaned back and looked again at the view across the eastern approaches of Victoria Harbor. Emma was sitting on the veranda of Lyemun Barracks on the northeastern corner of Hong Kong Island. It was, she had learned, the home of the Depot and Record Office of the Hong Kong Military Service Corps. She gazed at the scene and was grateful that the Colonel had suggested they meet there. The officer's mess had spectacular views and a peaceful, indulgent, colonial atmosphere. It was a perfect place to enjoy a cold drink.

The colonel drank deeply from his glass of beer, sighed and said, "And how can I help you, Miss Templeton?"

"I understand you have been briefed as to why I am here, but I wanted to chat with you off the record, in the hope that you might suggest how I can make some progress." She shrugged. "To be quite honest, I'm not getting very far."

"I gather you are trying to get a handle on what drives the recidivism rate of our prisoners here in Hong Kong."

"Yes." She paused. "My understanding is that it is, in good part, due to the activities of the triad organizations."

"That wouldn't surprise me."

"The trouble is, the only triad members I have interviewed in the prisons have been very low-level operatives. I've not managed to learn much."

The colonel pursed his lips. "I'm not sure I can help you."

"Does the military ever brush up against triad activities?"

"Well, there are places where we have to be pretty sensitive."

"Really? Tell me more."

"One place is The Walled City."

Emma waited for him to continue.

"It's a small area, about six and a half acres, just behind Kai Tak airfield. About 35,000 people are crammed into more than three-hundred apartment blocks." He chuckled. "All of them have been constructed without a single contribution from an architect."

Emma was staggered. "How can that be? It's right in the heart of Kowloon City."

The colonel smiled. "I know. It all came about as a result of an accident in history. The Walled City was not included in the ninety-nine year lease that ceded Kowloon, Hong Kong, and the New Territories to the British in 1889. Evidently, this was because it was home to various Chinese magistrates and military personnel."

"Does the city have a wall?"

"Not any more. The Japanese dismantled it during World War II and used it as rubble to extend Kai Tak airport into the harbor."

Emma frowned. "So, who actually owns it? The Communists have taken over China now."

"Well, that's my point. Our military can't go in there; and we don't allow the Communist government access to it." The colonel shrugged. "So the triads have taken it over, and it has become a very fertile place for their activities."

She leaned forward. "Would it be possible for me to visit this place?"

"I wouldn't suggest it. It's not a nice place. And I certainly wouldn't be allowed to take you."

"So, there's nothing you can do?"

The colonel passed a hand across his stubble. "Well, I have to go to the prison on Lan Tau Island in a few days. It houses some of our worst offenders: many from the Walled City. You could come with me and interview them, if you like."

Emma's heart sank. She would doubtless just meet more junior gang members. But anything was better than nothing.

"Thank you. I'd appreciate that."

"Come to think of it," said the colonel. I think the governor of the prison there has some sort of link with this place."

"What? Lyemun Barracks?"

"Yes. I'm not sure of the details, but I think he may have witnessed the massacre that occurred."

Emma raised her eyebrows. "What massacre?"

"The Japanese executed one-hundred British soldiers here in 1941."

It was six o'clock before Emma managed to get back to the unit at Repulse Bay. She'd been interviewing people throughout the day and was keen to have a shower and change into something comfortable.

There was no sign of Elliot, so she was spared his teasing of her business attire. There was, however, plenty of evidence of him having been around. His stuff was strewn all over the kitchen bench. A small canvas bag with a round plywood base sat at one end. Emma presumed that the things cluttering the bench came from it. She fingered the different items, understanding only some of them. There was a ball of twine, some small brass shackles, pliers, a knife, and a strange leather object with a buckle on it. She could see that he'd been working with some thick black string, weaving it into a patterned toggle. It looked to be nearly finished.

Emma lined the items neatly up at the far end of the bench. As she did, she reflected again on the fantastic story he'd shared with her three days ago, of meeting a brother he never knew existed. When Elliot told her about the dragon head there was little doubt in her mind that his brother would have to be a senior member of the triads. She drummed her fingers on the bench. If only she could find a way to meet him and talk with him: it could be the break-through she was looking for in her work.

Her musings were interrupted by the phone. She picked up the receiver.

"Hello; Emma Templeton speaking."

A female voice replied. "Oh, I'm sorry. I may have the wrong number. I was hoping to speak to Elliot Gleeson." The woman spoke with a soft purr.

"No, you've got the right number, but Elliot is not here."

There was a pause. "Oh…are you his girlfriend?"

Emma was shocked at the question. "No, no. I just live in the room next door. We share an accommodation complex. Why do you ask?"

"I'm so sorry. I didn't mean to pry. My name is Kendal Shiffer. I was thinking of, er…having dinner with him." She rushed on. "I just didn't want any complications."

Emma forced a laugh. "You want to know what you could be letting yourself in for."

"Something like that. Yes."

Neither of them spoke for a while.

Emma was surprised when Kendal continued the conversation. "Woman to woman: what's he like? Have you known him long?"

There was no mistaking the sincerity in Kendal's question. Emma rather suspected that Kendal Shiffer had been hurt by earlier romances. She couldn't help but think, with some bitterness, that at least she'd had some.

"Hardly at all. I've only known him for four days."

"Oh."

A kaleidoscope of pictures crossed Emma's mind: Elliot on the beach, Elliot lying indolently across a balcony chair, and Elliot weak and helpless in bed.

She swallowed. "I can tell you that he steals my breakfast provisions and leaves his stuff lying around everywhere."

Kendal laughed.

"Elliot is also fun. He's anti convention and anti all things pretentious. Some of the fun is a smokescreen, however. Deep down, he's grieving the death of his mother."

"Oh, I didn't know that."

"He hides it well."

"So he is a man of secrets."

"Not really. It's just that he's protective of himself and others. He's naturally a bit adversarial, and hates people having control over him." She paused. "I also think he's an easy man to underestimate."

"An iron fist in a velvet glove?"

"No, he doesn't have a velvet glove. He has the multi-colored mittens of a child, all sun and fun, but the fist inside is no less real."

"Yes," said Kendal slowly. "I've seen something of that fist. He can take charge when he wants."

"Hmm, that's Elliot."

Kendal gave a soft laugh. "I thought you said you didn't know him."

"Oh no. I don't. Well, not really." Emma rushed on. "Um…may I be cheeky enough to ask: What are you like? Would it work between you two?"

"What do you think? You seem to be pretty good at summing people up."

"Elliot has told me a bit about you, but not a lot. And it was actually in the context of another conversation."

"Oh really. What did he say?"

"That you were blond, beautiful, and had legs that go right up to your arm-pits."

"Hmm, carnal but nice."

"He also said you were clever and headed up an investment company." Emma paused. "He was pretty taken with you."

"He told you that?"

"No, but I could tell."

"Well, Emma; thanks for your insight." She paused. "I think I'd like to meet you some day. I suspect there is quite a lot more to you than meets the eye."

Emma shook her head. "I doubt that. I'm five foot six with brown hair – brown everything in fact. I'm tragically unremarkable."

"Can you ask Elliot to call me?"

She gave Emma the phone number.

Elliot pushed the door of the unit open with his knee, and carried the shopping through to the kitchen area.

Emma was at the sink washing up her teacup.

"I've bought some glazed duck and some bok choy. My brother says I ought to try it."

"How did your meeting with him go?"

"Interesting. We're planning to meet his auntie tomorrow night to get some answers. Kai calls her a crazy Christian. I'm not sure what that means. Evidently, she teaches kids somewhere." He handed her the bok choy. "If you give these a light boil, I'll heat up the duck." He smiled. "I asked them chop it up. Wasn't sure I was up to doing it myself. The thing still had a beak."

"Small mercies. Thanks." She took hold of the bok choy. "This is nicely exotic. I was planning to make myself spaghetti Bolognese."

"You should be grateful I didn't bring back some one-hundred-year-old eggs."

Emma raised an eyebrow.

"Seriously," he said. The albumin is dark gray, and the yolk is black. Kai tells me they stick them in a tray of mud and ash." He wrinkled his nose. "I sniffed one. It smelled like ammonia and Camembert."

"Thanks for sparing me. By the way, you've had a phone call."

"Really. Who from?"

"Kendal Shiffer. She wants you to call her."

Elliot froze, and his heart began to thump. "Did she say why?"

"Well, she asked quite a lot about you. She wanted to know if you were safe enough to have dinner with. I told her you were feckless and irresponsible."

He couldn't repress a grin.

Emma pointed a bunch of bok choy at him. "I advise you to go carefully with that woman, Elliot. She's been wounded and is testing you out. You've probably only got one shot at persuading her to continue seeing you."

"Where's her number?"

"By the telephone."

"Thanks Em."

Elliot walked to the phone, took a deep breath, and dialed the number.

It was answered after the fifth ring. "Kendal Shiffer speaking."

Aah, the softness of her voice – the warmth of her...he swallowed. "I understand you are looking for another sailing lesson."

She laughed. "But only from someone safe and reliable."

"I assure you that I put an absolute priority on my students' well-being."

"Well, you now have a chance to prove it. I have a free evening tomorrow night. As I was rude enough to not be available last time, I'm offering to rectify it tomorrow."

Tomorrow. *Oh no!* Realization dawned. Elliot slapped his forehead. *No, no no!* He'd promised to meet with Kai and go to his auntie's house. He groaned in anguish. What was he to do?

"What's the matter, sailor?" Kendal's voice was soft, but Elliot managed to hear a slight waver in her voice." He gritted his teeth. The last thing he wanted to do was to disappoint this exquisite woman. Emma's words rose unbidden into his consciousness. *You've probably only got one shot at persuading her to continue seeing you.*

"The answer is yes. Of course," he said quickly. "I just need to reorganize some things."

"Is that a maybe or a yes?"

"That is a definite, enthusiastic, and very grateful yes."

There was a pause. "Hmm. I'll pick you up at 6."

The phone went dead.

Elliot rested his forehead against the wall and groaned. Why did life have to be so complicated?

"Are you okay?" Emma called over to him from the kitchen.

"Yes and no." He groaned again in anguish. "I've double-booked myself for tomorrow night."

"Then you need to make a phone call to fix it. I'll get you a lime soda."

Emma's words steadied him to the extent that he was able to dial another number on the phone.

A woman's voice answered in Chinese. Elliot said hesitantly, "Is Kai there?"

The voice came back. "You wait."

It was a long time before the phone came alive again. He heard Kai's voice, just one word. "Yes?"

"Kai, it is Elliot here. I'm afraid I have a problem with tomorrow night."

"What problem? We made an agreement."

Elliot squeezed his eyes shut, hating what he was having to do. "I know. I'm very sorry. I have a very important meeting with someone."

"You have a meeting more important than meeting my auntie?"

"No, no. It is not more important. It is just more time critical."

There was silence.

Eventually, Kai's voice came through. "I am very angry. Is this person you are meeting a man or a woman?"

Elliot cleared his throat. "Er, a woman actually."

"A woman!" shouted Kai. "How can this be more important?"

"Kai, Kai. She is very important. She is one of Hong Kong's top investors – very rich."

"Is she beautiful?"

"Very."

"Ahh. Who is she?"

Should he tell him? Would it be betraying a confidence? Then again, would not telling Kai, cause him to distrust Elliot? The questions swirled in his mind.

Before he could heed the warning bells in his head, he heard himself say, "Her name is Kendal Shiffer."

"Is she in Kowloon?"

"No, in Hong Kong, on Peak Road, wherever that is."

"Ahh, that is in Magazine Gap, just under Victoria Peak. Very rich area."

Elliot interrupted. "Kai, I'm very sorry. Believe me, I wouldn't postpone unless it was important." He paused. "How can I fix this'?

"You can't. I will fix it." With that, Kai abruptly ended the call.

Elliot slowly replaced the phone into its cradle.

Emma walked up beside him and handed him his drink. "I think you need this."

He grunted. "Thanks Em, but I think I'll have a shower." Elliot made an attempt at a smile. "It is where I do my best thinking. Then, I'll call auntie myself and apologize."

Emma watched Elliot walk away. She was still holding his drink. He cut a forlorn figure. The poor fellow was caught up in an extraordinary set of circumstances, and her heart went out to him.

And what was it he had called her? *Em.* She smiled. No one had ever called her Em, before now. She liked it.

The water in the saucepan was beginning to boil, so she switched it off, uncertain now when she and Elliot would be eating. She walked disconsolately into the living area. Her thoughts dwelt very much on Elliot, but also on her own need to interview his brother, Kai. Could it ever come about? And if so, how could she organize it?

The more she pondered the question, the more she was convinced that the key to the possibility was Kai's auntie. She sounded like a woman for whom goodness was important. Perhaps she could be persuaded to facilitate a meeting between her and Kai.

But how? She didn't have her number. Elliot had it, but it was in his pocket…and she certainly didn't want to ask him for it, or implicate him in any way in case things backfired.

Emma shook her head at Elliot's cheekiness in spying on Kai to get his auntie's number. He'd been scurrilous.

Unbidden, a terrible temptation began to form in her mind.

She dismissed it. But it came again and was insistent. *It's probably the only chance you'll get.* She shook her head, but the idea would not go away.

She could at least give it a try. After all, the chances of it succeeding were remote.

She went to her room and returned with her makeup bag. Wondering if she was doing the right thing, she took out the scissors and cut a single strand of her hair. Then, she opened the jar of foundation cream and picked up the tweezers. With great care, she cut tiny lengths of hair – less than an eighth of an inch long. Then she picked them up with the tweezers, dabbed them with a touch of foundation makeup, and stuck them on the inside of the holes on the fingerplate of the rotary dial phone. The stage was set.

Emma put away her makeup bag, found a pen and paper, and waited.

Elliot felt marginally better after his shower, but it didn't prevent him from staring at the phone with trepidation. Since arriving in Hong Kong, his whole world had been turned upside down and his identity challenged. Just who was he really? How could Kai be his twin brother?

He ran a tongue over his lips and began to dial the number on the napkin.

A woman's voice answered. "Hello."

Elliot froze. What should he say?

He put the phone down, leaned against the wall, and rubbed his temples. *Don't be stupid. Get on with it.*

With a sigh, he picked up the phone and called the number again.

It was answered immediately. "Hello. Who's speaking?"

Elliot swallowed. "Hello. I am Kai's brother Elliot. Are you his auntie?"

There was a pause, then Elliot heard her say, "Yes, I am. Hello Elliot. Kai has told me about you."

Elliot was amazed at how natural she sounded. He stammered, "I am...err, I'm looking forward to meeting you."

"Yes. You're coming tomorrow night with Kai."

"Well that's the problem," said Elliot. "Something important has come up, and I can't come. I'm very sorry. I wanted to phone and apologize in person because I want to see you very much."

"Do you wish to see me at another time?"

"Oh yes. Yes please," Elliot breathed out a sigh of relief.

"Organize it with Kai, then. There should be no problem."

"Thank you for your understanding." Even as he said the words, Elliot was conscious of one question that cried out to be answered. He continued to speak.

"Auntie," he paused, "are you really my Auntie?"

"I'm close enough to it, so yes dear, I am."

Emma was not surprised to hear Elliot say that he'd eat later, because he needed to go for a walk along the beach to think things through.

She thought that a walk would probably do him good, and bent down to switch off the oven.

Emma then picked up the piece of paper in front of her and sat down beside the telephone. A close inspection of the tiny bits of hair in the holes of the phone's fingerplate told her that six of the numbers had been used. She wrote them down.

Then she sat back and looked at what she'd already written on the paper when hearing Elliot dial the phone. The sound of the whirr of the fingerplate returning to zero after each number was dialed told her whether the digit dialed was bigger or smaller than the previous one. All she'd done was to rank the different sounds in size. Once she had factored in these figures with numbers had actually been used to dial, Emma was left with a simple mathematical problem.

Ten minutes later, she'd solved it. She had the phone number of Kai's auntie.

The question that now tormented her was whether or not she should use it. Guilt and curiosity twisted round each other like writhing snakes. Each paused occasionally to lunge at her.

Eventually, she could stand it no longer. She snatched up the phone and dialed the number.

A voice answered. "Hello."

"Oh, hello. My name is Emma Templeton. Am I speaking with Kai's auntie?"

"Yes," came the guarded reply.

"Please don't be alarmed. I'm a friend of Elliot's."

There was a pause. "How can I help you?"

"I've been sent to Hong Kong to help determine the level of threat posed by triad societies to the UK. There is concern about the spread of its, er..."

"...evil?" finished the auntie.

"Yes." Emma rushed on. "I don't want to put you in a difficult position..."

"Why would you be putting me in such a position?"

"Because, I very much suspect that Kai is a senior member of a triad society. Elliot has told me about the jade dragon pendants. He didn't understand their significance, but, er...I do."

"Oh, I see." There was a pause. "What is it that you want?"

"I would love the chance to speak with Kai, to try and understand the philosophy and thinking behind the triads." She rushed on. "I assure you, I don't have any connections to the police, and Kai would be quite safe. I'd just welcome the chance to learn from a senior member of the organization."

"But you must know that it is a very secret organization. No one would be allowed to tell you anything."

"Oh yes. I understand that, and respect that. I don't need any specific details about who, where, and what, I just want to understand the philosophy that drives it."

"I still don't think I can help you. There is no way I would ever place Kai in danger. He is a son to me, and it would be an act of betrayal."

Emma's heart fell. "I understand."

"What made you think that I would help you see Kai?"

"Because you, like me, are a Christian, and want to see a halt to evil."

There was a long silence.

Emma held her breath.

The auntie spoke. "I will not bring harm to Kai in any way, but what I will do is show you something of the power of the triad society in a place where it is best seen. Then, perhaps, you will know what to fear, and what to prepare for."

"Oh. Where's that?"

"I will show you *Hak Nam*."

"What is *Hak Nam*?"

"The name means, 'City of Darkness.' Its other name is 'The Walled City.'"

Chapter 10

The driver leaped out of his car door and managed to open the door for Kendal before Elliot could get to it. Elliot did, however arrive next to him in time to see her long legs unfold and swing round to get out of the car. Kendal's aqua-blue dress was cut very short and showed off acres of thigh. Elliot had needed to survive the tension of sitting inches from them for the last twenty minutes.

They hadn't talked much in the car. In truth, Elliot found himself in the totally unfamiliar position of feeling overwhelmed. The ready repartee he could normally conjure on any occasion deserted him. He held out his hand and helped Kendal to her feet.

She offered him a shy smile as she stood in front of him for a moment, chest to chest. Her hair flowed softly over her shoulders, just as he'd remembered it – golden honey.

Elliot risked saying something with candid honesty. "Kendal, you are amazingly beautiful, and I feel way out of my league."

Kendal looked at him without saying anything for a moment. Then she said, "Sometimes, my league does not treat people kindly." She smiled away any risk of embarrassment. "Shall we go in?"

Elliot offered his arm, and they walked toward the basement of

Sutherland House. There was a door with a sign above that simply said, 'The GoDown.' A smartly dressed, round-faced Chinese man stood at the door.

Kendal smiled at him. "Good evening Mr. Wen-ping."

"Missy Kendal. It is good to see you."

As the man opened the door for them, the raunchy sound of the Rolling Stones singing 'Brown Sugar' enveloped them.

"What is this place?" whispered Elliot.

"It's a place for badly behaving expats – quite fun. I thought we'd have a drink here before we walked round the corner to the Hilton."

"The Hilton!"

"Yes."

Elliot swallowed. He looked around him. The place was buzzing with Westerners all chatting and laughing. Even though some were still in business attire, the place had a laid-back informal atmosphere that Elliot approved of.

They picked out a table and began to walk toward it. Kendal, he noticed, attracted a few glances. It was little wonder. Elliot was trying not to stare at her himself. Every step she took, she turned into a seductive dance. Elliot shook his head. He was fairly sure she was unaware of the impact she was making. Marshalling his tortured sensibilities, he sat down.

"They serve wine here straight from the barrels," said Kendal. "What will you have?"

Elliot held up a hand. "There is only so much humiliation a man can take when a beautiful woman takes him to dinner. Please let him at least pay for the drinks."

A pretty blond English waitress came to their table. "Hi guys. What will you have?"

Kendal smiled at her. "Hi Lottie. May I have a whiskey sour?"

"And I'll have a beer," said Elliot.

The waitress left.

"You seem to know everyone," said Elliot.

"I've been taken here a few times. It's fun. The trick is to know when to leave. It can get rowdy."

The music was not quite loud enough to discourage conversation, but it discouraged intimacy. Elliot wondered whether this was the reason Kendal had chosen the location. Rod Stewart's 'Maggie Mae' was now booming from the speakers.

"How long has this place been open," he asked.

"About five years, I think. Do you like it?"

"Yes. It's nicely unpretentious."

"A bit like you," she said.

It was a pretty compliment, one that took a moment for Elliot to fully grasp. He smiled. "What made you risk going out with a sailor?"

"I saw some interesting qualities."

"I'm not going to ask you what they are."

"Good, because I wouldn't tell you."

"So, it's not just because sailors leave town?"

Kendal laughed. "That might be part of it. So don't press it."

He smiled. "You know that I'm madly in love with you, don't you?"

"No, I don't know that. But I do know that I have your attention."

"I'll settle for that – for now."

She smiled.

The lilting words of Don McLean's 'American Pie' filled the room.

Their drinks arrived. Kendal nodded her thanks and returned her attention to Elliot.

"Do you have family?"

Elliot instantly felt a pang of grief. He dropped his head. The innocent question had prized open the lid of a box he'd been trying to keep shut. How on earth could he even answer the question? He'd once thought he was an only child, but this was palpably not now the case. Elliot elected to speak only of his parents. "Dad died five years ago, and mum three months ago."

Kendal reached out a hand and placed it over his. "I'm so sorry. I didn't know."

Elliot sniffed. "Nah. It's okay."

Kendal did not remove her hand. She tilted her head and looked at him quizzically. "Tell me about your mum. What was she like?"

He leaned back in his seat, sliding his imprisoned hand free.

"I…I didn't mean to intrude."

Elliot waved a dismissive hand. "No, no. You're just being caring – being wonderful, actually. It's just that, er…I've not really verbalized…" he trailed off.

"You don't have to talk about it if you don't want to."

He grunted. "It's a weird thing, death, isn't it? Makes you think about why things bother to exist and why they die." Elliot shook his head. "Perhaps it's a good thing that we have to think about these things occasionally." He allowed his eyes to take in the laughter and hubbub going on around them. "Death is sort of…the final test for what you believe, isn't it?" He forced a laugh. "I'm not sure I've allowed myself to think much at all."

"What are you thinking now?"

Elliot wished she'd take his hand back. But she didn't. He sighed. "It's made me think that how I've been living to date is a pretty weak response to the miracle of existence."

Neither spoke for a while.

Kendal broke the silence. "My father died last year, and I'm still not over it." She smiled weakly. "I keep expecting him to come into the room. It's weird, isn't it?"

"Do you miss him?"

"Very much. It was one of the reasons I decided to learn to sail. I was tired of moping around."

"Do you think it'll work?"

She smiled. "It's certainly been a diversion." She changed the subject. "Did the major make it back to the yacht club without his rudder?"

Elliot chuckled. "No. He had to be towed in by the rescue boat. The bloke wasn't too happy."

Kendal smiled, then asked. "Why do you love sailing?"

"Dunno." He tried to think. "Two reasons, I suppose. The first is the community of crazies you meet when you mess about with boats. And the second is…" he tried to find the right words. "Um… the fantastic sensation of floating, and being driven through the water by the force of wind alone."

Kendal smiled. "Well, you certainly managed to share some of that the other day. I'm grateful."

"You're welcome."

Elliot edged his hand forward, pretending nonchalance, hoping. Sadly, the move was only met by another question.

"Do you plan to make a career of sailing?"

"Sort of. I really want to get into the world of yacht design. I've been trained in marine engineering, and I'm currently doing a type of apprenticeship with Camper and Nicholson at Gosport." He smiled. "They don't really pay me much at the moment, so I teach sailing for the RYA two days a week."

"The RYA?"

"The Royal Yachting Association." He changed the subject. "What about you? What's your ambition?"

Kendal smiled. "To survive."

"Survive?"

"Yes. Most people have an ambition to reach the top of their game before they retire." She shrugged. "With the death of my father, I was forced to the top straight away."

"Are you coping?"

"Barely. I'm good with numbers, and I love seeing possibilities, it's just that it all comes with a lot of responsibility. It can be over-whelming."

"Don't you have anyone to help?"

"Oh yes. Uncle Lachlan runs the company with me." She sighed. "That's part of the problem. "He doesn't really take me, or my contributions, very seriously. He'd dearly like to be in total control, so we have a bit of battle."

Elliot reached across and took her hand. "I wish I could say something helpful. But yours is a world I know nothing about."

Kendal laughed and removed her hand. "Yes. We are very different characters."

"Different characters? Why?"

She tilted her head. "If a bat and a ball cost $1.10 in total, and the bat costs $1.00 more than the ball. How much does the ball cost?"

"Ten cents," he replied.

She smiled. "And that's the difference between the two of us."

"What do you mean?" he retorted.

"Yours is the answer that intuitively springs to mind, but it's wrong. If the ball cost 10 cents and the bat costs $1.00 more than the ball, then the bat would cost $1.10 for a grand total of $1.20. So the correct answer is that the ball costs 5 cents."

"Oh." Elliot felt a little foolish.

Kendal shrugged. "You think intuitively. I get bogged down with details and numbers."

Elliot couldn't think of anything to say, so he rummaged in his pocket and produced a plaited string key fob. He handed it to her. "A gift for you. Something I made."

Kendal took it and turned it over in her hands. "And this also says a lot about you."

"Really?"

"Hmm. It's different, simple and real." She pointed to the fancy knot at the crown of the key fob. "This looks amazing."

"It's called a diamond knot." He smiled. "Probably the nearest I'll ever get to a real diamond." He didn't tell her it was generally considered to be the hardest decorative knot to make. Elliot had learned to perfect it many years ago.

Kendal put the key fob into her clutch bag and smiled. "Now let me give you something. Let's walk round to the Hilton."

Chapter 11

The taxi took Emma east along Tung Tau Tsuen Road and dropped her off at the corner. With some sense of trepidation, she crossed over and headed to the noodle stall thirty yards down the road. As she did, she looked up at the wall of scrappy high-rise buildings. Hundreds of tiny rooms seemed to be piled on top of each other like building blocks that had been badly stacked by a child. They rose about fifteen floors into the sky. Metal cages, all painted different colors, were bolted onto the outside wall allowing the occupants of the tiny rooms more space to breath.

Emma shuddered. It looked a desperate place.

She stepped into the open-fronted noodle stall. Two young men with bare chests and tattooed arms sat at a table shoveling food from bowls into their mouths. They put their bowls down and stared at her with an expression that hovered between arrogance and menace. However, the elderly Chinese lady sitting with them looked at her and smiled. Her eyes were full of lively interest and seemed to dance.

"You are Emma Templeton, I presume."

"I am. And you are…?" she paused. "What do I call you? I'm afraid I don't know your name."

"Just call me Mama-san. It's what they call me here." She nodded to the men sitting with her. "This is Ah Lam and Ah Kei. They live in the Walled City."

The elderly woman was dressed in loose trousers and a tunic that was buttoned up to her neck, despite the heat. She spoke to the men rapidly in Cantonese, then struggled to her feet with the aid of two sticks.

With a shock, Emma saw that she had clubbed feet. She stammered, "I…I don't wish to cause you pain or difficulty in showing me…"

The woman interrupted her. "No I am used to it. I just go slow." She smiled. "If I get very tired, the boys sometimes pull me along on a fruit-stall trolley. Come with me."

The two of them walked along Tung Tau Tsuen Road past a string of dentist shops. Emma had never seen so many false teeth displayed behind the windows. She was amused to see that one shop even had them on the ceiling fan.

Mama-san pointed to them. "There are many dentists and even some doctors here. They have been trained in China but cannot operate legally here without taking more exams. So they operate along the edge of the Walled City. Some are very good."

They came to a narrow gap between two shops. "This is where we enter. It is very dark. Don't look up. There is much filth that gets thrown down."

Emma gulped. She wanted to run, but it was too late now. "It doesn't look very inviting."

Mama-san laughed. "This is the good part. The worst part is on the other side where the illegal squatters huts are. That's where most of the heroin dens are, and probably most of the violence." She nodded to an old man squatting down by the entrance into the city. "How is the weather today?" she asked in Cantonese.

"It is fine, Mama-san."

"That is good."

She led the way into the narrow alleyway, saying as she went. "He is a *tin man toi*, a weatherman. He guards this entrance to the city."

Emma had no idea what that meant. It was hard to imagine anyone who looked less like a guard.

Mamma-san led her through a maze of narrow alleyways, all strewn with rubbish. Sometimes, a slimy fetid sewer ran down the middle. A tangle of dripping water pipes and electricity cables hung just above Emma's head. They were covered in the dust and rubbish of eons. Emma didn't dare look up. She also needed to keep her head down so she could be careful where she put her feet.

Emma squealed when she saw her first rat. It was big and bold, barely bothering to get out of her way when she passed.

Mamma-san kept up a running commentary. "You may wonder why I am so short." She laughed. "Despite my bad feet, I had to carry buckets of water up many flights of stairs each day when I lived here. Drinking water is supplied from just eight standpipes. Seven are on the edge of the city and there's just one inside."

Emma was aghast. "But how many people live here?"

"No one knows for sure. Some say it's about forty-thousand."

"You used to live here?"

"Yes, in my childhood and early adult life."

"But where did you play?"

Emma pushed past a woman making noodle parcels on a table she'd set up in the alleyway. A little boy was sitting at a small desk drawing. The desk had been lifted onto the top of the table. The boy had to keep his feet up to avoid putting them on the food and the flour underneath him.

"I played with the other children on the rooftop. We did our homework there, and we used to fly kites." She smiled. "They nearly touched the planes coming in to land at Kai Tak."

Everywhere Emma looked, she saw people desperately eking out a living. Sweat shops abounded. There was the clack of looms from garment manufacturers, and children were assembling plastic flowers or making candied sweets. It was all taking place in impossibly crowded spaces with no natural light.

Some of the people in the shops nodded to Mamma-san.

"The people here still seem to remember you," she said.

"And so they should. I come here three times a week to teach their children. I do it together with a missionary lady who lives here."

"But surely it's dangerous working here if it's controlled by triad societies."

"It was initially for my friend, but not any more. She has earned their respect."

"How on earth did she do that?"

"With love. She helps them get off heroin, and challenges corrupt police when they're falsely arrested."

"Oh."

As she stepped round some old bottle crates, another smell began to permeate the stench of crowded humanity. It was a sickly sweet odor.

"What is that smell?"

"Come and see." Mama-san beckoned to her. She was standing in front of a room that opened off the alleyway.

Emma could see men, young and old, lying on double-storied wooden platforms. Each of them had a metal tray containing cups and bottles beside them. All of them were smoking from long bamboo pipes. The pipes were surprisingly thick, about an inch-and-a-half in diameter. Those smoking them had glazed eyes.

"This is an opium divan." Mama-san pointed to a man placing something on one of the patron's trays. "Each opium divan is presided over by a *pahng-jue*." She spoke of it all in a shockingly matter-of-fact way. "Come. Follow me."

Emma followed her guide deeper into the darkness.

Mama-san stepped back to make room for someone who had come down a narrow flight of concrete stairs. As the man pushed past, she said. "There are no building regulations here. So stairs are simply squeezed into the spaces between buildings or borrowed from the building next door."

Up ahead, she saw a door open and five or six men slink out into the alleyway. As they did, two old women sitting on orange boxes called out to them in Cantonese. Emma caught a little of what they said.

"Come. I have girls. Very young. Very good. They are fully trained." The women reached out, trying to pull at the men's hands.

"What is this place?" whispered Emma. She caught a glimpse inside the room. It was quite small, about twelve feet square.

"It is a yellow film theater, what you call a blue film theater. They have fifteen minute sessions, sometimes including a live lesbian show."

"And the old women are pimps?"

"Yes. Girls as young as nine are sold to pimps by their drug-addicted parents. Others are tricked or raped by triad gang members and then sold into the sex trade." Mama-san squatted down and spoke to one of the women. As she did, she lifted up the woman's hand and turned it over. Emma couldn't hear what was being said. Mama-san laid her hand briefly on the cheek of the old woman, and then stood up. She turned to Emma. "Did you see how black and scarred the back of her hands were?"

"Yes."

"That's from injecting heroin. Old prostitutes act as mama-san to the young ones. They pimp for them outside the theaters and brothels."

Emma felt she'd seen enough. She ached to be out in the sun, the fresh air, in a place that didn't visit hell, degradation, and ruin on nine-year-old girls. Her stomach heaved. She was dazed, which was probably why she didn't see the man lying beside the alleyway. Wet sewage and rubbish lay around him. A small boy, presumably the man's son, was trying to lift the man's head. But the head simply nodded back onto his chest. Spittle dribbled from his mouth.

Emma stood back in shock.

The man was a living skeleton. Sunken eye sockets stared without sight from a sallow face.

Mama-san paused to speak to the child. She asked the child if he was coming to school.

The boy shook his head and pointed to his father. "I have to look after him and do my work as a *for-gei*."

Mama-san patted him on the shoulder and hobbled away.

"Mama-san, what's a *for-gei*?"

"It is one of the better jobs for a boy. He works in a gambling den collecting bets and pawning watches for clients." She beckoned Emma to keep following her.

A minute later, Mama-san was standing beside a wooden door that had an iron gate pulled down to protect it. Emma had noticed that almost all of Hong Kong's shops were protected by iron gates. However, it was unusual for one to be pulled down so late in the afternoon when business was at its peak.

Mama-san spoke to a young man sitting on an upturned plastic bin. The man got up, lifted the iron shutter, and opened the door behind it. She beckoned Emma to follow her and step inside.

Emma did so – and entered the pit of hell.

Men were sitting on wooden benches lolling against the supports, some were very young.

Mama-san whispered. "This is a heroin den. They are more discreet than the opium dens and more deadly."

Emma could see one young boy preparing to inject himself with a needle. He was heating heroin in a spoon with a cigarette lighter. Other clients were pouring sandy grains of heroin on a trough of silver foil and heating it. Emma watched in dreadful fascination as a man heated the heroin until it turned to dark treacle. He then put the outer case of a matchbox to his nose and mouth and began to inhale the fumes as the smoking treacle rolled from side to side on the foil.

Mama-san whispered. "He is chasing the dragon."

"Chasing the dragon?"

She nodded. "Smoking heroin."

As Emma watched, something of the dreadful attraction behind this self-degradation began to reach her. It seemed to call to her in her brokenness, promising relief. She began to feel the devilish attraction of chasing the dragon, of embracing escape.

"Get me out of here," she whispered.

Mama-san took her arm and pushed her toward the door.

Emma stumbled out of the den barely in control of her faculties.

As she stepped outside, the terrible attraction she'd felt inside began to dissipate. It left her emotionally exhausted. She simply had no strength left to process the horrors of all she'd seen.

Emma leaned against a grimy wall and wept. She wept at the ruination of lives; she wept for children who were only half alive, living ghouls with yellow eyes lost in a daze of heroin. She wept at the depravity of humankind – and her own weakness.

Mama-san put an arm around her shoulder. "You have seen enough. It is time to leave."

Chapter 12

"Where do you live?"

Emma barely heard the question. She was crouched over, holding a fist against her stomach. She wanted to retch.

They were standing outside on Tung Tsing Road. Mama-san rubbed Emma's back. "There, there. The Walled City is not kind to new people." She rubbed some more. "Let's get you home. Where do you live?"

"R…Repulse Bay," said Emma. "But I'm not sure I could bear to be alone, right now."

"Repulse Bay is not too far from where I live. Let me take you to my house and we'll have some tea. Then, we can talk until your heart is strong again."

Emma nodded her gratitude, and a short time later they were in a taxi crossing over to Hong Kong Island through the new tunnel. She didn't take any notice of where they were going until they were half way across the island, passing between steep ridges. As they drove, the ridges seemed to become steeper and the area more remote. 'Remote', she acknowledged, was a relative term in Hong Kong.

"Where are we going?" she asked.

"I live in Tai Tam. It is on the coast road east of Repulse Bay. The house belongs to my father, but he never goes there. I lived there for many years in order to look after his Number One Wife. She died two years ago, but he still lets me live there."

"Don't you have family of your own?"

"No one wants to marry a woman with deformed feet." She smiled. "But I have many children in the Walled City, so perhaps that is a good thing."

Emma didn't know what to say.

The taxi pulled off the main road and nosed its way down a narrow road.

Mamma-san interrupted her thoughts. "This is a quiet spot. Only local fishermen use this road."

The car pulled up beside a dignified Chinese-colonial house. It was roofed with glazed Chinese roof tiles. The deep ribbing made it look as if hundreds of bamboo poles had been laid side by side along the roof.

The house and its covered walkways were built around the edge of two compounds. One compound was laid out as an ornamental garden; the other was growing vegetables. Emma could see an old man in the middle of it chipping away with a hoe. He saw her looking at him and gave her a wave. She waved back. The man had been burned dark brown by the sun and had to be at least seventy years old.

Emma looked around appreciatively. The house had spectacular views across the bay and the moored boats to the mountainous hills on the other side of the water. She sighed. "This is a beautiful home."

Mamma-san pointed to the chairs on the patio. "Sit down and enjoy the view. I'll get some tea."

Emma sat down and nursed the stormy emotions within her. The scene before her was so much at odds with the horrors of the Walled City it was obscene. She felt she had no right experiencing such beauty when others were experiencing such hell.

The tea arrived, and Mamma-san sat down with her.

Both were silent for a long while.

Emma didn't know what to say or what questions to ask. Eventually she blurted, "So all of what we saw is controlled by the triads."

"Yes."

"I want to respect your loyalties, and do not wish to be a rude Westerner, but is there anything more you can tell me about the triads that might help me understand?"

Mamma-san sighed. "I can tell you very little. There is a code of secrecy which I have to respect."

Emma dropped her head. "Oh."

"But I can tell some things which might be considered to be general knowledge." She paused. "So, what questions do you have?"

"I understand that the triads originated as a nationalist movement dedicated to reestablishing Chinese sovereignty." Emma shrugged. "Has it completely disintegrated into gangsterism? Has it lost all of the values and spirituality it began with?"

Mamma-san nodded. "It has lost much of it. When people used to join the society, they were required to swear oaths during a ritual that included killing a chicken and drinking drops of its blood in a bowl of rice wine. Initiates wore special clothes, learned secret handshakes, and chanted Taoist and Buddhist prayers." She shook her head. "This is rarely done any more."

"So there is no spiritual foundation?"

"Oh no. Triads are very spiritual, but they are confused."

Emma raised an eyebrow.

"Gangsters are cruel and heartless, but they are also superstitious."

"Is Kai like this?"

"Yes," said Mamma-san slowly. "He worships many things including Guan Gong.

"Wasn't he a general who lived two thousand years ago in China during the 'Three Nation Period'?"

"Yes. He served under the warlord Liu Bei in the late Eastern Han dynasty. As time passed, Guan Yu became a Chinese deity and was given the name Guan Gong, meaning 'Lord Guan.' He is regarded as the epitome of loyalty and righteousness."

"Is that Kai's religion?"

"Oh no. He also worships Buddha and chants the Great Compassion Mantra of Guanyin." Mamma-san shrugged. "He is lost and is searching."

"How on earth does he expect to find an answer when he does what he does?" said Emma crossly.

Mamma-san steepled her fingers. "And there you have the conundrum. Despite their swagger and arrogance, most triad members are secretly miserable and filled with self-hate."

"Including Kai?"

"Especially Kai."

The two of them were silent for a while.

"Where does the name 14K come from?" asked Emma.

"I was told that the name came from the place where the society started in 1949: number 14, Po Wah St, Canton."

"Does it have a leader, or are there many leaders?"

"Both. There is a leader. He is a 489, a Dragon Head. But there are many leaders under him: each has their own area. The leaders relate to each other as 'cousins'."

"Where is Kai in this hierarchy?"

"I will not tell you – and I'm not even supposed to know."

Emma nodded. "Who can belong to these societies?"

"Almost anyone. Even rich business leaders can be members. Most have the title 'White Paper Fan.' In other words, they are administrators."

Mamma-san cocked her head at the sound of a car pulling up in front of the house. Then she put a finger to her mouth and urged Emma to be quiet. "Shhh."

Moments later, a figure stood in the doorway of the patio. A man spoke in Cantonese. "Who is this white foreign devil?"

The voice was so familiar to her. It was Elliot's voice, but with a slight American accent. The man stepped from the shadows into the early twilight.

Emma swallowed. He looked so like Elliot it was uncanny. This had to be his brother, Kai. The man was twirling something on his finger.

Emma realized with a shock that the man now standing before her was responsible, at least in part, for the depravity and suffering she'd experienced in the Walled City. The activities there were this man's stock-in-trade.

She clenched her fists. The warning signals in her mind that had controlled and moderated her behavior for so many years were now overwhelmed by a madness she was quite unfamiliar with.

Mamma-san cleared her throat. "Emma is making inquiries about my work with the children in the Walled City. We've just come back from there."

"Why is she making these inquiries?"

"She has been a student in Oxford and is studying Chinese culture in Hong Kong."

The man scoffed. "What can she possibly know about that? She's just a…"

His derision finally broke what was left of Emma's reserve.

She interrupted him, and spoke in Cantonese, "…a foreign devil?"

The man paused, raised an eyebrow, and continued. "An imperialist bully."

Emma broke in again. "A cheese eater."

Her comment caused the man to frown. "Are you another of these stupid Christians?"

"Yes."

He tossed his head. *Yau moe gau chor.*

Heat began to rise up Emma's neck that had nothing to do with the dying sun. She got to her feet and put her hands on her hips. "Don't you tell me I am mad. I have just come back from the madness and hell you have created in the Walled City." She waved a finger at him. "I live in the same apartment block as your brother Elliot, which is why I know who you are. And I understand enough about Chinese culture to know the significance of the dragon stone he wears around his neck, and that you have the other part."

Kai scowled and turned to his aunt. "What have you told her?"

Mamma-san lifted her chin. "I have told her nothing of significance." She paused. "I warn you, Kai; she is a scholar. Do not underestimate her."

Kai tossed his head.

His auntie tapped the chair next to her. "Sit down and have some tea. Question her yourself. I will go inside and organize something to eat."

Kai stared at Emma for a moment and sat down.

Emma had the impression that she was being comprehensively assessed. She was doing a good deal of assessing herself: they were like two cats circling one another.

She sat down.

Kai jerked his chin at her. "Why do you bring your Christianity to China? It is Western."

"Christianity goes wherever there is need. You have created a great need in the Walled City. So you tell me: What is better for the people there, your philosophy or my Christianity?"

"Christianity has nothing to do with China."

She pointed an accusing finger at him. "You are so ignorant of Chinese history, you don't deserve to call yourself Chinese."

The man's countenance darkened. "Don't you dare speak to me like that."

Emma was too angry to care.

"The ancient legends of China speak of the existence of 'Five Emperors' who lived 2852 BC to 2070 BC. Confucius wrote about the third of these emperors, Emperor Shun, in his Book of History. He describes Shun as the one who sacrificed to Shang Di, the 'Emperor of Heaven' – same as the Christian God." She waved a finger at him. "So don't tell me that worship of the One True God is un-Chinese. It has been integral to Chinese culture from its earliest history."

Kai furrowed his brow. "Is this true?"

Emma threw herself back in her seat in exasperation. "Of course it's true. And you should know it. Inscriptions on ancient oracle bones even speak of the worship of Shang Di during the Shang dynasty."

"How do you know this?"

"Because I don't let ideology and prejudice get in the way of truth," she retorted.

"You are rude."

"And you are ignorant of your heritage."

To Emma's relief, Kai started to laugh.

"Tell me more, Little Kitten."

"Little Kitten?"

"You scratch."

Emma was lost for words. She retreated to safer ground. "Every Chinese emperor has claimed a God-given mandate to rule. They renewed this mandate every year when they traveled to Mount Tai and sacrificed to Shang Di. This sacrifice was eventually moved to the Temple of Heaven outside the Forbidden City."

Kai shook his head. "But your Christ does not belong to China."

"Christianity is more Chinese than many religions and philosophies now practiced in China."

"How so?"

"Christianity arrived in China in 635AD. There's a monument saying that the Tang emperor, Taizong approved of the preaching of Christianity throughout the empire and ordered that a church be built in Chang An." She waved a finger at Kai. "And I might remind you, the Tang dynasty is regarded as a high point in Chinese civilization."

Kai put his hands up in surrender. "Enough of your scratches." He sat back. "Anyway, now we have Communism."

"Communism's devotion to equality is very much a Christian principle."

"But Christianity is not allowed. People's highest loyalty has to be to Communism."

"History has shown that trying to sit in a position over God has seldom worked out well. It simply causes resentment. People understand that every political system is tainted by the fallibilities of humankind. God, however, is not. Communism's greatest strength will come through fostering, rather than repressing, authentic Christianity. And why shouldn't it? Christianity is good for a nation. It encourages hard work, care, and honesty. So why foster resentment when you can foster co-operation?" She sat back. "Strong men force compliance. But wise men win hearts."

"It still has nothing to do with China."

"What?"

"Communists are not Christians."

Emma pointed a finger at him. "Your 'Young Marshal' Zhang Xueliang, the Communist hero who kidnapped Chiang Kai-shek, was a Christian." She waved a finger. "And the warlord, Feng Yuxiang, who went on to join the Revolutionary Committee, was a Christian. His people loved him because of his kindness. And Sun Yat-sen, whom Communists call 'Father of the Nation,' was a Christian."

Kai stiffened.

Emma nodded. "Yes. I think you know. Sun Yat-sen was also a triad. He was dedicated to the overthrow of the foreign Qing dynasty. He loved justice and freedom." She glared at him. "I didn't see much evidence of your justice and freedom in the Walled City."

Emma and Kai continued to argue until Mamma-san came in with a tray of food. She scolded them both. "I've been listening to you both squabbling like children for the last ten minutes. For goodness sake, stop and eat something."

Emma suddenly realized that she had been behaving in way that was completely foreign to her. The shock of it caused her to retreat into her controlled self again. She poured tea into the extra cup and handed it to Kai. The action was instinctive. It was what she would have done for Elliot.

Kai raised his eyebrows, but accepted the cup.

Chapter 13

E lliot's sense of apprehension was in no way diminished by the beauty of the drive from Repulse Bay to Tai Tam. The moon-silvered sea glittered between the steeply sided headlands visible only in silhouette. He was sitting beside his brother in the back of the taxi. Neither had spoken during the drive.

It was odd sitting beside him – to feel close, but not close. What would he learn about himself and his brother in the next hour or so, he wondered. What would prove true?

The car pulled up on the gravel next to a stately white colonial home. A light was burning in the front porch. It cast both light and shadow over the elderly woman sitting in a chair by the door. As the car stopped, she reached for two sticks and struggled to her feet.

Elliot got out of the car, paused, then stepped over to her. She watched his every move. Her eyes seemed to be alive, dancing with the life that was so palpably lacking in the rest of her body.

Kai walked just behind him.

The old woman transferred her two walking sticks to one hand and held out the other for Elliot to hold. It was the action of a mother.

Elliot felt, at that fleeting moment, the loss of his own mother and was conscious of a wave of emotion.

The woman massaged the back of his hand with her thumb. "So you are Elliot."

Elliot nodded, and didn't trust himself to say anything.

She let his hand go and reclaimed her walking stick. "Follow me. We shall eat."

Elliot found his voice. "Please don't go to any trouble. I have already eaten." He'd eaten spaghetti Bolognese with Emma an hour ago.

The woman was unfazed. "Pah. You are with your Chinese family now. We do everything with food."

She led the way through the hallway into the dining room. The table was richly decorated with flowers and set for three. The woman pointed to the head of the table. "You sit there, Elliot, at the head of the table." She smiled. "You have come home, and must be honored."

"Thank you, Auntie. It is a privilege to be here."

It took a moment for him to realize what he'd said. He'd called her 'Auntie,' quite unconsciously, and she hadn't turned a hair. It was bewildering.

He sat down.

Elliot didn't notice much about the food, only that a smiling Chinese man came from the kitchen bearing a new dish at regular intervals. Before they began to eat, Auntie bowed her head. Elliot used this time to take off his jade dragon pendant and lay it on the table. He was desperate to know its meaning.

Elliot was surprised when Kai followed his example, and laid his ivory locket beside it.

When Auntie opened her eyes, she glanced at the pendants, and nodded. "Now eat."

It was twenty minutes before she sat back in her chair and looked at both Elliot and Kai.

"Did you know that Emma Templeton was here last night, Elliot?"

His mouth dropped open. "What? She was here?"

"Yes."

Elliot gripped the edge of the table. "She didn't mention it. And we've just had tea together."

"I imagine she had her own reasons for that. We met at the Walled City. She was looking at the mission work there. Emma didn't cope well with what she saw, so I brought her back here to talk about it." She drew a breath. "Kai visited unexpectedly while she was here."

Elliot directed a sharp look at his brother. "Did Emma leave this place okay? How was she?"

Kai was crumbling a piece of bread between his fingers. "She talked too much."

"You didn't…"

"…hurt her? No I didn't, not that she didn't deserve it. She was very rude."

Elliot shook his head. He couldn't imagine Emma ever being rude. He turned to his brother. "Never hurt her, d'ya hear? Never hurt her. Promise me that."

Kai lifted his chin. "Is she is under your protection?"

"I…I suppose so."

Kai nodded. "Very well."

"Seriously, Kai." he swallowed. "I'll tell her to keep away from you and Auntie if it will help."

Kai waved his hand. "No, don't do that. I find her…interesting."

"Interesting?"

Kai tried a smile that only half worked. "She…makes you think."

For a while only a clock on the mantelpiece added to the conversation.

Auntie cleared her throat. "I think it is time for me to tell you a story – the story that has brought you both here tonight."

"My father was born in Canton in 1910. He married my mother twenty-one years later, and I was born the next year." She shrugged. "I was deformed, so he was not very pleased with me. Anyway, my father had a profitable war trading around the Pearl

River between Canton, Hong Kong, and Macau. He could smell where the big profits could be made, so he moved his operations to Hong Kong. By this stage, he was a senior member of the 14K triad society.

"My father had many affairs and this caused my mother to threaten suicide. She didn't kill herself, but she became ill. My job was to look after her, both when we lived in the Walled City and when we moved here."

Elliot furrowed his brow. "Is she still here?"

"No. She died five years ago."

"Oh, so this beautiful home belongs to you, now."

"No. It belongs to my father." She smiled sadly. "It would be seen as dishonorable if his wife and daughter did not live in a house that showed his wealth."

"Go on," he prompted.

"Just after the War, my father met the woman who was your mother. She was seventeen years old at the time." Auntie looked at Elliot. "Her parents were Mr. and Mrs. Gleeson."

"What?" said Elliot. "My...my parents? Er, this girl was my sister?"

"Not quite. Listen."

Elliot forced himself to be quiet.

"My father beguiled this young girl with an offer to work as a hostess in his business, taking high rollers to the floating casinos in Macau." Auntie reached across and took hold of Elliot's hand. "You must understand Elliot; your mother was an only child and had been indulged. She wouldn't listen to her parents." She squeezed his hand. "Anyway, my father seduced her, and she gave birth to twins – you two. Your mother died in childbirth."

Elliot shook his head. The story was unbelievable. So many questions clamored for answers.

Auntie continued. "Mr. and Mrs. Gleeson were devastated of course and threatened my father with the police." She sighed. "Sadly, my father is not one to take kindly to threats. He simply said that he'd kill you both if he was reported."

Elliot saw Kai lower his head. It was obvious he was not

enjoying being reminded of his father's first response to him as a son.

"Go on, Auntie," Elliot prompted.

"My father put a proposition to the Gleesons. He suggested they take one son and raise him as their own, and Father would keep the other as an insurance that they would never go to the police." Auntie shrugged. "The Gleesons knew they were never going to be able to have another baby, so they agreed. Mr. Gleeson worked as a bureaucrat at the Governor's office and was able to organize the necessary papers."

Elliot frowned. "But how did he falsify a birth certificate? That needs a doctor."

"My father threatened the doctor who delivered you with death if he didn't provide one."

Elliot blew out his cheeks. "So my parents...were actually not my parents."

"No. They were your grandparents."

"And you are not my auntie; you are my half-sister."

"It is better that you think of me as your auntie. It will mean I can scold you."

Elliot didn't smile. He picked up his jade pendant. "Where did this come from?"

"Your father had those made and gave one to each of you." She smiled sadly. "It wasn't really an act of kindness. It was to remind the Gleesons he retained total control over one of their grandsons. It was a statement of power. As you know, the dragon head is a symbol..."

"...of the triads," finished Elliot.

Auntie nodded.

Elliot pointed to Kai. "If your mother..." he paused, "*our* mother died, who raised you?"

"I did," said Auntie. I've cared for him, scolded him, and bandaged his wounds ever since he was born."

Kai lifted his chin. "Which one of us was born first?"

Auntie pointed to Elliot. "You were born first, Elliot by just seven minutes."

Kai turned to Elliot with another attempt at a smile. "So I suppose you think you can boss me around, big brother?"

Elliot closed his eyes. He was desperately trying to come to terms with what he had just heard.

The clock ticked.

After a while, he lowered his hands. "So, this creature, this monster who is my father – what's his name?"

Kai answered. "He has a number of names. But most people simply call him Mr. K."

"Is he still alive?"

"Yes. He lives in Kowloon. But do not go near him. He is a very dangerous man." Kai put a hand on Elliot's forearm. "Promise me you will not go near him."

Elliot didn't know what to say. He simply shook his head. "It's crazy."

Kai shook his arm. "Promise me!" he insisted.

Elliot snatched his arm away. "Okay, okay."

Auntie smiled. "You are fighting like brothers already." She nodded. "That is good."

Chapter 14

E mma emerged from her bed-sit to discover that Elliot had prepared her breakfast along with his own. He hadn't yet eaten it, presumably choosing to wait for Emma to join him. The man himself had his little canvas bag open beside him and was stitching a piece of leather with a needle and a leather pad that he'd strapped to his palm.

She smiled. Emma loved that about Elliot. The idea that he was meant to live independently of other people in the unit complex never seemed to have occurred to him. He naturally expected the two of them to eat together, and organized things so they did. It was a new experience for her. On the occasions she was not eating in a college dining hall, she'd only ever catered for herself. She shook her head. It was like living as a family.

"What's that thing on your hand?" she asked.

"Good morning to you, too," he said. "It's a sailmaker's palm – used to help with stitching through tough material."

"What are you making?"

"A leather case for your sunglasses. You were complaining of them getting scratched the other day."

"Oh."

Elliot took off his sail-maker's palm. "Let's eat. Do you want coffee?"

Emma nodded.

They ate in companionable silence, but it was a silence that failed to hide a number of questions she was burning to ask.

"You haven't told me how your evening with Kendal Shiffer went."

Elliot put down his spoon. "Ah, the lovely Kendal." His eyes looked into the middle distance seeing nothing, Emma suspected, but memories. They seemed to be pleasant ones. She was conscious of her stomach tightening.

Elliot continued. "She's the most beautiful woman I've ever met." He grinned. "Seriously classy. Absurd, really. She's very much at home in Hong Kong and seems to know everyone worth knowing in its society. And yet she chose to hang out with me." He paused. "But do you know…despite everything, there's…" his voice trailed off.

"There's what?" said Emma with rather more force than she'd intended.

"There's a sort of loneliness about her."

"Really?"

"Hmm. I suspect that beauty and brains are not always easy to live with."

She raised an eyebrow. Elliot may display a carefree persona, but he could also be perceptive. She would need to be careful. He was looking at her now over the rim of his coffee cup.

"Why didn't you tell me you had met up with Auntie and Kai?" he asked.

Emma had been expecting the question. She shrugged. "I wanted you to have your own experience of meeting them – untainted by my experience. All this is very much your story. It's not mine, so I don't want to intrude."

"Hmm."

"What do you mean, 'Hmm?'"

"And you just happened to meet Auntie in this Walled City place?"

Damn the man. "Well, I did meet her there. And it's not all that unlikely. Of course the Walled City is going to be of interest to me. It's the center for a lot of criminal activity – the sort of stuff I'm researching. And your auntie works there as a teacher." She changed the subject.

"You do know, don't you, that Kai is involved in triad activity at a fairly senior level?"

Elliot sighed. "Yes. I know he's involved with the triads, but just how senior he is, I've no idea."

Emma reached out toward him, but didn't quite make contact. "Please be careful, Elliot. Don't allow yourself to get drawn into your brother's world. It's brutal, cruel and dangerous."

Elliot smiled. "Am I seriously being lectured on gangland safety by a young woman who has barely left home – an Oxford academic?"

His words stung. "I may know more than you think," she said defensively.

"Hmm." He put his coffee mug down. "Perhaps you do."

It was time to move the conversation on again. "I'm trying not to pry. But what did you learn last night? I'm intrigued. How is it possible for Kai to be your twin brother?"

For the next ten minutes, Elliot gave an account of all that had happened and all that he'd learned the previous evening.

When Emma reached for her coffee again, she found it had cooled. She walked to the sink, tipped it out, and put the kettle back on for another.

Elliot was rocking his empty mug around on its base. "Kai is very different from me."

Emma took the mug from him, put it beside her own, and put a spoon of instant coffee into both. "You're a sailing instructor, and he is a gangster, so that's probably not surprising."

"Nah. It's more than that," he said.

She leaned back against the sink and looked at him. "Well, from my brief experience of him, I don't think he's very different from you at all."

"What do you mean?"

"Both of you are only half alive."

Elliot sat himself up straight. "What are you talking about?"

"The two of you are both lost."

Elliot furrowed his brow.

Emma was far from sure she should have begun this conversation. But it was too late to pull back now. She'd allowed his patronizing comment about her lack of experience in life to reach her. So, what was it she wanted to say, or should say? She searched for a metaphor that Elliot might understand.

"You are like boats that have been cut free from their moorings. They don't know what they should do, or what they were built for. Neither knows they were meant to sail with the wind and travel to distant destinations. They just float along the river, allowing what they bump into to define their meaningless life." She put her hands on her hips. "You particularly. For you, it's just 'eat, drink, and be merry for tomorrow we die.'"

"What do you mean by that?"

Emma turned her back on him and waved a hand in frustration. "It's a quote."

"Oh. Right."

An army Land Rover, driven by a corporal called George, arrived to pick up Emma and the colonel at the ferry terminal. The two of them had taken a Star ferry from Central to the island of Lan Tau in order to visit Tong Fuk prison. It was the only prison for adult inmates that Emma had yet to visit.

The colonel assumed the front seat beside the driver, leaving Emma to nurse her thoughts. Most of them surrounded her conversation with Elliot that morning.

Her musings were interrupted by the colonel. "You may be in luck, Miss Templeton. I heard yesterday that a senior member of the *Ging Yi* triads has recently become an inmate at Tong Fuk. I've organized for you to speak with him."

"Really? What's his name?"

"His name is Suen Jai."

Thirty minutes later, she was speaking with the governor of the Tong Fuk correctional institution. The governor ran his eyes over Emma and didn't quite repress a sigh.

Emma asked him about the correctional services on Lan Tau Island.

He replied mechanically, "A new prison has just been opened on Lan Tau Island. It is a low security prison for young offenders. But our prison here at Tong Fuk is much bigger, and we house adult prisoners. I understand you want to interview some of them."

"Yes please. You have a new prisoner here, Suen Jai."

"Aah. The wily Suen Jai." He grunted. "Yes, we have him here, and not before time, I might add."

"I'd hoped he might be able to tell me something of the nature of his organization."

The governor gave a sardonic laugh. "Good luck with that. I doubt he'll tell you anything he doesn't want you to know."

"Oh, that's a pity. I'm trying to understand the power organizations like his have that persuades so many young men to reoffend."

The governor rubbed his scalp. "Well, he certainly has power. A goodly number of people in here answer to him."

The colonel and the governor strode on ahead, deep in conversation. Emma trailed behind. She saw a shelf in the corridor containing jars of formalin in which various animals had been preserved. It was an odd thing to see in a prison. Emma stared at one flask in particular that contained a snake.

She shuddered and turned to catch up with her two colleagues. However, when she looked up, they were nowhere to be seen. There was just an empty corridor and a few closed doors.

Emma hastened down the corridor and opened the first door she came to. With a shock, she discovered that it led into a huge hall. About a hundred men were sitting at tables packing various objects into small cardboard boxes. As soon as they saw Emma, they all jumped to their feet and stood to attention.

Emma's mouth dropped open in horror. She gulped, smiled, and shut the door.

Emma leaned against the wall, willing her heart to slow down. *Good grief! The discipline here is terrifying.*

The next door along the corridor opened, and the governor stepped out. "We're in here, Miss Templeton. I've organized some tea."

An hour later, Emma entered a room with a desk and chair behind a wall of iron mesh. One yard beyond this wall was another barrier of mesh. A middle-aged Chinese man sat behind it on a plastic chair. He wore a congenial smile. Emma thought he looked like someone you might expect to be selling knick-knacks at a market stall. He certainly didn't look like a gang leader.

The man stood up when Emma entered.

Emma smiled at him and acknowledged him with a small but distinct bow.

For an instant, a frown crossed his face. But a second later, the smile was back in place.

Emma turned to the interpreter who had entered the room with her.

"Could you explain to Mr. Suen Jai that my name is Emma Templeton. I have come here from England to help the British government find better ways to stop prisoners reoffending and going to jail."

The interpreter translated Emma's words into Cantonese.

Suen Jai nodded.

Emma continued. "Please tell Mr. Suen Jai that I have been in Hong Kong for three weeks talking to prisoners, and I am grateful to be talking with him. I would value his opinion."

Again the interpreter relayed Emma's message.

Emma smiled at the man sitting behind the mesh and said in English. "Mr. Suen Jai, you understand a little English?"

The man nodded slowly. "A little bit, only."

"That is good, because I want you to speak to me in confidence without the need of this interpreter. Do you think we can do this?"

The interpreter translated the question to the gang boss.

Suen Jai shrugged. "I try. But I may say it first in Chinese – just to help me think."

"That is okay." Emma turned to the interpreter and asked him to leave.

Once she was alone with Suen Jai, Emma summoned what she hoped was an encouraging smile. "Do you have a family, Mr. Suen Jai?"

The man spoke in Cantonese. "*I would like to force you to your knees and rape you like a dog.*" Then he smiled and said in English. "I have two sons, both good boys."

Emma managed to keep her smile, although she was convinced she was looking like an imbecile. She forced herself to speak. "Congratulations. Sons are good. No father wants a son to go to prison many times, do they?"

Suen Jai replied in Cantonese, speaking obscenities that were shockingly vile and calculated to instill fear. All the time, he was smiling. Then he switched to English. "No, it is very bad for young man to go to prison. Make father very sad." He put a hand on his heart.

Emma desperately wanted to look down at her notes, to look anywhere rather than at the face of the man who had just defiled her mind with the most horrendous, degrading images imaginable. But she was determined not to give him the power to win or to expose the game she was playing.

"Yes, very sad," she said.

"You married, Missy Templeton?"

"Oh no. I only finished studying at university two months ago. I've been very busy."

Suen Jai grunted approvingly. "You very clever."

Emma acknowledged his compliment with another bow. All the time, she was thinking how she could continue to keep one step ahead of the monster before her.

"The triads send many young men to prison. What can the government do to stop this?"

The gang boss once again lapsed into Cantonese. *Can't stop us, you stupid bitch. Wherever Chinese people go, triads go. We grow like a tree. You cut off a branch; another grows. Ambition, greed, and addiction define the human condition. We just give it shape.* He nodded ingratiatingly and said in English. "Maybe if the government helps the poor more and gives more teaching – things will get better."

"I agree," said Emma. "That is the conclusion I have been coming to myself. You are wise."

Suen Jai inclined his head.

Emma pressed on. "Maybe we should have more police too?"

The gang leader shook his head. "Your police...many bad men."

Emma leaned back. "Surely, the police are not bad here in Hong Kong?"

Suen Jai threw his head back and laughed. It was not a nice sound. "We give police people to arrest for drugs. We pay these people and look after them while they are in prison. They have good time. They get drugs easy here." He shrugged. "So everyone happy."

"Then, why are you in here?"

Suen Jai rubbed his fingers together. "Not enough 'tea fee.'"

"Tea fee?"

"We give police tea fee so they do things...or maybe not do things."

Emma conjured a look of shock. "Do you mean bribes?"

Suen Jai shrugged. "This is Hong Kong."

"But this is terrible. This has to be stopped."

Emma had actually learned enough in the last few weeks so none of what she was being told about the police surprised her. But what she really wanted to know was whether the triads had coordinated plans to export their activities overseas. She drew a deep breath.

"I would not like bad triads and bad police to spread to England. What can we do?"

"We are already there, fool. We send drugs to the UK, and we send drugs and Philippine prostitutes to Australia. You can't stop us. We keep coming like waves on the sea. You are stupid and weak." He pretended to think for a

moment, and said in English, "Ah Missy Templeton, triads are like plants. They like their own country and their own soil. They are not easily uprooted." He shook his head. "There is very little triad activity in your country."

"But how important is triad activity here? Did the triads help cause the Communist riots here in Hong Kong a few years ago?"

"*Of course we hate you foreigners and your arrogant ways. But no, we didn't ferment the riots. We didn't have to. All Chinese people resent being subject to imperialist overlords.*" Suen Jai clicked his fingers as if trying to summon the right words. "No. We no like Communism. It is strict. It makes it hard for us to operate. We need a Western society to make good money."

Emma nodded. "I understand. I am sorry Western society is so corrupt." She stood up. "I thank you. You have been very helpful and very wise."

Suen Jai stood up, smiled, and said in Cantonese, "*You are a fool.*" In English, he added, "It is good to speak to clever lady."

Chapter 15

Emma said almost nothing during her trip back from Lan Tau Island. She couldn't get the horrific pictures Suen Jai had spoken of out of her mind. They shrieked at her sensibilities, wounded her spirit, and scarred her mind. She felt unutterably defiled and wanted desperately to be cleansed of the filth.

But at least she'd not betrayed her knowledge of Cantonese with the dreadful test Suen Jai had sprung on her. She had, in fact, managed to learn a great deal, and now felt she had enough to write a report for Mr. Egerton in London. It would make sobering reading. She would type it up in the next few days, then fly back to the UK.

Emma knew that she'd been playing a dangerous game, particularly with Suen Jai. He'd pretended to speak English poorly, but his use of words, 'uprooted' and 'operate' left Emma in no doubt that the gang boss actually spoke English very well. It had been a game of cat and mouse.

Emma felt no sense of victory. She wanted to cry for her loss of innocence and the images that now tormented her. Barely knowing what she was doing, she ran from the lift, unlocked the door to the apartment, and barged inside. She didn't stop until she was in her bathroom. Her fingers fumbled as she unhooked the waistband of her dress. Emma yanked at it in frustration. Finally, her gray dress fell away. Not waiting to take anything else off, she dived under the shower, desperate for its cleansing.

Then she wept.

Eventually, the anguish of her soul subsided to a point where she could reach beyond herself for help. She sank to the floor of the shower cubicle, leaned against the wall, and prayed.

Wash me, Lord, in your peace.
Banish this wretched evil from my mind.
Replace the nightmare of what I've heard with your presence,
and let me experience the healing of your love.

It wasn't a particularly sophisticated prayer, but it was enough for her to begin feeling a peace that was beyond words.

Her weeping eased to a whimper.

Emma heard the shower curtain twitch and opened her eyes in alarm.

Elliot was standing there looking down at her.

"Are you all right?"

Emma was appalled and drew her knees up tighter against herself. "What are you doing here?" she cried.

"Well, the front door was wide open, and the door to your room was wide open… and I heard you crying." He looked at her. "What's the matter?"

His concern did nothing to help her sensibilities. She began to cry again – deep soul-shuddering sobs wracked her body.

Emma was only slightly aware of Elliot stepping into the shower cubicle. However, she became fully aware when he sat down beside her under the water and put an arm around her shoulder.

Emma curled up against him and over the next five minutes, allowed her grief to exhaust itself.

Elliot rubbed his head with the towel as he made his way from the lift to the front door of his unit. He'd felt the need for an early morning swim before the heat of the day took the edge off the freshness it gave. Emma would probably still be asleep. She'd stayed up late last night pecking away at a typewriter. He could hear her going hard at it through the closed door. If her account of what she'd needed to endure yesterday was anything to go by, she'd certainly have something to write about. However, getting the information had cost her dearly. He shook his head. Emma was a conundrum. She was tough, determined, yet vulnerable – so terribly vulnerable.

Elliot opened the door and froze. Two men were standing in front of the kitchen area. One of them was a policeman. Emma was behind them, hugging her cotton dressing gown to herself. Her hair was disheveled, and she was looking pale.

"Who are you?" he asked.

The man in civilian dress lifted his chin.

"I'm detective sergeant Morrison." He waved an arm at his colleague, "And this is senior constable Marsh."

Elliot nodded to them both. "Hello. Would you both please show me your identification?"

The two men fished in their pockets and produced their identification wallets.

As Elliot inspected them and handed them back, a dreadful sense of unease began to chill his heart. "How can we help you?"

The detective spoke. "Are you Elliot Gleeson?"

"I am."

"We'd like a few words with you please – alone if you'd like."

"What about?"

"About your relationship with Kendal Shiffer."

Emma interrupted. "I…I can go into my room if you'd like."

Elliot put his hand up. "No. Please don't go." He wanted Emma to be with him to face whatever was coming. He turned back to the detective. "I don't really have a relationship with Kendal. We've only just met. We're just beginning to explore a friendship. Why do you ask?"

The detective pursed his lips. "Because Miss Shiffer was kidnapped yesterday morning." He paused. "You were one of the last people, outside her normal circle of contacts, to have seen her."

Elliot felt the room begin to spin. "What?" He stumbled forward and sat himself down on a dining room chair. "You're not serious?"

"Very serious," said the detective.

Emma broke in. "If you two sit down at the table with Elliot, I'll get everyone a cup of tea?"

Elliot put his head in his hands. "Tell me what happened," he demanded.

"Kendal Shiffer's car was run off the road at 7:45 yesterday morning. Her driver was knocked unconscious, and Miss Shiffer was bundled into a taxi that was following her car."

"What knocked her car off the road?"

"A car coming from the other direction – stolen, we've discovered."

Elliot rubbed a hand across his face. "Good grief." He thought of Kendal, so beautiful and beguiling, her soft skin kissed by the sun and warmed to a tan, and groaned. The thought of anyone hurting her or defiling her was more than he could bear.

The detective appeared unmoved by his grief. "What exactly is your relationship with Miss Shiffer?"

Elliot spoke between his fingers. "I taught her sailing last week."

"When, exactly?"

"A week ago yesterday. We enjoyed each other's company and agreed to go out to dinner, um...three nights ago." He lifted his head. "That's it."

The detective looked at his notes. "Ah, yes. You went to the GoDown and then to the Hilton."

"Yes."

"You've had no contact since."

"No."

"Where were you at 7:45 yesterday morning?"

Emma interrupted. "He was teaching me to swim down on the beach here. Elliot was still here at 9am when I left to catch the bus to Central. I had some work to do on Lan Tau Island."

"Is that right, Mr. Gleeson?"

"Yes."

The detective looked at Elliot and then Emma. "Just for the record, can I ask what the relationship is between you two?"

Elliot looked at Emma.

Emma dropped her head.

"We've become friends," said Elliot. "We share the facilities here – and have done for nine days."

"Friends; is that all?"

"Yes," said Emma, quickly.

More questions followed concerning the nature of Elliot's work, but it was evident that this was purely routine.

A few minutes later, the policeman and the detective left.

Elliot paced up and down the tiled floor of the apartment. Every few moments he would groan in anguish. Kendal, so precious, so vulnerable, so captivating with her honey-blond hair, now in mortal danger. It was crushing and obscene.

"Who? Why?" he shouted, banging his fist against the wall. "No! No!" he groaned! Elliot flopped into an armchair and covered his face with his hands. He was dimly aware of Emma laying a hand on his shoulder for a fleeting moment. Then she sat opposite in a chair.

"Why?" he groaned again.

"Oh Elliot," said Emma. "I'm so sad – sad for Kendal and sad for you."

He groaned again.

Emma sighed. "From my research, I can tell you that Kendal's abduction has the classic hallmarks of triad activity. I know of two other people who were kidnapped in a similar fashion."

Elliot lifted his head. "Did they survive?"

"One did."

"No! No! Don't tell me any more."

Even as another wave of anguish swept over him, a dreadful thought began to suggest itself. Elliot shook his head, but it wouldn't go away. It was a terrible thought, and a condemnatory one, for it accused him. The very idea that he could have contributed in large part to Kendal's abduction was appalling.

"Emma," he said. "I…I have a terrible feeling…" he trailed off.

Emma lifted her head. Elliot was shocked to see that she had been crying. But he was so traumatized by the thought that afflicted him that he didn't comment. "Emma, I told Kai about Kendal when I called to apologize for standing him up on our visit to Auntie." He looked at Emma's tear-ravaged face. "Do you suppose…" He cleared his throat. "Do you suppose that Kai could have kidnapped Kendal?"

"Did you tell Kai that she was very rich?"

"Yes."

"Oh! Um…did you tell him where she lived?"

Elliot covered his face again. "Yes," he said through his fingers. "I told him the street she lived on."

Emma got up from her chair, crossed over to him and laid a hand on his shoulder. "Then you can give the police a good angle to explore."

"Yes. Yes, of course." He threw his head back. "But if I'm wrong, I will have ruined my relationship with my…" he paused, "family."

"Elliot. I don't think you have any choice. You've got to do something."

"Yes I do." He got to his feet. "I'm going to visit Auntie. She only teaches three mornings a week so there's a good chance she'll be in."

Elliot retrieved the number from his room and dialed the phone.

It was answered fairly quickly by someone speaking Chinese. Elliot asked if Auntie was in, but was again answered in Chinese. He slapped his forehead in frustration.

Emma, who was standing by his side, took the phone from him. "Here give me that." A moment later she was gabbling in Chinese.

His mouth dropped open. The idea that little Emma, who had barely lived outside of Oxford, could speak Cantonese was ridiculous.

She put the phone down. "That was the cook. He said that Auntie is there. I've asked him to let her know that we'll be there in forty minutes."

Elliot shook his head. "No. This doesn't concern you. I'm not sure what I'm heading into. It mightn't be nice, or even safe. I don't want you to get involved."

Emma crossed her arms. "Well, I am involved, and that's it." Her voice brooked no argument. "Besides," she added in a more conciliatory tone, "there aren't many people who know more about triad societies than me."

"But...but you're just a..."

"An academic?"

He nodded.

Emma poked him in the chest. "There's a whole lot about me you don't yet know, mate."

Elliot watched as Auntie sat back in her patio chair and looked across the sparkling water of the bay. He suspected that she was not actually seeing any of it. She appeared to be lost in thought as she tapped her fingers against her mouth. It was as if she was afraid to speak.

Elliot had recounted what happened to Kendal, and voiced his dreadful suspicions about Kai. "Is it possible that Kai could be behind this?" he'd asked. "He was certainly angry that I would put a priority on meeting her over him the other night."

Auntie nodded slowly. "Yes, I have to say; it is possible. But he would not have kidnapped her just because he was angry. He's not stupidly vindictive. However, your mention of Miss Shiffer may have brought her to his attention."

"...as a potential kidnap target?" added Emma.

"Yes."

Elliot put his hands on his head in anguish.

Auntie looked at him. "This woman, Kendal Shiffer, she was your girlfriend?"

"No, er, yes. I'd...er, hoped."

The old woman turned to Emma and spoke to her in Chinese.

Elliot wondered what on earth she was saying. He was obviously being cut out of the conversation. He saw Emma drop her head and say, *m-hai, m-hai.*

Auntie nodded and switched back to English. "Elliot, I am more sorry than words can say. Please understand that. But I must ask, will you be going to the police with your suspicions?"

Elliot could plainly see the pain of the idea in her eyes. He bit his lips. "I don't know what else I can do?"

"Kai is your brother."

"I know."

"If he is innocent, this is not something he will forgive." Auntie paused. "And if he is guilty, it will definitely be something he will not forgive. Loyalty is everything in Chinese culture."

It was strange to Elliot that Kai could be spoken of as someone so Chinese whilst, he, his twin brother, was so obviously not. But he knew that the disquiet in his soul had nothing to do with Kai's ethnicity. The fact was, he'd just discovered his brother, his twin. He was no longer the only one in his family. And something of Kai was already deeply connected with him. Elliot instinctively understood him and shared his heart.

Emma interrupted his thoughts. "I imagine, Auntie, that you are in a moral dilemma. Kai is a son to you, and you would want to protect him as a mother. And yet, as a Christian, you abhor evil. I'm so sorry you have had this thrust upon you."

Auntie nodded. "It is very sad, but it is life." She drew in a deep breath. "But this is one of those defining moments, moments that test the value of who you are and what you believe." She slapped the side of the chair. "I simply will not sit idly by and allow evil to win." She turned to Elliot. "So you must do what you must do, with my blessing."

Elliot could not look at her. "Thank you, Auntie."

For a while, no one said anything.

Emma broke the silence. "Is there another way we can explore?"

"What?" he demanded.

"What if we could speak to Kai?"

Auntie immediately shook her head. "No. If Kai is doing this, then it means that his father's directions are behind it. Kai will not, and cannot, go against his father." She gave a barely suppressed shiver.

Elliot was casting around for ideas, any idea. "What if we could find Kendal?" The stupidity of his suggestion mocked his sense of helplessness.

Emma, however, picked up on the theme. "Auntie, would you have any idea where Kai might have taken Kendal if he was responsible for her kidnapping?"

"Oh that is easy dear. He would have taken her to the Walled City."

Elliot's head snapped up. "Really? Why can you be so sure?"

"Most of the rooms in there have no windows. It is a place where police are not routinely active, and…" she trailed off.

"And what?" prompted Emma.

"And it is a place where Kai has total control."

Elliot rubbed his eyes with the heel of his hands. "But how can we find out?"

"And what do we do once we have found out, if we don't want to involve the police?" added Emma.

More silence followed.

A fishing boat chugged past noisily, heading out into the Pacific.

"There might be a way," said Auntie slowly.

"What?" demanded Elliot.

"The children. I teach the children in the City. Nothing happens there that a child somewhere doesn't see. The City is their playground."

"But you can't endanger the children," protested Emma.

"Certainly not, dear. But I can ask a question." She smiled at her. "The trick with children is to ask the right question."

Emma frowned.

Auntie patted her hand. "What if I were to say: 'What parts of the Walled City have the bosses recently told you not to go to?'" Auntie wagged a finger. "Just make sure you obey them, children. I don't want any of you hurt."

Chapter 16

"You must be joking. I'm not paying a single dollar to a low-life like you. You don't have the balls to carry this through, and I'm very confident the police will get you."

The phone cut dead.

Kai frowned. This was not the normal response to a ransom demand. He'd delivered a number of them in his time, and knew. There was normally a demand for proof of life, which he was willing to supply, followed by negotiation and threat. But Lachlan Shiffer of Shiffer Investments hadn't asked for it. In fact, he hadn't even bothered to respond to his first telephone call giving him instructions to go to a certain phone booth for more information.

Lachlan Shiffer had simply ignored it.

Kai had been forced to call again and threaten to send body parts of his niece to him in the post. But he'd just been rebuffed again.

Kai weighed the telephone receiver in his hands before he placed it back on its cradle. Something was wrong. What he'd just heard on the phone made no sense at all. No sane person would treat a ransom demand in such a cavalier fashion. Kai rubbed the back of his neck.

Well, he'd just have to bring hell down upon him. The repercussions would be gruesome, merciless, and highly demonstrative. No one scorned the 14K and got away with it. Kai shook his head. Anyone with half a brain would never doubt that a triad organization would carry out its threat. Something pricked his consciousness into unease. Lachlan Shiffer's words and actions had been provocative in the extreme. The big question was why.

He sighed. If he was going to get any answers, he'd have to question Kendal Shiffer, and that posed its own problems. Kendal knew his brother, Elliot, so even if she heard Kai, let alone saw him, she'd know who her abductor was. The woman would then be able to inform the police. He would need someone else to question her. However, he wanted to be close enough to direct the questioning and hear the answers.

Kai walked out of the shop and across to where a coolie was squatting down beside his rickshaw. He nodded to the man and climbed into the seat. There were not many rickshaws left in Hong Kong now. They were being phased out because they were thought to be inefficient. It was a pity, because Kai liked them. They made up in flexibility what they lacked in speed. Their main limitation was that they only had one seat, which made it impossible for him to travel with a bodyguard. Kai pulled the rickshaw's canopy up over his head to protect himself from the sun and sat back. The wiry coolie picked up the pulling looms and began to tow him through the narrow streets toward the Walled City, frustrating a good deal of other road users as he went.

Kai had not been involved in the kidnap personally. Ah Ming and his team had carried it out with their usual efficiency. Kai liked to keep his distance from the victim, so he knew he was breaking one of his own rules by going to the place where she was being held. His role in any kidnap scenario was usually restricted to doing the negotiations. He was good at it.

The coolie dropped him off on Tung Sing Road. Kai ducked through the traffic and slipped through a narrow gap between two shops into the fetid gloom of the Walled City. He threaded his way through the narrow passageways, his feet instinctively avoiding the filth running down their middle. Kai stepped round an addict crouched against the wall, lost in his own Nirvana, and made his way up two flights of concrete stairs.

One of his men, Daih So, was on the landing, sitting on a wooden box. He was smoking. Kai glanced at his hand.

No warning signals.

Good.

He walked over to a steel door. It had once been painted green, but most of it had peeled off, leaving behind blisters of rust.

Kai rapped on the metal.

After a moment, he heard the hatch covering the inspection hole slide open. A bloodshot eye peered at him for a moment before it was snapped shut. The door bolts shrieked as they were pulled open.

Kai entered the room. The walls, floor, and ceiling were all made of concrete. Someone had once painted the walls white, but now they were covered in grime. It was the home of a couple who were heroin addicts, but their habit was not so bad that they couldn't function. The man and his wife backed away against a wall when he came in.

Kai lifted a questioning chin.

The woman pointed to a curtained area at the back of the room.

He stepped over and peered round the curtains keeping most of his face hidden.

Kendal Shiffer lay on a thin mat on the floor. The handcuffs on her wrists had a piece of chain attached. The other end was attached to a ringbolt embedded in the wall. Kai wrinkled his nose at the smell of feces, urine, and disinfectant that came from the portable toilet in the corner. A plywood packing-case stood on its end on the other side of the room. The Shiffer woman would have been carried up inside it. The box stood beside her like a coffin. Kai thought grimly that it might very well become one.

The woman seemed to be in a drugged sleep. She certainly should be. The couple had been given enough drugs to keep her sedated, but they sometimes stole the drugs for their own use.

Kai swung the prayer tassel round his finger as he looked at the woman on the floor. It was the first time he'd seen her. He was mildly curious to learn what she was like – why Elliot had put such a priority on seeing her. She was in shadow, so Kai moved the curtains to allow light from the single globe behind him to reach her.

The first thing he saw was a tangle of blond hair falling across her shoulders and over her face. *Wow!* he thought. She certainly had a striking body. Her business skirt had ridden up revealing long legs and curving thighs. The woman's breasts were full, pressing hard against her shirt.

Kai nodded appreciatively. He squatted down and ran a finger along her legs. No wonder she had turned his brother's head.

The thought of his brother disturbed him. He'd been angry at his impudence in prioritizing this woman over him, but to kidnap his woman…well, if Elliot held even the faintest suspicion he was responsible, it would destroy any relationship they might otherwise have. A few days ago, he wouldn't have cared. But the idea that he had a twin brother, however culturally different, was something that now filled him with wonder.

Dammit! Why wouldn't Lachlan Shiffer simply pay up the money? One million Hong Kong dollars was not exorbitant. Then it would all be over by the end of tomorrow and things could get back to normal.

He pulled the edge of the woman's skirt back in place to make her more modest. He'd done what he could to ensure the Shiffer woman wouldn't be too traumatized. He thought guiltily of his own feelings of lust, and distracted himself from them by barking at the couple behind him. "Has the woman been sexually molested?"

"No. No, Goko. No. No one's touched her."

"Make sure no one does – on my orders."

"Yes Goko."

"You have the keys to the handcuffs?"

"Yes, they are in here on the shelf."

"Give them to me," he ordered.

The man reached over to a shelf and handed him the key.

Kai put it in his pocket. Then he reached forward and picked up the woman's hand. It had long slender fingers.

Fingers...Hmm. He tried to block out the mental image of fingers being cut off by bolt cutters. Something in him screamed at such defilement.

Kai shook his head in irritation. *Dammit.* He was being sabotaged by scruples more and more these days. It was ridiculous. He was Goko of the 14K. His job was to exert power and instill fear.

Kai caressed the woman's hand.

Unbidden, the words spoken by the 'Little Kitten' Emma, played again in his mind. They had haunted his conscience ever since she'd spoken them. *I don't see any evidence of the high ideals of the early triads...You do nothing that pleases God...You simply destroy what God creates...You will not be remembered well, either by God or by history.*

He stood up and punched the wall with his fist. Its surface was rough and wet. A water pipe somewhere was leaking.

Once he had steadied himself, he squatted down again beside the woman and brushed back her hair. When he saw the sleeping innocence and perfection of her face, he held his breath. Something again screamed in his soul. *How could this person not be created by the gods? Which god would ever approve of her mutilation and death?*

His question was met by silence. He lowered his head. He was dammed, and it was as simple as that.

"There is no hope," he said, savagely. Kai wanted to take out his prayer tassel and hurl it against the wall.

He was startled to see the woman's eyes begin to flutter, trying to open.

She said in a weak voice, "Elliot?" Then they closed again.

Before he could think about what she'd said, he was interrupted by a voice behind him.

"How long will this woman be staying here?" asked the man.

"Until I say so," snarled Kai. He felt in his pocket for his prayer tassel. "Just make sure you look after her."

The phone rang as Emma was helping Elliot wash up the evening meal dishes. As Elliot's hands were in the sink, she stepped across to the phone and picked it up.

"Hello. Emma Templeton speaking."

"Hello Emma."

Her heart skipped a beat. She gripped the phone with two hands. "Auntie. Have you learned anything?"

"Yes dear, I have. I think I know where Kendal Shiffer has been taken in the Walled City. Can you and Elliot come over tonight?"

Chapter 17

E lliot plucked at the unfamiliar shirt and wished for the umpteenth time that he didn't have to wear the sleeves rolled down. The taxi lacked air-conditioning, and he could feel the sweat patches growing under his arms. But Hong Kong's oppressive summer was not the only reason for his perspiration. He knew that in a few minutes, he would be undertaking a course of action that was as unlikely to succeed as it was dangerous.

Auntie sat beside him in the back seat of the taxi. She was the one who had given Elliot the shirt. It was one of Kai's. She patted Elliot on the arm and pointed out of the window to a grim wall of apartment blocks. Iron cages clung to their sides from which poles holding people's washing protruded. There was no redeeming aesthetic feature to be seen.

"That's the Walled City," she said.

"It looks forbidding."

Auntie nodded. "It is. And yet even within its horrors and secrets, there is a sense of community." She pointed up ahead. "That's where we'll park and wait for our man."

Elliot nodded.

The taxi pulled into the curb. With the little breeze that had been generated by the moving car now denied him, Elliot began to sweat profusely. He looked at Auntie enviously. She didn't seem to be affected by the heat at all.

Elliot glanced round to check on another taxi that had pulled in behind them. No one had yet objected to either taxi being illegally parked. The chaos of Hong Kong's traffic flowed past and people ignored them as they busied themselves going in and out of the shops.

A full ten minutes passed before Auntie sat herself forward. "Aah, there he is." She pointed to a man dressed in blue trousers, white shirt, and a blue postal cap. He carried a canvas sack over his shoulder.

Auntie called out to him through the car window in Chinese.

The man came over to the car. When he recognized Auntie, he bobbed his head in respect.

The two of them gabbled away for a while. Eventually the man nodded.

Auntie leaned back in her seat, took out her purse, and extracted fifty Hong Kong dollars. As she did, she spoke to Elliot quietly under her breath.

"This man is the postman for the Walled City. He is probably the only person who knows his way around every part of it. He's agreed to deliver a letter for me before he does his normal round. I've told him that it's a vitally important one – so important that you will be going with him to see that it is delivered into the hands of the recipient." She glanced at him. "Understand?"

"What's the letter actually about?"

She waved a hand, dismissively. "It's just an invitation for residents to send their children to our school." She smiled. "But he doesn't know that."

Elliot nodded. "Does this man know Kai? What will I say if he speaks to me?"

"He knows of Kai and will have seen him a few times. But I doubt that he's ever spoken to him. People don't unless they have permission to." She patted his knee. "Just walk a few steps behind him. The alleyways are narrow, so you'll have to anyway. That will discourage conversation."

"But what if I want to say something to him?"

"Just use sign language. Pretend you don't deign to favor him with words. Be arrogant."

Elliot rubbed the sides of his temples. This was madness. The absurdity of what he was attempting hit him afresh. Fear and self-doubt gripped his heart. He forced himself to picture Kendal in his mind.

The memory of her devastating smile gave him all the motivation he needed.

He began to get out of the car.

Auntie restrained him for a second. "Don't forget your finger tassel."

Elliot nodded, and opened the door.

"I can't be seen with you from this point on." Auntie added quietly. "But I'll be praying for you."

He got out of the car and pulled out a short length of chain. Twelve hours ago, it had been Emma's silver bracelet. Elliot had threaded a split-ring onto one end, and a wooden bead on the other. He slipped his forefinger into the split-ring and began to twirl the bead around.

The wretched thing nearly flew off his finger, but he managed to catch it in time. He tried swinging it again, this time with more success.

The postman looked at him cautiously from under his hat.

Elliot flicked a hand at him indicating that he should move on. The man turned and began threading his way through the morning shoppers until he came to a gap in the wall of shops. It was no more than three feet wide. Elliot followed the postman through the gap into another world.

The alley was dark and wet. A dirty tangle of pipes and cables ran just above his head. Every now and then he had to step round a stack of old fruit boxes. He stepped aside to allow a child carrying a huge hessian sack on his back to come past. He could not have been more than ten years of age.

Elliot tried not to allow himself to be too distracted by what he saw going on in the tiny sweat shops just off the alleyway, or imagine what might be going on behind the doors that were closed. His one task was to remember the route he was walking as the postman weaved through the maze of alleyways.

An old crone sitting on a milk crate gabbled at him in Chinese.

A wave of panic swept over him. What on earth should he do? *Be brutal and arrogant.* He lifted his hand in what might have been the beginnings of a back-handed slap.

The woman cowered away.

Elliot kept walking.

The postman stopped at the bottom of a flight of concrete steps. Elliot waved him on. The steps were crude. Damp patches smelling of urine covered the landings. As they came to the top of the second flight of stairs, Elliot saw a young man lounging across the top step of the landing. He was dressed only in shorts and plastic sandals. His torso was covered in tattoos.

The postman stepped past him and crossed the landing to a rusting green door. Elliot followed behind, twirling his finger tassel. The young man spoke to him briefly. Elliot acknowledged him by a small lift of his chin.

The postman took out Auntie's letter and knocked on the door.

Elliot took the letter from the man's hand and waved him away. The postman bobbed his head and scurried away.

Nothing happened.

He rapped on the metal door with the wooden bead.

The action seemed to have the desired effect, because he heard a scuffle inside and the rasp of the inspection hatch being opened. He couldn't see anything of the person looking at him other than a tired, yellow-tinged eye.

Bolts scraped, and a moment later the door swung open.

Elliot was faced with an elderly woman who cringed and bowed in front of him. A man, possibly her husband, stood behind her. The stench from the room nearly made him gag. Elliot looked around.

A portable paraffin stove stood on a filthy bench top. There was an untidy pile of bedding alonside one wall. His heart sank. There was no sign of Kendal. But he could see that the back of the room had been curtained off. He stepped over to it and snatched back the curtains.

And there was Kendal, curled up in a fetal position: her hair tangled, and her clothes crumpled and soiled. A chain was fixed to a pair of handcuffs. He stared at her, appalled. A second later, he was on his knees feeling for a pulse in her carotid artery.

Mercifully, he could feel one – steady and strong.

Kendal's eyes blinked and tried to focus on what was happening. She lifted her head, but then let it drop back to the mat.

Elliot gently lifted her head and held it against his cheek. "It's okay. I've got you," he whispered.

She tried to speak, but managed no more than a moan. Her head lolled against him. Carefully, he laid it back down to the mat. As he did, another emotion began to surface within him. Kendal's degradation in this hell-hole filled him with fury. He balled a hand into a fist and held it against his forehead as he fought down the urge to lash out at the couple behind him and beat them both senseless.

No, no. Elliot forced himself to relax. He had to stay in control if he was ever going to get Kendal out safely – and doing that required him to put the fear of God into Kendal's captors. His lips were compressed into a straight line. That, at least, was no problem – he was very angry. Elliot stood up and ripped the curtains fully aside.

The man standing behind them cowered back. Elliot pointed to the padlock holding the chain onto the handcuffs and clicked his fingers impatiently. The old man groped along a shelf behind him, found a key, and handed it out to him.

Elliot ignored it and pointed again to the padlock.

The man bent down and unfastened it. As he backed away, Elliot pointed to the handcuffs and clicked his finger again.

The man shook his head, gabbled in Chinese, and pointed to Elliot.

Something was wrong.

Every moment of delay increased the chances of Elliot

attracting suspicion. He'd just have to cope with the handcuffs. Elliot bent down, scooped Kendal up into his arms, and carried her to the cooking bench. He knocked some of the pots and pans to the floor and laid her half down so he could release one arm to drape a tea towel over her hands. Then he picked her up again.

The towel threatened to fall off, but the old woman pulled it straight and tucked it round her wrists.

He carried Kendal to the door and gave it a kick. The man leaped forward and opened it.

Seconds later, he was carrying her across the landing to the triad sitting on the top step. The young man put down the pornographic magazine he was reading and stood up with a bewildered frown.

If it came to a fight, Elliot knew he was ready for it. Anger still seethed within him. He could feel the length of steel pipe down his trousers. It was attached to a wire hooked over his belt. But if he used it, he'd have to drop Kendal.

No, he decided, it was better to bluff it out.

Keep the initiative.

Elliot jerked his head sideways indicating that the man should get out of his way.

To his relief he did so, but the man began to follow Elliot down the stairs.

Elliot turned, shook his head, and pointed with a finger back up the stairs.

The man said something in Chinese, but Elliot had already turned back and was going down the stairs.

Mercifully, he was not followed.

Elliot felt ridiculously conspicuous carrying a semi-conscious woman through the dank alleyways. The fact that no one challenged him did not speak well of the place. When anyone looked his way, he scowled at them. All, without exception, turned away.

Finally, he saw sunlight at the end of the alleyway. Thirty yards…twenty…ten…and then he was out on the pavement. The people crowding the path immediately stepped away from him in alarm.

Elliot hooked Kendal up and put her face next to his cheek in pretense of affection. It seemed to ease the concern of some of those around him.

A taxi moved up from where it had been parked forty yards down the road and swooped into the curb beside him.

The back door opened.

Elliot could see Emma in the back seat beckoning to him.

He blundered across to her and lifted Kendal into the car.

Emma hoisted Kendal on top of her to make room for Elliot to sit beside them.

He dived into the seat as Emma barked a command to the taxi driver.

However, the car did not move.

As Elliot turned to shut the back door, he saw with horror that Kai was there. He had wedged his thigh against the car door to keep it open.

The two brothers looked at each other, saying nothing.

Elliot was sick to the stomach. However, as he stared in disbelief, Kai put his hand in his pocket and held something out to him.

It took a moment for Elliot to realize what it was. It was a small blunt-looking key – the key to the handcuffs.

Slowley, he reached forward and took it.

Kai nodded. "She's free. Leave the police out of it and don't take her home. I'll call." Then Kai closed the door.

"Go," screamed Emma at the driver.

Chapter 18

The doorbell rang. Emma felt a surge of relief and leaped to her feet to open the door.

Mamma-san stood there leaning on her two sticks. She wasted no words. "Is everyone all right?"

"Yes, Mamma-san. Come in. Thanks so much for coming. It's just that neither of us know what we should do with Kendal. How do we help her?" Her voice faltered. "Neither of us have experience…with drugs."

"Hmm. Sadly, I have. Let me have a look at her." She waved one of her sticks to acknowledge Elliot and then followed Emma into her bedsit.

Kendal was lying on the bed, still in her clothes. Emma had tried to clean her up, but she still smelled appallingly bad.

Mamma-san busied herself checking her vital signs and stroking Kendal's hand. "Let's get these clothes off her and get rid of them. I need to check any injection points for infection and see if there is evidence of sexual violation."

Her matter-of-fact voice was both reassuring and deeply disturbing.

A short time later, they had Kendal stripped and in the bath. By this time, she was in and out of consciousness. She'd lift her head, and then let it fall down to her chest again.

Mamma-san spoke to her constantly, assuring her that she was safe and that she was loved. Emma was deeply moved by her words. Mamma-san had never been a mother, but was naturally more of a mother than any person Emma had ever met. Something deep within her instinctively reached out for that love.

When Kendal was fully clean and placed in Emma's bed, Mamma-san sat beside her and stroked her hair. "Oh, you poor dear. You are safe now – with people who love you. Elliot is just outside, and Emma and I are looking forward to getting to know you properly when you wake up. Now rest in God's love and sleep."

Mamma-san got to her feet, reached out for Emma's hand, and gave it a brief squeeze. "You did well, Emma." She turned back at Kendal and continued to speak. "There is no sign of any infection, but it is very early yet. Sleep is what she needs most now." She paused. "I had a brief consult with my friend, Sai Wing, before I came. He says that it is important that she drinks a lot, so make sure she does. Evidently, she will be nauseous and perhaps a bit irritable when she's fully awake, but she hasn't been on heroin long enough for addiction to kick in." Mamma-san reached for her shoulder bag and extracted a bottle of tablets. "Give her one of these three times a day."

"What are they?"

"Chinese medicine. The ingredients are all natural – part nutrients, part antibiotics. Sai Wing says they're very good."

Emma nodded.

Mamma-san reached for her walking sticks. "We can let Elliot in now. I suspect he'll want to see that all is well."

Emma went to the door and opened it.

Elliot was outside, pacing up and down the hallway.

"You can come in now. Kendal's cleaned up and in bed."

He leaped for the door, eased past her, and crossed over to the bed. Emma caught sight of him kneeling down and reaching out to stroke Kendal's cheek before she closed the door.

Emma took the plastic bags containing Kendal's soiled clothes to the lift and went down to the basement where she deposited them in one of the large communal bins.

She had only just returned to the apartment, when the phone rang. With some misgiving, she picked it up. "Emma Templeton speaking."

"Ahh, that is good. You are at Repulse Bay. Is the Shiffer woman with you?"

Emma recognized his voice straight away. It was Kai.

"Why should I tell you where she is?"

"Is she safe?" Kai demanded.

Emma furrowed her brow on hearing his concern. "Why should you care? You kidnapped her."

There was a pause. "Yes."

"So give me one reason why I shouldn't report you to the police."

"I could say: because it would result in 14K hunting you and Elliot down," he paused. "But that wouldn't be the truth."

"What is the truth?"

"The truth, much as it pains me to admit it, is that I regret doing it."

"Oh."

Nothing was said for a while.

Kai broke the silence. "Is Kendal Shiffer recovering?"

"We think so. Auntie has checked her over. She's sleeping now."

"Auntie, I might have guessed." He paused. "I'm going to ask you something that may seem a bit weird."

"What?" Emma was not disposed to be charitable to Kai in any way. She was appalled at what he'd done.

"Can I come over to your place in Repulse Bay and talk?"

"Certainly not. I'm about to call the police."

"That would be unwise."

"Why? Because you'll hunt me down?"

"No."

"Then why?"

"Because Kendal Shiffer is still in danger."

"What?"

"You heard."

"Why?"

"Can I come over – right now?"

Emma rubbed her forehead. Anxiety and outrage battled within her. What should she do?

"Will you be safe?" she said eventually. It was a stupid thing to ask.

"Yes, unless you scratch me."

It was a poor attempt at humor and totally inappropriate in the circumstances, but it broke her mental impasse.

"Alright. Come."

"Bastard!"

Emma laid a restraining hand on Elliot's arm. But he was not so easily mollified. With dismay, she saw Elliot clench his fists and step toward Kai. He had just come into the front door with Mamma-san. She had volunteered to wait for him in the foyer – presumably to speak to Kai before they all met together.

"No!" Emma yelled.

She shocked herself with her own vehemence.

Elliot stopped in his tracks.

Emma knew that they needed to get the next bit of the conversation out of the way before anything more fruitful could occur. She decided to take the initiative.

"Why did you kidnap your own brother's girlfriend?"

It was a brutal question.

"Is the Shiffer woman your girlfriend?" asked Kai.

Emma looked at Elliot.

"Yes," he said.

Kai shrugged. "She was rich, and she interrupted my plans to meet with you."

"Your plans!" exploded Elliot. "You arrogant, self-centered, evil bastard."

Be careful with your language," barked Kai. "Your woman is free because I decided to let you go."

Elliot looked as if he might explode.

Emma again sought to defuse the situation by taking the lead. "Didn't you care about your brother at all?"

She had the satisfaction of seeing her question hit the mark.

Kai nodded. "The idea that I had a brother hadn't really reached me when I planned it." He shrugged. "And it was all meant to be over by now."

"With the ransom paid?"

"Yes."

Elliot jutted out his chin. "And just how much were you trying to extort, you bastard?"

"Just one million Hong Kong dollars."

"How much is that?"

"About a quarter of a million pounds Sterling," said Emma.

Silence hung in the room. The late morning traffic could be heard growling along Repulse Bay Road.

Mamma-san broke the silence. "I need to sit down, so can I ask everyone to do the same." She smiled at Elliot. "Perhaps you could get us all a cup of tea, dear."

Emma suspected that Mamma-san was giving Elliot something to do so that he wouldn't explode. It was a clever move.

Mercifully, Elliot made his way to the kitchen area.

Everyone sat down.

When they were seated, Kai called across to Elliot. "Did anyone in the Walled City challenge you or suspect that you were not me?"

"Why do you ask?"

"Just answer me," said Kai impatiently.

Elliot turned back to the kettle and switched it off. "No. The guy on the top of the stairs was a bit confused but didn't investigate. Why?"

"Because if it was known you had impersonated me and taken a captive from me, I would be honor bound to kill you."

The shock of what he said hung in the room.

Emma forced herself to say something quickly. "But no one did find out, and we haven't told anyone."

Kai nodded. "That is good."

She decided it was time to turn the heat back on Kai.

"Why did you help us get away?"

Kai shrugged. "A number of reasons."

"Such as?"

Kai pointed to Mamma-san. "I am suspicious of your prayers, old woman. Something's messing with my mind."

Mamma-san was unmoved. "If God is messing with your mind, then you are fortunate that he persists with you."

Kai turned to Emma. "And you haven't helped."

Emma looked up in surprise.

"What did I do?"

Kai waved his hand irritably. "All your talk of honor and God."

"Oh."

"And one other thing," added Kai.

Everyone looked at him.

"What?" demanded Elliot.

Kai drew in a deep breath. "Kendal Shiffer is..." His voice faltered. "...a very beautiful woman, the most beautiful I have ever seen."

Emma was finding the conversation bizarre. Treachery and truth were dancing together in the most extraordinary way.

"What do we tell the police, and what do we tell Kendal's family?" she asked.

"We have to get her home, that's for sure," nodded Elliot. "And I suppose we'll have to tell the police that she's been found, so they stop looking. I haven't seen anything on TV about her kidnap, so I expect there's some sort of suppression order. But, make no mistake, they'll be looking for her."

Kai looked at his brother. "That would make things very difficult for me."

"Why?"

"Because it would be known that 14K did not carry out its threat."

"I couldn't care a bloody fig. Why would that matter anyway?" said Elliot crossly.

Kai turned to his brother. "It would probably mean that I would be killed."

The brutal savagery of Kai's world bludgeoned Emma's sensibilities yet again. She was appalled.

"And there's one other thing," added Kai.

"What's that?" she asked.

"Lachlan Shiffer, of Shiffer Investments, wants Kendal dead."

Chapter 19

K ai shook his brother's hand from his arm. "It's true," he insisted. "No one would dare any triad to not carry out a threat." Kai shrugged. "We have a reputation to protect."

Elliot snorted in anger. "Damn your reputation."

Kai looked at his brother, gauging whether or not things were heading for a fight.

Emma interrupted. "Do we know anything that might suggest this is true? Could Lachlan Shiffer be trying to goad 14K into killing Kendal? It seems too fantastic." She turned to Elliot. "Has Kendal shared anything about her uncle with you?"

Elliot's chin was thrust out in defiance, and he was still dark with rage. Part of Kai's mind was trying working out where he would have to hit his brother first.

"Elliot!" Emma's voice demanded attention.

With some relief, Kai watched his brother turn away and throw himself into an armchair.

Kai glanced at Emma and gave her a nod of appreciation. She'd succeeded in diffusing the situation yet again.

"I hardly know anything," Elliot said.

"What do you know?"

"Just that Kendal's father died last year and that Kendal is now sharing the running of the company with her uncle, Lachlan." He shrugged. "She told me the company is doing pretty well. Evidently, there's some sort of investment bonanza happening in Hong Kong at the moment."

Emma got to her feet as Mamma-san hobbled in from the kitchen and relieved the old woman of the tray she was holding. The girl handed both himself and Elliot a mug of tea. This simple action did much to reduce the tension in the room even further. Mamma-san sat herself on a dining chair with obvious relief and continued the conversation. "Money can do strange things to people. If he'd once caught a whiff of the possibility of having the company to himself, he might have become addicted to the idea."

"How do we find out?" asked Emma.

Kai had already been giving the subject some thought and was ready with an answer. "We call him and find out."

"What?" Emma exclaimed.

Kai shrugged. "If he won't pay to ransom Kendal back, we'll ask him if he will pay to have Kendal killed. Simple."

Elliot passed a hand over his face. "I don't believe I'm hearing this."

Kai nodded. "I will go now and call."

"Why can't you phone from here?" asked Emma.

Elliot answered for him. "Because the call could be traced."

"Yes." Kai turned and headed toward the door.

His brother leaped to his feet. "Oh no. I'm not letting you out of my sight. I'm coming with you. I want to hear exactly what is being said."

Kai shrugged. "Suit yourself."

He saw Emma lay a hand on Elliot's arm. "Don't you have to teach sailing later this afternoon?"

"Yes. But I can go after lunch. I only have to get to Middle Island at the end of the beach, so I've got a bit of time."

Mamma-san interrupted. "Go and make your phone call, and bring back some lunch. I doubt there is enough here to feed us all."

Kai felt odd walking along the foreshore with his twin brother. They looked so alike that he felt everyone must be looking at them. It was not a comfortable sensation .

His brother interrupted his thoughts. "There should be a phone in the foyer of the Repulse Bay Hotel."

"No. You and I stand out and might be remembered. We'll use the phone in a café. No one will remember seeing us, and no one will say that they remember even if they do. People value a trouble-free life."

"And you are capable of handing out trouble, I suppose," said Elliot sourly.

"Yes."

Neither spoke for a while.

In the end, Kai elected to use a phone located in a general store. It was screened by a shelf which gave them a degree of privacy. He took out a notebook and dialed a number.

A secretary answered and asked his business.

"I want to speak with Lachlan Shiffer. It concerns his niece."

"Are you the police?"

"Yes."

There was a pause before Lachlan Shiffer came on the phone. "Yes?" he demanded.

At this point, Elliot grabbed at the handset so he could also hear what was being said. Kai wrestled it back to a position that allowed him to speak. "Mr. Shiffer, I represent the 14K triad society. Do you understand what that means?"

"It means you're a bastard."

"It means you will die unless you do what I say."

There was a moment's silence before Shiffer replied. "What do you want?"

"I want to know what you want. You are trying to make us kill your niece. That much is clear." Kai pictured Kendal's beautiful face and long tanned limbs. Anger rose up within him. He said through gritted teeth, "And we are happy to do so – at a price."

"What price?"

"One million Hong Kong dollars – the same price that was asked for the ransom."

"That's ridiculous. I could let out a contract for one fifth that amount."

"For two-hundred thousand dollars?"

"Yes."

"14K will accept that contract. We will supply proof, and you will pay within twenty-four hours. I will come and collect the money from your office personally."

"Aren't you afraid of being recognized?"

"Oh, I very much hope I am, for whenever you see me, you will be reminded that I have continued to let you live." Kai paused. He needed Shiffer to be terrified. "Your disrespect of 14K means that you have come very close to death. If you are wise, you will not give us the pleasure of killing you. Yours, I assure you, would not be a comfortable death. We'd need it to be a warning to anyone else who might be tempted to play games with us."

Kai saw his brother look at him with incredulity.

He returned his attention to the phone. "Two-hundred thousand, then?"

There was a pause. "Yes. But it's two-hundred thousand to whoever fulfills the contract. You may not be the only one I offer it to."

Kai was shocked at the man's stupidity. "Why do that? We are the ones who have your niece."

Elliot looked fit to explode.

Kai took sole command of the phone and turned away in time to hear Lachlan say, "But I have no proof of that."

"Do not play with me Mr. Shiffer – if you value your life. We can show you proof."

For a moment, nothing was said.

Lachlan eventually broke the silence. "How long will you need…to get the evidence to me?"

"Have the money with you within the next five days and keep it in your briefcase. I will be in contact in a week."

Kai followed Elliot through the front door of the unit, carrying the bag that contained their lunch: crispy egg noodles and fried noodles with pork. As he entered the living room, he was alarmed to see Kendal sitting on the sofa between Emma and Auntie. She looked wan but otherwise seemed well. Hardly any vestige of drug-induced sleepiness remained. She was wearing a dressing gown, presumably Emma's. Ruffled golden hair fell over her shoulders.

Kai's heart gave a lurch.

Emma got to her feet. "We've told Kendal everything that's happened." She worked her lips as if searching for words. "She's not found it easy, so go gently with her."

Kai watched Kendal's eyes flick between Elliot and him. After a second's confusion, they settled on Elliot.

His brother lifted a hand in salutation, as if not trusting himself to say more. Kai could understand. He was probably feeling guilty about passing on Kendal's details to him.

Kendal turned and stared at Kai.

She looked beautiful…and angry.

He stared back – defiant. But even as he did, Kai couldn't help but feel just a little disorientated by her. She was statuesque, proud, and looked powerful.

"So it's all true," she said.

Kai said nothing.

Kendal got to her feet, stepped across to him, and slapped him hard across the face.

Kai barely reacted. After a tense silence, he said, "Yes. I organized your kidnap, and Elliot impersonated me to rescue you. But I caught him as he was getting away."

Elliot broke in. "Kai actually helped you to escape…in the end."

Kai looked at his brother crossly. "Are you trying to excuse my actions?" He heard his own voice. It sounded arrogant and dangerous. He knew he sounded like that when he felt under pressure.

"Why did you let me go?" she asked.

"Because you are the most beautiful woman I have ever seen, and I knew the gods would not be pleased."

Kendal pursed her lips. "You speak of gods, do you know what I've had to endure?"

A sickening alarm rose within his belly. "Were you sexually molested?"

"No, I don't think so. But it was still a nightmare." She paused. "Didn't you care, even a little bit?"

"No. Not then." He lifted his chin defiantly.

"But now?"

Kai did not answer.

"Damn you." She pounded his chest with a fist. Then she punched him with two hands. A moment later, she was pummeling his chest, raining blows on him as if banging on a door.

Kai did not flinch. He welcomed the pain.

Finally, Kendal ran out of strength. She put her hands over her face and burst into tears. Heart wrenching, shuddering sobs escaped her.

Kai caught her as she began to sway.

As she fell against his chest, she instinctively clutched at his shirt, balling it in her fists as she wept.

Kai held her upright with one arm. He wanted to encircle her back with the other but could not bring himself to do so. He stared at his free hand for a moment, perplexed over what he should do with it. But the hand had a mind of its own. It pressed Kendal against his chest. He could feel her breasts against him.

Further thoughts were interrupted by Elliot clearing his throat. "We, er...actually have another problem."

Emma looked across at him. "What's that? Does Lachlan..." her voice trailed off.

Elliot nodded. "Yes. Lachlan has offered two-hundred thousand dollars to have Kendal killed."

Kendal's wailing immediately increased in intensity.

Auntie prized Kendal away from Kai and held her to her own bosom, rocking her gently and cooing words of comfort.

Emma asked quietly. "Why would your uncle wish you dead, Kendal? What's going on?"

Auntie maneuvered Kendal to the couch and sat her down.

Eventually Kendal's weeping subsided, and she began sniffing. Emma handed her a handkerchief.

Kai couldn't stop the fleeting thought that using a handkerchief was a disgusting Western habit. He watched Kendal fight to get herself back under control and restore a degree of dignity. She dabbed at her eyes and allowed her hair to fall forward so that it obscured much of her face.

She shook her head and said softly. "Oh Lachlan. Why? You idiot. It didn't have to come to this!"

Emma prompted her to say more. "What's going on, Kendal?"

Kendal sniffed and shook her head. "Lachlan is not great at investing. In fact, he wouldn't be employed with us at all if he wasn't part owner of the company." She sighed. "He's way too conservative in his investments and has lost people a lot of money. The Board now insists I also sign off on all the accounts he manages." She lowered her head. "He doesn't check the facts and invests in the wrong things, sometimes on the basis of the rumors he hears in his club."

Emma nodded. "So, there's been trouble between you two."

"Not just between the two of us. Lachlan has managed to put a lot of the staff offside. But I'd never have thought he would..." she lowered her head and began to cry.

Emma reached over and put a hand on her shoulder. "We'll sort it out. Nothing's going to happen to you while we're looking after you."

Silently, Kai agreed. He vowed that nothing on earth would ever hurt Kendal again if he could stop it. The irony of what he promised himself, given his recent behavior, was not lost on him. He shook his head. It was bewildering.

Emma continued to speak. "But we do need to find a place for you to hide until we can sort this out with the police."

Kai frowned and shook his head. "Going to the police may not be a good idea. There are many being paid by triads." He paused. "I pay some myself."

Emma nodded. "I'm afraid I agree. With the level of corruption that currently exists in the police, we can't guarantee Kendal will remain safe even if we do go to them." She shrugged. "Although it's highly unlikely that any of the police would turn a blind eye to a murder plot, we just can't be sure." She looked at Kai. "But the main reason we can't go to the police is that you would be arrested. We have to find a way to stop Lachlan ourselves."

Kai wasn't sure what to think. He just knew he felt uncomfortable. He glanced at Emma. The woman had surprised him again with her knowledge of police corruption. She was a strange one, Emma. He brought his thoughts back to the matter in hand. "We have to find a place where Kendal can hide. Can she stay here?"

Elliot shook his head. "I don't think so. Someone could come at any time to claim the third bedroom. And besides that, a cleaner comes in every second day."

Emma looked at Auntie. "Could she stay with you, Auntie?"

The old woman also shook her head. "Sadly, no. I have sharp-eyed servants and am visited most days. I'm afraid I couldn't promise to keep Kendal's whereabouts a secret." She paused. "However, I do know of a place where she could be kept for a week or so without anyone noticing."

"Where's that?" asked Emma.

"Tai-O. It's a fishing village on a little island just off the Western end of Lan Tau Island."

"Lan Tau, where the big prison is?"

"Yes." Auntie smiled. "They call Tai-O 'The Venice of Hong Kong.'"

Emma tilted her head. "Really? Why's that?"

"The village is built on sticks over the water."

"Wow!"

"The friend I work with in the Walled City sometimes goes there when she needs a few days to herself. The fishing family she stays with always welcomes her because she was responsible for getting their son off heroin."

Emma nodded appreciatively. "She sounds quite a lady, this friend."

"She is."

Kai frowned. "How will we get there? The police will be looking for her."

Elliot picked up a map on the coffee table and began unfolding it. "Show me where it is."

Auntie leaned across and stabbed a finger on the map. "There."

"Wow. It's certainly remote." He looked again at the map. "It looks to be about twenty-four nautical miles from here."

Kai knew nothing about nautical miles. "So?" he asked.

Elliot looked up at him. "So I reckon I could sail you there. It would be about four hours sailing each way. If we set off at 5am, I'd be back in time to teach that afternoon."

Emma leaned forward. "Do you have a boat that's able to get there? It's a fairly long way."

"I've got the use of a Swan 36 this month. I use her to teach offshore stuff. She'll do the job easily."

"How many people can it carry?" asked Emma.

"Why?"

"Because there's no way Kendal can be by herself in Tai-O. I'll be going with her."

Elliot raised an eyebrow. "Can you get time off?"

"Yes. I'm my own boss, and I've nearly finished typing up my report." She shrugged. "My work here is pretty much done."

Kai saw Kendal reach for Emma's hand and give it a squeeze. He cleared his throat. "So, who will be going?"

"Just Elliot, Kendal, and myself." Emma looked quizzically at Kai. "Are you all right with that?"

Damn the woman. She sees too much. "Yes," he said. He drank from his mug of tea to wash away the lie.

Auntie got to her feet. "Let's not get ahead of ourselves. I need to make a few phone calls."

Elliot pointed to the phone. Auntie heaved herself to her feet and shuffled across to it.

The conversation between the rest of them continued in fairly desultory fashion until Auntie rejoined them.

Kai was not surprised when she announced, "It is okay with the fishing family, Mr. and Mrs. Lund." She smiled at the girls. "You can stay as long as you like from tomorrow night. I've said that I will supply a bag of rice and a box of fresh vegetables. The Lund's will provide plenty of fish." Auntie laid a hand on Kendal's shoulder. "I must warn you that the conditions will be pretty basic. You'll be sleeping in hammocks, but at least you will be over the water so it'll be cool."

Kendal lifted her chin. "What about toilets and showers?"

"There's a toilet block on shore with a squat hole and a shower."

Kai saw Kendal blanch, but she said nothing.

Auntie turned to Elliot. "Mr. Lund fishes at night. That means he'll be free mid-morning to motor out to you in his boat when he sees you to collect Emma and Kendal. He says it would be less conspicuous than you trying to bring your big pleasure boat in."

Elliot nodded and looked at his watch. "Right, I've only got fifty minutes before I have to leave. Let's get planning."

Kai had the helpless feeling of knowing he had little to contribute to the plans. He told himself that he could at least ensure that the plans were sound. Besides, he reminded himself, he had other things to occupy him. How on earth was he going to find the funds 14K expected from the kidnap of Kendal? His very life might depend on the answer.

Chapter 20

E lliot rose early the next morning. He lit the gas under the kettle for a cup of tea and made his way up the companionway steps. After removing the washboards that sealed the hatchway, he stepped outside into the cockpit. It was still dark.

He'd spent the night aboard *Soleil* so he could have her ready to sail the moment the girls joined him. The fuel tanks had been topped up the night before, and all he had to do now was to remove the sail covers and have another look at the marine chart to remind himself of the salient features of their journey.

It was no hardship for Elliot to live aboard a yacht. He loved them, and *Soleil* was a particularly well-appointed boat. She was a thirty-six foot sloop made of fiberglass. He was familiar with her design as it had been revolutionary in its time. It had a spacious cabin that was able to sleep seven people. The salon featured a U-Shaped settee. When the table in front of it was raised, six people could sit down for a meal. When it was lowered, the settee converted into a double bed.

Elliot had studied the design carefully over the last few weeks and believed it could be improved. He felt that the open spaces down below could prove dangerous to people in rough seas. There were simply not enough places people could wedge themselves in and be secure. It was an old conundrum. A designer always had to balance how much a design catered for the comfort of life on board when the boat was safely moored, and how much it was designed for life at sea. Personally, Elliot always favored what was required at sea. After all, that was the boat's primary purpose.

Fifteen minutes later, the sail covers were off, and the jib lay ready to hoist on the foredeck. He made his way back to the cockpit, picked up his mug of tea, and nursed his thoughts.

They were stormy and disturbing.

The threat to Kendal's life was a shocking and difficult thing to process. Just as disturbing was the memory of Kai's words that had betrayed his affection for Kendal. Elliot's emotions tumbled over each other and taunted him as he brooded.

Eventually, the false dawn started to give way to the real thing. Shafts of light began to highlight the eastern flanks of Middle Island. The island's steep sides soared upward from the still waters thirty yards away. He could now see the white walls of the yacht club. Its patrons needed to climb a long flight of stairs to reach it and could justifiably feel they'd earned a beer by the time they got to the top. The club was just a satellite of the Royal Hong Kong Yacht Club and therefore only had basic amenities. It was nonetheless a handy facility to have as it enabled sailors to sail on the south side of Hong Kong Island in less congested waters. Elliot thought that it was in an ideal location and had little doubt it would develop significantly in the future. *Perhaps Kendal's investment company would have a hand in it.*

Thinking about Kendal took him back to the dark places to which his thoughts had taken him earlier. He was far from sure how things would turn out for her, particularly given what she would have to endure during their voyage over to Tai-O.

Elliot was rescued from his brooding by the sight of Emma and Kendal walking along the far shore. They were carrying Elliot's duffel bag between them. He'd lent it to them to carry their belongings. Moments later, a wiry old Chinese man was propelling them across the water using a single oar over the stern of his sampan. His strokes caused the boat to waggle from side to side as it crossed over to where *Soleil* was moored.

Kendal was wearing clothes he didn't recognize. Emma must have done some shopping for her the previous afternoon.

Elliot helped them aboard and gave them a brief tour of the boat.

After that, not much was said. It was as if each of them was fearful of what lay ahead.

Soft cat's-paws of wind occasionally ruffled an otherwise calm sea. There was hardly any wind which meant they would have to use the vessel's motor. He estimated they would probably be at Tai-O before the southerly wind picked up and allowed them to sail. He sighed. At least that would give him a rollicking sail back to Middle Island.

They were virtually the only boat moving on the water. It was too early for pleasure craft, and all the fishing boats had long since returned to harbor. The 'putt, putt' sound of the fishermen's single cylinder diesels taking them out to their fishing grounds could be heard in the early evening. They fished at night using lights. Elliot had watched them from the balcony at Repulse Bay. They looked like fireflies resting on the water.

The only vessel they passed was a motorized junk. Her high stern made her look as if she was lifting up her skirts. Red tassels adorned her square prow, presumably to ensure good luck.

The little engine drove *Soleil* easily through the water past the steep northern slopes of Lamma Island. Elliot could see a village on the Western end of the island. Everything looked peaceful.

Elliot, however, was not at peace, although he did his best to appear as though he was, as he stood at the helm. The boat's wheel was mounted on a binnacle in the center of the cockpit. This did not leave a lot of room for crew, but with just the two girls, there was plenty of room.

Emma was holding Kendal's hand.

Elliot cleared his throat. "There's tea in the cupboard above the sink if you want a cup."

"Great," said Emma. "I'll make us all a brew."

As she went down the companionway, Kendal pointed to a large straggly island that was looming up to the north. "That's Cheung Chau Island isn't it?"

"Yes, it is."

She smiled. "Have you heard about its famous Bun Festival?"

"No."

"It's a crazy thing. Young men climb sixty-foot tall bamboo frames to pluck buns from giant phallic-shaped bun-towers enclosed within them. Evidently, they use about sixty-thousand buns."

"Wow! I'd like to see that. When does it happen?"

"You've missed it this year. It happens in May."

It wasn't much of a conversation, but Elliot was pleased that Kendal had made the effort. She was looking terrific even though she was pale. The apparent wind caused by their forward motion caused her hair to lift occasionally and blow across her face.

Elliot felt his heart constrict.

Emma handed up mugs of tea from the companionway, and they drank in silence, each seemingly content to listen to the drumming of the motor and the whoosh of water down the side of the boat.

All too soon, *Soleil* was passing the rocky island of Shek Kwu Chau. The nautical chart had also listed its other name, Coffin Island. Elliot thought it quite appropriate given what they would soon be doing.

Twenty minutes later, Elliot broke the silence. "Okay team. This is about as isolated as we're ever going to be, so this is where we do our thing." He turned to Emma. "Will your camera be able to work okay here?"

Emma reached into the bag beside her and produced a white plastic camera. "Yes," she said. "It's a Polaroid 'Swinger,' so it'll give us instant shots."

Elliot hadn't known that such cameras even existed. "Very impressive. Just make sure you show Kendal in the shots and nothing of the boat."

He reached down and switched off the engine leaving *Soleil* to bob impatiently until she gentled down and got used to the quiet.

Then he made his way forward and began rigging the spinnaker boom out to the side, canting it forty-five degrees into the air. The main halyard had been threaded through its outside end and led back to the cockpit. After rigging guy ropes so the boom could not move, Elliot opened the stern locker behind the cockpit and pulled out a long length of chain. It rattled onto the floor at his feet. He turned and said, "Well, this is it." He glanced at Kendal. "Are you still up for this?"

Kendal nodded.

"Okay. Let me remind you what's going to happen. I'm going to wrap this chain around you, clip the main halyard to the chain, and winch you overboard." He took a deep breath. "Emma will take a series of photos of you apparently being drowned. Then we'll bring you back on board."

Kendal nodded and said in a voice that was almost steady, "Are you sure I'll be safe?"

"Yes. You'll have a safety rope tied to your feet. If the main halyard breaks, we'll still be able to haul you back on board."

"Will I need to hold my breath?"

"No. If your head goes under, it will only be a dip of a few seconds. I'll be watching carefully."

Kendal stood up. "Okay then." She drew a deep breath. "Let's get this over with."

Emma held out her hand. "Wait. We need these shots to be shocking and compelling. If you are photographed in clothes that may be recognized as not belonging to you, Lachlan might get suspicious." She grimaced. "I'm sorry, but I think you need to at least strip down to your underpants and bra."

Kendal turned to Elliot. "What do you think?"

Elliot swallowed. "Um, I think she's right. If we're going to do it, we have to make it as convincing as possible. It's got to be...horrible."

She turned back to Emma. "You said that I should at least strip down to underpants and bra. Does that mean that being naked would be better?"

Emma worked her mouth, but it took a while for the words to

come. "Um, it would show a level of degradation consistent with a brutal killing," She paused, then hurried on. "But in no way am I suggesting you should."

Kendal lifted her chin. "I'm prepared to do anything it takes to make this convincing." She looked at Emma and then Elliot, as if daring them to say otherwise.

No one said anything.

Kendal nodded and began to undress.

Elliot watched, appalled at what Kendal was having to put herself through. He dammed Lachlan to hell and back, and at that moment wanted to inflict terrible violence on him.

He also needed to cope with sexual tension. It appalled him in the circumstances, but there was no denying it. His body tightened. It was impossible not to notice Kendal's magnificent body. It was exquisite proud breasts, narrow waist, and beautiful curving thighs.

She was naked except for her panties.

Elliot moved forward with the end of the chain.

For a few moments, the two of them stood still and looked at each other.

Elliot saw the battle between fear and bravery in her eyes – and something else. She didn't flinch as he looked at her.

He swallowed.

Kendal bent down and began to remove her panties, but it was all too much for Elliot. "Stop," he said. He reached out a hand. "I… I'm not sure I can do this…if…" he did not finish the sentence.

Kendal pulled her panties back up and said nothing.

Emma broke in. "I think you look convincing enough as you are."

"I'm ready," said Kendal.

Elliot took out the handcuffs that had sat uncomfortably in his pocket for so long and put them on Kendal's wrists. Then he began to wrap the chain around her torso. What made the operation even more terrible was that Kendal turned around on her feet to assist him. More than once he had to stop, lower his head, and psych himself up to continue. It was the hardest thing he'd ever had to do in his life. The chain pushed hard against her breasts, disfiguring them.

Eventually, it was done.

Elliot tied the end of the main halyard to the chain behind her back and then guided her until she stood on the side deck. He returned to the main winch and, without ceremony, began to wind it in as quickly as he could.

Kendal screamed as the halyard pulled her overboard and swung her out so that her legs trailed in the water. *Soleil* listed over under the weight and dropped Kendal into the water up to her thighs.

Elliot could see the chains pressing into Kendal's flesh.

Mercifully, her screaming stopped.

Emma began to take her photographs, but it was not a quick process. It took time for each individual film to be developed.

Elliot dropped Kendal lower and lower in the water until she was up to her neck. When that photograph had been taken, he yelled, "That's enough. I'm bringing you back in."

He loosened one of the guys tethering the spinnaker boom so that it could swing in and bring Kendal back to side of the boat. Then, with Emma's help, he hauled her back into the cockpit.

Kendal lay on the floor, sobbing.

Elliot found that he too was weeping.

After a while, he helped Kendal to her feet and unwrapped the chain. They had left red welts across her torso. Elliot traced his fingers over one just under her breast, bowed his head and tried to blink away his tears.

He was amazed to hear Kendal say, "I'm okay, Elliot."

How could she be okay? He removed the handcuffs from her wrists and, in a flash of anger, threw them into the sea.

Emma took Kendal by the hand. "Kendal, I'd like to take one more shot of you in the water with no rope holding you up, with only the top of your head showing. Do you feel up to getting back in the water for another minute?"

Kendal nodded and without a word, climbed over the guard rail and eased herself back into the water.

Three minutes later, she was back on board. Emma guided her down the companionway into the cabin.

Elliot called after them, "I won't start the engine until you've finished having a shower. You'll find it works pretty well. Just follow the instructions printed on the bulkhead." He then trailed the chain up to the foredeck and set about reattaching it to the anchor-line from where it had been taken.

Emma poked her head up from the companionway when he returned to the cockpit. She said hesitantly, "The photographs are good."

He nodded.

She continued. "I'll stay down here a while with Kendal."

"Could you make her a cup of tea? Use plenty of sugar, even though she doesn't take it. It's good for shock."

Emma nodded and disappeared.

He glanced around him. The steep hills of Lan Tau Island were to the north, and to the west, were the uninhabited Soko Islands. Elliot felt a puff of wind on his cheek. Moments later, it was followed by another. The wind was now darkening the surface of the water, raising it up into tiny ripples. It was as if it too no longer needed to hold its breath.

Emma called up from down below, "Kendal's finished her shower. Once she's finished her tea, she's going to lie down in one of the bunks. I'll settle her and then come and join you."

Ten minutes later, Emma was with Elliot in the cockpit. *Soleil* was now scything through the water. She was under power, but Elliot gauged that it wouldn't be long before there was enough wind to sail.

In the hope that it would help take Emma's mind off the trauma they'd just been through, he invited her to take the wheel. She agreed, and after a few tentative turns back and forth, got the feel of the boat and was looking comfortable. In fact, she seemed to relish being on the helm. Elliot wondered how she would fare when the boat was under sail. He found himself looking forward to finding out.

Ten minutes later, he hoisted the main and jib. They flapped and banged until he hauled them in. *Soleil's* sails caught the wind. She leaned over and surged forward. With some relief, Elliot switched off the engine. The only sound was that of *Soleil* shouldering her way through the waves.

Elliot took a deep breath. There was something pure and elemental about being driven through the sea by wind alone. And right now, he desperately needed to feel something pure. The terrible process of acting out Kendal's murder had rocked him to the core. It was shocking to see someone, particularly such an exquisite woman, being humiliated, terrorized, and dispatched as if they were of no worth. What sort of evil would countenance such a thing?

He curled himself up on the cockpit bench where he could keep an eye on Emma at the wheel. She was doing well.

The thoughts within him churned and tumbled, exhausting him and giving him no peace. Eventually, he gave them voice.

"What sort of utter bastard can order the murder of someone like Kendal − of anyone, come to that?" he blurted. Elliot shook his head. "I don't get it. I simply don't understand that level of evil."

Emma glanced at him. "Fundamentally, evil is the absence of empathy. More specifically, it is the absence of God's love."

Elliot raised an eyebrow. This was not where he expected the conversation to go. He felt awkward. "God's love?"

She nodded. "Yes. If you don't acknowledge God, there's no fundamental morality, meaning or purpose. And the end-point of that is to collapse back to the world of the animal kingdom with its lust for predation and power." She paused. "...as every godless despot in the last century has shown."

Elliot scoffed. "I don't think I lack morals − and I'm an atheist."

Emma waved her hand dismissively. "You're simply trading on the moral capital built up by centuries of Christian culture. It will be eroded in time, driven by the lie of self-liberation." She sniffed. "Elitism and oppression is the logical endpoint of atheistic thinking. A world where there is no morality beyond that which pleases the self, will not be a kind one.

Elliot buried his hands in the pockets of his smock top. "I don't do any of those…bad things."

"No, but by floating lazily down the atheistic path of society, you're helping to bring it about."

Elliot grunted and turned away. "I've never really thought about this stuff."

"Hmm. An atheist can never be too careful in maintaining their ignorance."

"What do you mean?"

"Atheism shuts down serious thinking about why the universe exists."

He laughed. "I thought the Enlightenment won the right for us to open our minds."

"Open your mind?"

"Yes."

"Have you seriously explored the claim of God coming to us in history as Jesus?"

"Not really."

"And that's an open mind?"

Elliot crossed his arms. "How the hell can anyone know what is actually true?"

"I think having the humility and courage to seek is probably where it begins."

"Hmm." He looked away.

Emma added hesitantly. "Anyway, I…I hope you find the truth."

"You'd care?"

"Yes."

Soleil surged along the south coast of Lan Tau Island on her favorite point of sailing, a beam reach with the wind blowing against her side. She seemed to rejoice in being set free to dance with the elements. It wasn't long before they reached the south-western corner of the island and changed course to head north. *Soleil's* motion changed because the wind was now behind her. She rolled from side to side as she made her way up the western coast. Tai-O Island could now be seen up ahead.

Elliot made sure Emma was comfortable on the wheel and then

ducked down the companionway to check on Kendal. He found her curled up on a bunk. She was facing the hull, as if trying to hide.

"Hi," he said. He felt it a woefully inadequate thing to say. Elliot swallowed and tried again. "How are you going?" He brushed her hair back from her cheek, and laid his hand on it for just a second.

Kendal moved her hand and laid it on top of his. "I'll live."

"Well, I'm glad of that." He paused. "You did well."

"I was terrified."

"Yes. The photos show it."

She turned over and lifted herself up on an elbow. "Can I see them?"

He shook his head. "No, I don't think so. The images would haunt you for too long."

"Oh." She paused. "Will you destroy them...when you can. I couldn't bear..."

"Yes. I...I'll look forward to doing it."

She managed a shy smile. "Did I disturb you too much?"

"You did." He didn't risk saying anything more and changed the subject. "We're coming up to Tai-O. I've spotted a boat making its way toward us. It will probably be Mr. Lund, so you'd better get ready to jump ship."

Kendal swung her legs over the edge. "Okay."

Elliot made his way up to the cockpit and took over the helm. A nuggety little fishing boat with a rounded canvas canopy on its deck came barreling up toward them. He waved at the man in the boat and turned *Soleil* into the wind so that she hove to. Once he'd hung out fenders on the starboard side, the fishing boat edged alongside. The man at its helm threw Elliot a line. He was dressed in a dirty vest and shorts.

Once the boat was made fast, the man stood up and tapped his chest. "Me, Mr. Lund."

Emma spoke to him in Cantonese.

The man beamed and motioned for her to pass Elliot's kit bag over to him. The girls followed after.

Elliot untied the lines that held the boats together, but was reluctant to let go of the last one. He held on to it and crouched down to speak with the girls. "I've got the day off tomorrow, so I'll be able to visit with Kai when he comes to bring the rice and vegetables that Auntie's organized."

Emma nodded and held out a plastic bag. "Don't forget these, she said. It's the photographs."

Elliot took them and nodded. He glanced up at the village of Tai-O. It was still well in the distance. The thought came to him that he would have no idea where to find the girls when he came with their supplies tomorrow. "Here," he said, unhitching one of *Soleil's* fenders. "Take this and hang it out the window of the house you're staying in. Then we'll know where to come."

She took the fender and managed a smile. "Are you sure you'll be able to handle *Soleil* okay on your own. She's a big boat."

"You're kidding me, right?"

She smiled.

Elliot threw the line to the fisherman.

"See you tomorrow," he shouted.

Chapter 21

There was nothing pretty about the little workboat. Elliot leaned against its boxy cabin and braced his legs in order to ride the motion of the boat. It had been surging along at a goodly pace for the last two hours, piloted by a cheerful young Chinese man.

The boat looked like a high-heeled slipper. Its graceful sheer rose up to a high stern. Nothing much else about it was graceful. A boxy cabin with peeling paint sat on its deck amid an assortment of metal drums, plastic cans, and bamboo poles.

That morning, Elliot had gone to Auntie's house in Tai Tam to join Kai who had spent the night there. With the help of a servant, the two of them carried sacks of rice and boxes of groceries to the fisherman's wharf and loaded them on the boat.

Elliot looked across to the mountainous western coast of Lan Tau Island. They'd made good progress and would be in Tai-O within the hour.

Kai was sitting close by on the deck with his back against the stubby mast. He'd not said much during the morning and seemed to be wrestling with some inner demon. Elliot noticed him fingering the ivory locket hanging round his neck. He risked a comment. "What's on your mind, Kai?"

Kai closed his eyes and tilted his head back with every appearance of weariness. When he eventually spoke, he said, "The dragon stone weighs heavier than it used to."

"What do you mean?"

Kai waved a hand. "It does not matter."

Elliot did not pursue it. In truth, his own mind was also in turmoil. He was still unable to get over mental images of Kendal wrapped in chains, and the evil that had made it necessary. Elliot clamped his jaw together as he replayed the memory of it.

He'd given the photos to Kai. His brother had looked at them, nodded, and said nothing. Elliot shook his head. How on earth could you say nothing about such a thing? Kendal had had to endure a terrible nightmare because of the avarice and ambitions of her uncle. He let the anger in him spill over into words. "Kai, when you go to see Lachlan with the photos, promise me that you will give him hell."

Kai lifted his head. "What do you mean?"

"I want Lachlan to suffer." he paused, "for everything he's caused Kendal to go through."

His brother looked at him with an unreadable expression. "I don't think you are used to saying such things."

Elliot crossed his arms. "Well, I'm saying them now."

Kai nodded slowly. "Be careful what you wish for."

"What do you mean?"

"Life is not good on the dark side. Do not go there, or wish for it."

Elliot lapsed into silence and nursed his brother's rebuke. The irony of being lectured on good and evil by a leader of a triad gang was not lost on him. Reflecting on evil made him recall his conversation with Emma. After a moment, he asked, "Do you believe in God?"

Kai looked at him balefully. "I am trying to find him."

"Why?"

"Because I am empty."

"I've never really looked," Elliot admitted.

Kai shook his head. "Can it be that you've never thought of these big things?"

"Not really."

Kai tilted his head back. "Then you are truly empty."

Elliot coughed a derisive laugh. "You've just said that it's you who feels empty."

"I am empty, yes," he paused, "and I am a bad man. But at least I know it."

Tai-O Island was now visible up ahead, and Elliot was able to see some of the details of the village. It clung to the island's shoreline in front of steeply sided hills. He was looking forward to seeing the village, not least because Auntie had told him that Tai-O was not only famous for its fishing but also for its history of piracy.

As they entered the tidal creek separating the island from the mainland, the features of Tai-O became clear. Much of the village was built on stilts over the water. The shoreline was encrusted with a dense collection of untidy wooden shacks. Many had wooden ladders enabling those living above to climb down to their boats. Tarpaulins, buckets, and washing hung from everywhere. Just occasionally, a TV aerial could be seen. They looked incongruous above the rickety village that, in all other respects, seemed to belong to a previous century.

Boats of all sizes were tethered below the wooden platforms. All of them had blunt, wedge-shaped fronts. The bigger ones sported canopies built of canvas, wood or tin. Some had cabins perched on top of their high sweeping sterns. Elliot couldn't help but wonder what life must be like living on a twenty-degree slope.

He glanced along the line of huts and saw *Soleil's* fender hanging from an open window. "There," he said, pointing to it.

The young boatman nodded, throttled the engine back, and glided the boat into the wooden ladder underneath it. As they approached, Emma and Kendal came to the window and waved. Elliot was relieved to see them both looking relaxed.

Mr. Lund appeared at the opening by the ladder and helped to haul the boxes and sacks up into the hut, voicing his appreciation at

Auntie's largesse as he did. "Your Auntie velly good! Number one good guy."

The room at the top of the ladder doubled as the girls' bedroom and living area, as well as being the main thoroughfare to the rest of the shack. Mrs. Lund came in from the back, welcomed them, and returned to the kitchen area to make them all tea.

Elliot looked around the room. Emma and Kendal were sleeping in hammocks behind a curtain. Each had been equipped with a mosquito net that hung from a cord above them. "Are the hammocks comfortable?" he asked.

"Very," said Emma. "You can hear the water under the floorboards. And even though you can hear the noise from the community around you, it's very peaceful."

"It looks a bit cramped," he said.

"Yes, but we're left pretty much to ourselves, except for meals," she said. "Life is slow here and reduced to its bare simplicity." She smiled. "There's something cleansing about it."

Kendal, he noticed, was wearing Emma's caftan. She plucked at it occasionally, pumping it in and out to air herself in the enervating heat. The sea breeze had yet to kick in.

"Where's our boat-wallah?" asked Elliot.

Kai sniffed. "He stayed on his boat. He lives there."

Mrs. Lund arrived with the tea and, after serving it, left them alone. Emma voiced their thanks.

The four of them sat on benches either side of a Formica-topped table sipping their tea. Elliot noticed that Kai was continuing to brood. He wore a permanent frown and seemed distracted. Eventually, Elliot couldn't bear it any longer. "Okay, mate. Out with it. What's the matter? You've been in a foul mood all morning."

Kai formed his mouth into a thin line, as if forcing himself to say nothing.

Emma's brow creased with concern. "What's the matter?"

Kai looked at her and sighed. "I have a problem."

They waited for him to say more.

He nodded to Kendal. "14K know I have kidnapped you. Some of them are waiting to be paid for their services." He lowered his gaze. "And my father, Mr. K, is waiting for his money to be paid to him."

Elliot frowned. "How much?"

"We demanded one million." He shrugged. "We don't negotiate. Mr. K needs to be paid half of that. So…"

"Half a million," finished Elliot. "Wow!" He paused for a moment before saying doubtfully, "Do you have enough in personal savings to cover that?"

Kai shook his head. "I can only cover half."

"So we need a quarter of a million."

"What happens if you don't pay?" asked Emma.

"I get questioned. My father has already asked to see me." He shrugged. "If my answer is not satisfactory, I am killed. 14K are very sensitive about people not paying money that's due them. It's the one thing they won't compromise on."

Emma's mouth dropped open. "Gee!"

"So you see, I have a problem."

Elliot tapped the table. "When do you need to pay this half million?"

"Tomorrow, ideally. Certainly, no longer than the day after."

Emma laid a hand on top of Kai's. "Then you've got to go into hiding. You've got to run for your life."

Kai snatched his hand away and slapped the table. "I will not run. It is not honorable."

Everyone was silent for a while.

Elliot blew out his cheeks. "How on earth can we get hold of another quarter of a million? We can't get it out of Lachlan in two days. We don't have the time."

Kendal looked at Kai. "I'd be prepared to lend you money against what we might recoup from Lachlan, but I can't operate my account." She shrugged. "I'm meant to be dead."

"How much money can we scrape together between us right now?" asked Emma.

Elliot leaned back. "Almost nothing from me. I'm skint."

"I have some," said Emma. "But I'd need to get to a bank that has a reciprocal arrangement with my bank in the UK. And all that would take time."

Elliot turned to his brother. "How much do you have?"

"I have twelve thousand dollars."

"What?"

"Twelve thousand?"

Elliot was incredulous. "You carry that sort of money around with you?"

"Quite often. Money is useful. It helps get things done."

Emma sighed. "Twelve thousand is a long way short of two-hundred and fifty thousand."

For a while, the only sounds came from the water lapping against the posts and some women laughing and chatting nearby.

Kendal lifted her chin. It was a regal gesture that accentuated the nape of her neck. "I might be able to turn that twelve thousand into a quarter of a million."

Everyone turned to her.

"Can you get me to Macau?" she added.

Elliot frowned.

"What: the old Portuguese settlement?"

"Yes."

"Why?"

"Can you get me to the floating casinos there? I'd normally travel by hydrofoil, but we don't have that option."

Elliot scratched his head. "Macau belongs to Portugal. You'd need a visa and a passport."

"I know. But I'm dead, remember."

"How on earth can you turn twelve thousand into two-hundred and fifty thousand?" said Emma.

With just a touch of haughtiness, Kendal replied, "I count cards." She smiled. "I'm rather good with numbers."

Elliot looked at her doubtfully. "How good?"

"I used to advise my father when he played. I got him banned from his first casino when I was eighteen."

"Oh."

Emma glanced at him. "But how can we get Kendal to Macau?"

Kai pushed himself back from the table. "Our boat-wallah can take us. He'll be glad to make more money."

"What? It would take ages to get there, wouldn't it?"

"Not really," said Elliot. "We're actually pretty close to Macau. I've seen the chart. Tai-O is on one side of the Pearl Estuary, and Macau is on the other. It can't be more than twenty nautical miles away." He did some calculations. "That's about three hours motoring at six knots."

Kendal nodded. "So you could get me there in time to play the tables this evening?"

"Yes."

"And I could get back in the early morning, which would give you time to get back to Hong Kong by tomorrow lunchtime?"

"Yeah. I suppose that would work."

"But what about the passport visa thing?" said Emma.

Kai waved a hand. "Pah! We won't need them if we go in the fishing boat. I go to Macau all the time without one."

Elliot nodded. "So: who's going to go? Kendal, obviously…"

"And Kai must go," said Emma. "He knows the ropes."

"Okay," said Elliot. "What do we need to do to get ready?"

Kai got to his feet. "I'll check with the boat-wallah. He'll have to make sure he's got enough diesel."

Kendal pointed to Kai. "Do you have a bank account?"

"Not one that is…er, regular."

"If we're going to deal with a casino, you'll need to open one before you go. I saw a Hong Kong and Shanghai Bank in the village yesterday. All you need to do is provide proof of identity."

In the end, all four of them decided to walk into the village. They threaded their way through the huts until they reached the narrow road that took them to the village center. The street was crowded with people doing their shopping and hawking their wares. Mangy dogs scavenged among them.

The biggest village shops were concentrated around the ferry that linked the island to the mainland. Elliot had never seen a ferry quite like it before. It was a broad, flat-bottomed punt. A rope that spanned the creek had been threaded between upright poles fastened to the side of the ferry. This arrangement stopped the punt from being swept sideways by the tide, and allowed the boatman to concentrate only on pulling the punt across the twenty yards to the other side. Elliot watched the sinewy man as he labored under his conical hat.

Slimy steps led down to the ferry. Beside the steps was a white building with a sign emblazoned on its front, 'The Hongkong and Shanghai Banking Corporation.'

Kai pointed to it. "I'll go in there with Kendal." He turned to Elliot and Emma. "You two stay outside."

Elliot wasn't sure what he felt about Kai taking charge, but nodded nonetheless.

He and Emma found a nearby food stall and ordered a coke.

They watched as people pushed past one other to get onto the punt.

"A curious feature of the Chinese psyche is that Chinese people don't value anyone or anything much beyond their own doorstep," Emma said. "They certainly don't queue politely like the English."

"I wonder why that is?"

Emma didn't answer.

Half an hour later, Kendal and Kai joined them.

"Now what?" said Elliot.

Kendal answered straight away. "Now I need to buy a dress, or at least a skirt. And preferably shoes."

Emma frowned. "Will you be able to get them here?"

"I think so," Kai said. "I saw a brothel." He smiled. "There's always a place selling dresses if there is a brothel."

Elliot shook his head in disbelief.

Kendal got off her stool. "Emma and I will go to try and find a dress that will fit." She sighed. "It mightn't be easy. I'm bigger than most Chinese."

A mental image of Kendal trying to get into a tight dress momentarily disturbed Elliot's sensibilities. He cleared his throat. "We'll wait for you back at the fishing shack."

Chapter 22

K ai watched sourly as the sleek white hydrofoil thundered past
them. The wretched thing must be going five times their
speed in the fishing boat. He would dearly love to be aboard it so he
could get to Macau quickly. Being tossed about by the drunken
movements of a slow-moving fishing boat had long since lost its
appeal.

He read the name on the hydrofoil: 'Flying Dragon.' It was
certainly flying – even though it was a large vessel. He shook his
head. There was something very strange about seeing a large boat
suspended above the water, held up only by fins.

Kai was sitting with his back against the front bulkhead of the
deck cabin. The only positive thing about this was that Kendal was
beside him. She had experimented with going into the cabin, but
hurriedly came back on deck, driven there by the noise, diesel
fumes, and the none-too-tidy domestic arrangements of the
boatman.

Kai luxuriated in being alone with her. She was wearing a
caftan, while he was bare chested. This wasn't, he reminded himself,
because he wanted to show off his physique. It was because his
white shirt had been washed and was now fluttering from one of the

cables that held the mast up. Nonetheless, he was in no rush to put the shirt back on.

Kendal insisted that they dress appropriately for the casino. She'd not only bought a dress for herself, but had bought him a pair of black trousers and some socks and shoes. Evidently, Emma had told her what size she thought Elliot's feet were.

He glanced at her as she arched her back and stretched. It was such an innocent movement, but it showcased her femininity in a way that caused him to hold his breath. Kendal settled herself back against the cabin and said, without looking at him, "Why did you open a bank account in your brother's name and not your own?"

He blinked. There'd been no subtle introduction to her question. It hit him squarely between the eyes. "I didn't think you noticed."

"I did."

"You have sharp eyes."

She waited for him to continue.

"I, er…" He gathered his thoughts and tried again. "It's wise for me to remain anonymous, right now." He shrugged. "Mine is, er…a life lived in the shadows."

"How did you get Elliot's wallet?"

"I stole it." He shrugged. "I needed details of his identity for the bank."

She smiled. "Have you given it back?"

"Yes. I just said it had dropped out of his pocket."

They lapsed into silence.

The coast of China was becoming more distinct up ahead of them. They would be in Macau in another forty minutes.

Kendal broke the silence. "Do you really have to pay half a million to your father?"

"Half a million – or a dead body." He shrugged. "Either is regarded as fruitful. A body helps the next victim to pay more."

"And in this case," she said slowly, "it would have to be my dead body."

"Yes."

She paused. "You weren't ever…tempted?"

He glanced at her. "No."

Kendal smiled. "I don't think you're very good at being a triad."

Kai said nothing.

"So tell me Kai," she said, "what is it that you really want?"

He leaned back and closed his eyes. What he wanted was to kiss Kendal, to run his hands over her and make love. Before he realized he'd said it, he heard himself say, "I want you."

Amazingly, Kendal didn't react. She looked at him and nodded. "You understand power," she said. "But I don't know if it is the power of lust or love?"

This was not the sort of conversation Kai was familiar with. He was used to dominating conversations, particularly with women. He said slowly, "I think you also understand power. But for you, it is different."

"In what way?"

"You love the power to transform."

"Transform?"

"Yes, you love transforming places like Hong Kong. It excites you." He tapped his chest. "I love power over people."

She looked at him doubtfully. "Hmm, I'm not sure that's really true."

He grunted. "It's probably less true now than it used to be," he conceded.

"So tell me: other than myself, what is it that you really seek?"

"In life?"

"Yes."

He lowered his head. "You cannot give me what I seek."

She waited for him to say more.

Kai sighed. "Because I don't know what that is."

Kendal nodded. "Give me some words that come closest to describing..." she trailed off.

Kai closed his eyes and leaned back. "Peace. I want peace; peace and honor." He looked up at her. "I daren't hope for forgiveness."

Nothing much was said in the next twenty minutes.

Kai eventually broke the silence. "How do you see things

working when we get to Macau? Do you want to advise me as I play the tables, or do you want to play them?"

"Are you used to playing blackjack?"

Kai sniffed. "No. I prefer *fan tan*."

"Then it's probably easier if I play."

"How do you count cards? Is it difficult?"

"It can be. There are a number of ways of doing it. But at its simplest, it's just a case of keeping track of how many cards have been dealt which have the value of 10."

"What do you mean?"

"Well, in Blackjack, the odds become favorable to the player when there are more aces and 10 value cards remaining in the shoe. Card counting is simply keeping track of the ratio of low cards to high cards that have been played. If there are more low cards, the advantage shifts to the player. If there are more high cards, the casino's advantage increases."

The city of Macau was now becoming visible. Kendal pointed to the round hotel tower of the Casino Lisboa. "That's one of the casinos my father was banned from."

Kai laughed. "The world does not like anyone winning."

"But Macau must at least offer the illusion of luck. Its very survival depends on it."

He raised an eyebrow.

"The British were rude enough to take over Hong Kong and develop it as one of the great deep water ports of Asia. It stole most of Macau's trade." She shrugged. "Macau had to developed itself as a gambling center to stay alive."

"Well, I hope I manage to stay alive." He hadn't intended to sound so negative, but it was too late. His comment had the effect of killing the conversation.

Kai got to his feet and walked down the side deck in order to talk to the boatman. "Bring us round to Inner Harbor and drop us near *Rua das Lorchas*," he said.

"Where's that?" the boatman asked.

"I'll show you."

The boat chugged past the two islands just off the Macau Peninsula and made its way up Inner Harbor. Macau city cluttered the bank on the right, and the hills of China rose from the water half a mile away to the left. The boatman pointed to the long line of junks moored just offshore from the city and said in Cantonese, "I'll anchor there and wait for you. Watch where I go so you can get a sampan out to me." He paused. "What time will you come?"

"No idea."

The boatman nodded.

Kendal walked down the boat and made her way below in order to change. For better or worse, the time had come to play the game that life had dealt them.

When Emma returned from carrying the tea tray back to Mrs. Lund, she found Elliot inspecting a hammock.

"These canvas hammocks are similar to those traditionally used by the British navy. They've got twelve cords at each end."

"I don't know about that, but I can tell you that they're comfortable to sleep in. Try it out. Mine's on the left."

Elliot pressed on her hammock and then sat down tentatively on it. Once he was satisfied as to its strength, he lay down. "Hmm. It's great."

Emma didn't want to talk about hammocks at all – and suspected Elliot didn't either. The number one subject burning in her heart was whether Kai and Kendal would be successful in getting the funds necessary to protect Kai. The ethics of gaining the funds through gambling bothered her, but there didn't seem to be any alternative. She sighed.

Elliot noticed. "Worrying about Kai and Kendal?"

She nodded. "Yes. It's a huge thing they're attempting."

"Crossing one of China's largest river estuaries in a small boat; entering illegally into another country; and having to win a quarter of a million Hong Kong dollars in a casino: what could possibly go wrong?"

She smiled. "Yeah, hard to imagine how anything could."

They were silent for a while.

The warm light of the western sun slowly surrendered to the deep blues of evening as twilight fell. Emma listened to the sounds of community around her. It was the sound of chatter, barking dogs, pots being banged and scrubbed, and mothers calling their children to bed. With time, the noise quietened down and peace, of a sort, descended.

The only disturbance came when Mr. Lund came in and hung a hurricane lamp up so they could have some light. It threw deep shadows across the ceiling joists. The man came back a minute later, passed through their room to the door on top of the ladder, and climbed down into his boat. Moments later, they could hear the engine puttering away taking him to his fishing ground.

Emma glanced at Elliot and couldn't work out whether or not he was asleep. Rather than disturb him, she climbed into Kendal's hammock.

Her troubled thoughts were interrupted. "Are you going to sleep?" said Elliot.

"I'm not sure I could."

"Me neither."

She paused. "Are you wishing you could have gone with them?"

"Yes."

"To protect Kendal from your brother?"

Elliot pulled down the side of his hammock so he could see Emma better. "The trouble with you, Emma Templeton, is that you see too much."

"Oh." She wasn't quite sure what to make of his comment. "Anyway," she continued. "I'm glad you stayed here."

"With you?"

"With me."

She let the ambiguity of her reply play among the lamplight that flickered on the beams above her. It was high time to change the subject.

"What do you want to do in life Elliot?"

"What: when I get back to England?"

"In life."

"Oh I dunno. Design yachts, I suppose. Perhaps develop a sailing school." He smiled. "Get through life with the minimum amount of grief."

Emma frowned. "Really?"

"Yeah. Why?"

"If your highest hope in life is simply to live as pleasurably as possible before you die, then you are terribly vulnerable."

"Vulnerable to what?"

"Having no hope or meaning to throw in the face of suffering when it comes."

Elliot looked doubtful. "I'm…a rationalist."

"Is it rational to believe that the universe came from nothing as a result of nothing?"

Elliot rubbed his forehead. "With all the different religions, how can you know what's true?"

"Perhaps because the true one came to tell us."

Elliot shook his head. "Nah. I don't buy it. Christianity is a western religion. It has no place in China."

"Really?"

Elliot nodded.

"The Christian gospel has the Jewish Old Testament as its heritage. Its stories lay down the principle of a lamb being sacrificed to symbolically take away the sins of the people."

"So?"

"Did you know that Jesus is referred to as the 'lamb of God?'"

"No."

"He's called that because he came to die to pay the price for our sins."

"I still don't…"

Emma interrupted him. "The Chinese word for 'righteousness' is *yi*. It's made up of two characters, one placed over the top of the other. The top character is 'a lamb.' The bottom character is 'me.'" She paused. "That means the Chinese character for righteousness is literally, 'the lamb over me.'" She looked across at Elliot. "Tell me, does that sound like God is not interested in China?"

Elliot held up his hands in surrender. "I shouldn't mess with an Oxford graduate."

Emma was disturbed by the rather shocking thought that she hoped he would.

Elliot continued. "Here, let's swap hammocks so you can sleep in your own."

When she climbed into her own hammock, she could smell the faint odor left by Elliot.

It was a pleasing smell.

Kai was still in shock and feeling more than a little self-conscious as he stood on the dock. Outwardly, he was watching the fishing boat chug out to the line of junks moored offshore. Inwardly, he was trying to get over the sight of Kendal. She had changed into an emerald green, figure-hugging *cheongsam*. It showcased her figure powerfully, not in a showy way but in a way that accentuated her class and poise. She was breathtaking.

He stood beside her in his white shirt and new dark trousers, conscious that he must now play a most unaccustomed role – that of being in support.

Evening was beginning to fall over the city, leeching out its color and replacing it with the twinkle of urban lights. The streets, however, seemed to be as busy as ever. He liked Macau and had occasionally done business with his counterpart here. The interests of 14K had grown rapidly within its gambling culture.

In many ways, Macau was a picture of Kai himself; it was part Asian and part Caucasian. Four-hundred years of Portuguese colonization had left a distinctive mark on the city. Colonial houses stood neatly alongside cobbled streets. The Portuguese passion for religion was also very evident, not least in the ornate facade of St. Paul's Basilica that stood on the hill in the middle of the city. Evidently, the rest of the building had been destroyed by fire. He wondered briefly if that was all religion was – a facade. But that thought led him to think of Auntie. He smiled and conceded that what you saw was what you got with her.

He dragged his thoughts back to the matter in hand and risked looking at Kendal. "Which casino are we going to?"

"It's probably safest to go where there's no chance of anyone remembering me or my father." She bit her lip. "It also needs to be reputable, one that's used to big money. I think that means we go to the Casino Macau Palace."

"What: the floating casino?"

"Yes. It's one of the original ones and has a good reputation."

Kai nodded and turned round to hail a bicycle rickshaw.

As they were peddled along the foreshore, Kendal continued to talk tactics, as much, Kai suspected, to reassure herself as him.

"We're starting off with a fairly low capital base."

Kai raised his eyebrows. "Low! Twelve thousand dollars!"

"Yes, low. So, it will take us some time before we earn enough to play with serious money. I'm afraid it will be a long night."

The rickshaw dropped them off in front of a three-story casino. It was an impressive building that had been built like a pagoda.

They filed across the companionway to the entrance. "Where will we begin?" he hissed.

"The gambling becomes more exclusive and more expensive as you go up the different stories in the boat."

"So where do we start?"

"In the middle."

"And finish on top?"

"Hopefully."

The bottom storey of the casino was full of people. He was not surprised: Asia was addicted to gambling. Rickshaw drivers in shorts and vests stood alongside people in dinner suits. *Fan tan* was popular, as was baccarat, but Kendal had come to play blackjack.

He led Kendal through the crowd to the stairs. As he climbed them, misgivings about what they were attempting to do began to eat like an acid into his heart. If this didn't work, his life was forfeit. An absurd thought flitted across his consciousness; maybe that wouldn't be such a bad thing. At least he'd be rescued from the torment of living with himself. This negative thought was shattered as soon as he glanced at Kendal. She radiated beauty and life. And having seen it, he couldn't imagine ever being without it.

"What do you want me to do while you're playing?"

Kendal furrowed her brow.

He continued on. "What actually is my role?"

"You watch over me." She laid a hand on his arm. "You look after me."

Kai nodded. He was always going to do that. What he'd hoped for was something more specific.

"Are you scared?" he asked.

"Don't you prod this exterior of mine too hard. I'm likely to run from the place screaming."

Kai nodded. "Don't worry. I've got your back." He felt he'd never uttered a truer word.

She searched his eyes. There was something in them – a pleading. "But what if I lose your money?"

He cleared his throat and said hoarsely, "It changes nothing. I'll still have your back."

Elliot was awake, and he wished he wasn't. He was lying in the hammock fully clothed so that he'd be ready the instant anything might happen. The galling thing was, he was awake, and Emma was fast asleep.

The hurricane lamp was still burning. He'd put it by the window to guide the boatman when he returned – *if he returned*, he thought sourly. He glanced over at Emma and watched the steady rise and fall of her chest. He wished that she was awake and he could talk to her to stave off the gnawing anxiety of waiting. She was always good to talk to.

The idea of Kendal being in danger from anyone, quite apart from the amorous advances of his brother, caused him to fret and anguish. He hated having to rely on Kai to look after Kendal. Dark thoughts turned over and over in his mind obsessively, uselessly, to a point of exhaustion.

He tried to take control of his thoughts and forced himself to reflect on the extraordinary fact that he had a brother – a twin. It was amazing, and yet, curiously unsurprising. At one level, everything was new. But on another, it was as if he'd known Kai all his life. He felt he instinctively knew him, and yet he was a total stranger to Kai's world of violence, depravity and abuse.

As he explored his feelings about Kai, he became aware that he cared for him – certainly enough to be protective. He wondered if it was simply a big brother thing, but he was under no illusions that he was also in fierce competition with him over Kendal. He sighed, amazed that he should have to worry about it at all. It was impossible to conceive of a more unlikely, ill-matched couple. And yet… Elliot clenched his fists. This was not a competition he was prepared to lose.

He looked over again at Emma and again wished they could talk.

Then he heard it, the faint *blonk, blonk, blonk* of a diesel engine. Was it a returning fisherman – perhaps Mr. Lund, or could it be Kai and Kendal?

He glanced at his watch. It was nearly 5am.

He listened again, barely daring to breathe. The sound gradually got louder until he was certain: it was Kai and Kendal's boat. He'd had to listen to the wretched engine for three hours yesterday and knew its sound.

Elliot reached across and gave the edge of Emma's hammock a shake.

She came awake almost instantly. "What's the matter?" she said, rubbing her eyes.

"The boat's coming back."

He eased himself out of the hammock, went to the table by the window, and picked up the hurricane lamp. Moments later, he was standing by the doorway above the ladder leading down to the inky black water. The lantern's light had destroyed his night vision, but his hearing remained acute. The engine noise became louder.

Hardly daring to believe they were back, he began to wave the lantern slowly back and forth.

Then, there it was. The engine suddenly stopped and the bluff, weather-beaten nose of the workboat nosed into the pylons below.

Kai and Kendal were standing in the bow. Kendal gave a brief wave and began climbing up the ladder – slightly hampered by the shopping bag she was holding.

Elliot pulled her into the doorway and wrapped his arms about her, barely believing she was real. He buried his face into her hair and said urgently in a muffled voice, "Are you okay? Are you safe?"

"Yes, yes," she laughed.

Kai came in through the door behind her.

"How did you go?" asked Emma.

Kendal pried herself away from Elliot, turned and raised a triumphal fist into the air. "Two-hundred and twenty thousand dollars has been deposited in the Hongkong and Shanghai Bank."

Emma squealed and threw her arms around Kendal.

Elliot couldn't believe it. "You managed to deposit two-hundred and twenty thousand dollars at night?"

Kai rubbed his eyes wearily. "We are talking Macau." He obviously thought the answer sufficient, but Elliot wasn't sure he was any the wiser.

The girls were now dancing up and down hugging each other causing the floor of the shack to bounce.

Unsurprisingly, Mrs. Lund came bustling through from the back. She asked with some alarm, "You okay?"

"Yes, yes," the girls assured her.

The old woman smiled in relief. "You want tea?"

"No, no. Please go back to bed," said Emma.

Elliot pulled Kendal back to him and inspected her. Her hair was disheveled, and she had dark smudges under her eyes. She stumbled slightly as he pulled her to him. He caught her and held her. The adrenaline was wearing off leaving her stupid with weariness.

He kissed the top of her head.

After a moment, she pulled away and said, "I need to get some sleep."

Emma came across and took charge of her. "Do you want to wash first?"

"I'll wash in the morning."

Elliot grunted. "It nearly is morning." He pointed to Kai. "And you and I need to get going."

Kai rubbed his temples. "Don't ask me to get back onto that bloody boat."

"Sorry mate. I've got to get back to Middle Island by one o'clock, and you need to get your finances sorted out before you visit…" He didn't go on. It was as if he could not bring himself to use the word 'father.'

Emma looked back at him. "Have a cup of tea first. I'll make it. And I'll see if I can find us something to eat."

Moments later, he could hear her clattering around the kitchen with Mrs. Lund who had obviously decided not to go back to bed.

Elliot looked at Kai. "How will you make up the thirty-thousand dollar shortfall?"

His brother shrugged. "I will visit someone."

Elliot wasn't sure he liked the sound of that. "Who?" he asked.

"It does not matter."

"If it involves you, it does matter."

The two of them stared at each other – daring each other, belligerent, like two wildebeests preparing to lock horns.

Kai was the first to back down. He sighed. "A man who supplies drugs to ships going to the UK." He sniffed. "He'll find out today that the price of my protection has risen."

"…by thirty-thousand dollars," added Elliot.

"Yes." Kai shrugged. "It is small change for him."

Elliot shook his head. He was getting the feeling that he'd woken up in a bizarre parallel universe.

Emma came back in carrying a tray of teacups. Mrs. Lund was behind her carrying a bowl of rice cakes. Emma smiled. "Anyone for tea?"

Elliot sighed. It was surreal.

Chapter 23

"You're late."

The Dragon Head glowered at Kai as he stood to attention before him.

Ah Keung was standing to the left of his father, just behind him. It was not a good sign.

"A thousand apologies, sir. I was on Lan Tau Island, dealing with a complication."

A tendril of smoke from the joss sticks in the shrine wafted like a wraith across the room, reaching out to him.

"Is this complication one that threatens 14K? Does it involve the police?"

Kai knew that his father was good at smelling a lie, so he decided to keep as close to the truth as possible. "No sir. 14K is safe. The problem was that the victim did not have parents, only an uncle. It took longer to persuade him to pay."

His father banged his fist down on the desk in front of him. "You told me to expect payment two days ago and have not told me otherwise. That is a dangerous thing to do. I thought you had failed me."

"Forgive me sir. I was too optimistic. Some people have yet to hear of 14K and learned to fear us."

"That is why I would have been very content if you had delivered a body, suitably defiled." He leaned forward and shouted. "We need to be feared. Do you hear?"

"Yes sir."

A long silence followed.

The smell of the joss sticks assailed his senses. Kai found himself nauseated by their cloying smell. It was odd. Their smell had never troubled him before. He'd always found comfort in their aroma and the spiritual blessings they promised.

His father interrupted him. "Have you failed me?"

Kai swallowed. It seemed such an innocent question, but one which had such terrible consequences. He lifted his chin. "I have never failed you, sir."

"Make sure you never do." The Dragon Head steepled his fingers and looked at him. "You seem to be becoming lost in the head these days and less committed. I don't like that. Neither do I like it when the money promised me does not arrive." He slapped the desk. "And when I see both lack of commitment and lack of money, I think dangerous thoughts."

Kai bowed. "I understand sir. But I have not failed." He held out a piece of paper. "I have here a deposit slip showing that half a million has been paid into your account."

Ah Keung came forward, took the slip, and gave it to the Dragon Head. The old man inspected it and laid it down in front of him. "Half a million?"

"Yes sir."

"And you have the other half?"

"Yes."

Kai started to sweat. Technically, his father could demand all the money, but it wasn't something that he did often; only when the Dragon Head needed to signal displeasure. Being late with a promised payment could easily cause that displeasure. If his father demanded the other half million, Kai knew he was doomed. He simply hadn't got it. Silently he pleaded, *Please don't. Please don't.*

His father looked at him sourly. "I suppose you will use the other half million on frivolous luxuries."

"I plan to invest it, sir."

His father snorted scornfully.

Kai thought it prudent to change the conversation.

"As you know, sir: your other son is back in Hong Kong. We met accidentally at the Aberdeen floating restaurant." He swallowed. "It was a shock."

The old man nodded. "I had heard." He paused. "How much does he know?"

"He and I have learned something of our story from Auntie." He paused. "I was wondering if you had plans to see him."

His question was met by a long silence.

"Does he wish to see me?"

Kai repressed a shudder. In no way did he want Elliot exposed to any of the hell that was his life. "No. He has not expressed any desire to do that. But he has asked what his surname is."

Kai knew that Elliot had wondered no such thing. He, however, had. Kai therefore decided to use Elliot as an excuse to ask a question he'd never dared to ask himself. He was aware, however, that he was playing a delicate game. Kai had no qualms about talking about Elliot's existence. In fact, it would have been suspicious if Kai had not mentioned him. But Kai wanted to do everything he could to ensure Elliot had nothing to do with his father.

The old man scowled. "He has asked about his Chinese surname?"

Kai cleared his throat. "Yes sir. He wants to know who he is."

But it was Kai who wanted to know about his heritage, for he knew nothing about his ancestors. He'd realized many years ago that there was no honor or goodness in his father, but he held on to the hope that he had honorable ancestors in China. Perhaps he had a surname. The Emperor and those acting on his behalf conferred surnames on a family. To have one was a sign of honor. Those who didn't have them were considered to be uncivilized. Ever since Kai had been old enough to concern himself with notions of honor, he'd hoped he had a surname.

His father leaned back in his chair. "I am the Dragon Head of 14K. That is honor enough."

"But does he have a surname, sir?"

His father banged the table. "I am the Dragon Head of 14K," he shouted.

Kai shouted back, "Does he have a surname?" Even as he yelled, he was shocked at his audacity.

The Dragon Head nodded to Ah Keung, who stepped forward and slapped Kai across the face.

Kai reeled before the blow, then pulled himself upright and stood to attention.

Another long silence followed.

His father pursed his lips and said slowly, "He has no surname. You have no surname. You have 14K. It is better."

"Yes sir."

Another silence followed.

His father grunted. "Can you make your brother useful to 14K? Can he be recruited?"

Kai shook his head. It was the very last thing he wanted for Elliot. "No sir. He is not ambitious, intelligent, or brave." Kai felt the injustice of his words acutely as he said them. In reality, Elliot had shown himself to be extraordinarily courageous and resourceful.

The Dragon Head waved dismissively. "Then I want nothing to do with him. Keep him away from me."

"Yes, sir."

The Dragon Head put the tips of his fingers together.

"What do you know about a woman called Emma Templeton?"

Kai's mouth dropped open in surprise. He was tempted to say 'nothing,' but realized the danger of doing so. Instead, he said, "She shares accommodation with my brother in Repulse Bay."

"I know. I just wanted to hear what you would say."

Kai breathed out slowly. It had been a narrow escape.

"Why do you ask about this woman, sir?"

"I'm hearing reports from our brothers in prison. She's been asking questions about our activities."

"But this is not new, sir. It happens from time to time."

His father nodded. "But I am told this woman is tenacious. And I am troubled that she has appeared on the scene before we had warning of her."

"Do you think she has learned anything important?"

"I don't think she has managed to dig too deep. Evidently, she doesn't know much about Chinese culture and doesn't speak Cantonese."

Kai's eyes opened wide, but he managed to stop himself from speaking too quickly. He swallowed, and said, "Really? All I know is that until a few months ago, she was an academic at Oxford University. I've met her. She is young and naive. It's difficult to imagine how she could be a threat."

His father grunted. "Until I know that to be the case, I've given instructions that I be kept informed of everything she does." He pointed to Kai. "And you too are to report anything significant to me."

Chapter 24

"If one monkey held hands with two others to form a team of three, how many teams could you make from all these monkeys?" Emma watched as the children ran to the blackboard in order to count the monkeys Kendal had drawn on it.

The blackboard was bolted on the side of the ablutions block not far from the shack where they were staying. It was obviously a place that served as a community facility, not least because the standpipe providing water for the local huts was located there.

The insatiable curiosity of the children at having two Western girls living among them was the cause of it all. Their unabashed staring had given way to questions, and this in turn had become friendship.

Emma loved them, and it wasn't long before children were competing with each other to hold her hand. She solved the problem by sitting them down and telling the fairy tale of 'Jack and the Beanstalk.' Kendal followed on with a quiz involving numbers.

The children's innocence and enthusiasm provided welcome relief from the anxiety Emma felt over the pressing realities of murder and kidnap.

After promising to meet with the children next day after lunch, Emma and Kendal were allowed to return to their hut.

"Whew!" said Kendal as she flopped down into a chair. "They're fabulous, but they do exhaust you." She glanced at Emma. "You're a born teacher. They loved you."

Emma raised her eyebrows. "Really? It all seemed pretty natural."

"Trust me; it's not. You've got talent."

Emma crossed over to her hammock and climbed in. "I wonder what the boys are up to – and if they managed to get everything sorted out."

"Hmm. We'll find out when we call them at Auntie's after tea."

Emma smiled. Even Kendal had taken to calling Mamma-san 'Auntie.' She was not surprised. Her very character seemed to invite it.

That morning, while Kendal was still asleep, Emma had gone down to the fish dock with Mrs. Lund to help put the fish Mr. Lund had brought back for market on display. Following the success of Kendal's visit to Macau, there was now nothing particular she had to do, so she delighted herself in finding joy at doing the small things, like brushing Kendal's hair.

She couldn't remember anyone ever brushing her own hair. This thought led her to wonder about Kendal's mother. Emma felt emboldened enough to ask, "Did your mother brush your hair when you were young?"

"Yes. But she died when I was fifteen. Leukemia."

"I'm so sorry."

"Hmm. It wasn't great. And Dad died last year. So, I don't have any parents."

Emma sighed. "I don't think I've ever had parents."

"Really? How come?"

"They sent me off to boarding school as soon as they could, and then they divorced and remarried. They hardly keep in contact."

Kendal looked at her in shock, and for a while the only noise came from the water underneath them slopping underneath against the piles.

Eventually, Kendal asked, "But do you have a boyfriend?"

"No. Things are not too great in that department either." Emma did not dare ask if Kendal had a boyfriend. She was not sure her heart was ready to hear the answer. Instead, she asked a more tangential question.

"Do you think you will marry?"

"Sometimes I think so. Other times, I think it could be a complication that would detract from what I really want to achieve."

"Wow, it would be a tragedy if you didn't – with your beauty."

Kendal sighed. "Beauty is a mixed blessing. Men are demanding creatures. They can frustrate you to a point that being a lesbian is a real attraction." She smiled. "I tried it for about thirty minutes when I was fifteen, but didn't take to it."

Emma laughed. "So we're trapped. We're heterosexual and single."

"But are we happily single, or not? That's the question that's hard to answer."

"At least you're able to make the decision. You can choose any guy you want. Things are a lot less certain with me." Her comment came out with slightly more bitterness than Emma had intended. She hurried on. "You've caused quite a stir with Kai and Elliot. They're both smitten with you."

Kendal shook her head. They're so similar it's bewildering. It's frighteningly easy for your affection for one to subconsciously transfer to the other." She paused. "But there are also differences."

Emma sat herself upright. "How do you think they are different?"

"Kai is more direct. There's nothing half-hearted about him. He declares his love and tells you that you are beautiful. He's like a barracuda; he goes for the kill – straight for what he wants."

"But hopefully, he doesn't devour you in the process."

"Yes. That's the danger."

Emma swallowed. "And Elliot?"

Kendal paused. "I'm not sure. What do you think?"

A knife turned in her heart. "I…I hardly know him."

"I'm not sure that's true. You told me quite a lot about him when I first spoke with you. Do you remember?"

"Yes."

"So tell me more."

In truth, it wasn't hard to say things about Elliot. Emma had thought about him a lot – too much, in fact. But she wasn't at all sure that her heart would let her speak about his qualities to Kendal. She sighed. But saying nothing would simply look perverse and reveal a sensitivity she didn't want exposed. She steeled herself and said, "Kai is a wolf disguised as a wolf. Elliot is a wolf disguised as a sheep."

"Is that all?"

"Pretty much. Elliot works to project a facade of being a feckless larrikin. But in reality, he's a leader. He's anti-convention, sure, but he's also fiercely loyal." She shrugged. "Elliot instinctively champions the underdog, largely, I suspect, because he knows what it's like to be one."

"I thought you said you hardly knew him." Kendal looked at her speculatively. "You don't fancy him, do you?"

Emma was shocked by the question. She scrabbled mentally for a way to deflect it. "Both Kai and Elliot are smitten with you, Kendal. You must know that."

"Hmm. I suspect that they're smitten with my appearance. Neither of them really knows me on the inside."

"And what is on the inside?"

Kendal laughed. "A complicated mess. I have lots of fears and frightening ambitions. I'm scared of what I think I can do…and frightened that I can't do it." She took a deep breath. "I desperately want to honor my father by continuing his business, but I am not sure I'm ready to carry the responsibility."

Emma nodded. "If you're wise enough to know your limitations, you're probably not going to make too many mistakes."

"You really think so?"

"Yes." Emma paused. "Why don't you find yourself someone who will mentor you?"

Kendal coughed a laugh. "There aren't many who can mentor me in my line of business."

"I'm not talking about a business mentor, I'm talking about a life mentor."

Kendal looked at her doubtfully. "And who's going to do that?"

Emma shrugged. "Why not ask Auntie?"

"Auntie?"

"Yes." Emma gave the idea time to percolate in Kendal's consciousness, and then changed the subject. "On the subject of business: what is it that has poisoned Lachlan to the extent that he wants you dead?"

Kendal's jaw tightened. "I'm afraid it's a long list." She shrugged. "We just don't think the same."

"Really? Give me an example."

"Well...um, our most recent spat has been over the premises where our offices are located."

"Go on."

"Shiffer Investments occupies the top floor of an eight-story building on Jaffe Road in Wan Chai. It's an old building and its owners are about to have it re-clad to make it look modern." She sighed. "Lachlan is okay with it, but I think it's a waste of money. The building is far too small to have any future in Hong Kong. I want to buy the building from its owners, pull it down, and build something that's at least forty stories high."

"Wow. Why forty stories?"

"The expense and technology needed to go higher increases dramatically beyond fifty stories."

Emma raised her eyebrows. "So, you really know about these things."

"It's my job."

"Wow."

Kendal continued. "But Lachlan won't hear of it." She shook her head. "It's such a lost opportunity."

"What would you do with all the extra space?"

"Businesses would rent the lower ten floors, and I'd put luxury units above them."

"Well," said Emma, "Elliot and Kai are working on a plan to get Lachlan completely out of your life."

Kendal shook her head, as if in disbelief.

Emma pressed on. "Can you tell me some stories about Lachlan's disastrous business dealings in the past?"

She grunted. "There've been quite a few. Why do you want to know?"

Emma chewed on her lower lip. "It might be useful when planning our next move."

Elliot tucked the last of the exam papers into a folder, then leaned back and stretched. He was sitting at an outside table on Auntie's veranda at Tai Tam. Both he and Kai had decided to stay with Auntie so they could plan their next move together and be on hand when the girls phoned from Tai-O. The other reason Elliot had jumped at the chance to stay with Auntie was so he could get to know her better and question her about the things that Emma had said to him.

His time in Hong Kong was drawing to a close and, in sailing terms, things had worked out well. He wasn't surprised. The Royal Hong Kong Yacht Club was a distinguished club that had operated efficiently for many years. All he'd needed to do was to formalize their procedures and upgrade competencies in a few areas. The exam papers for senior instructors that he'd just marked indicated a high level of understanding.

Elliot's instinct was to keep the requirement for exams to a minimum, but he knew they were nonetheless important. Instructors had to know how to organize a sailing regatta well and how to run their training courses safely. Experience had taught him that instructors generally fell into two groups. Some were sailors who needed to be shown how to teach; others were teachers who needed to be shown how to sail.

He glanced at his watch. It was 10am. Kai was not yet awake, so he was on his own in the house with Auntie and the servants. He'd worked on the exam papers for two hours and was now restless for something physical to do. Quite what, he didn't know, so he went in search of Auntie.

He found her in the kitchen talking to the cook.

"Hello, dear," she said. "Would you like a cup of tea?"

"No thanks, Auntie." He wasn't sure how to put what he wanted to say in words. "Um…can I talk with you some time about some…stuff."

"About what, dear?"

Elliot fiddled with the pestle and mortar sitting on the kitchen bench. "Er…about Christian stuff." He shrugged. "Emma's been saying things…"

"Certainly, dear. Do you want to chat now?"

"No. I need to do something physical – burn off some energy…"

"…and some anxiety, I expect."

Elliot nodded. "The girls don't plan to call until tea time tonight. I need something to do until then."

Auntie nodded and leaned forward to peer out the window. "Ah, there he is." She turned to Elliot. "Sai Wing is in the vegetable garden. It looks as if he's starting to clear half of it for a new planting. Why don't you give him a hand, and we can talk sometime this afternoon."

"Thanks Auntie."

Elliot threw his tee-shirt over the back of a chair on the veranda and walked over to the vegetable garden where an old man, burned nut brown by the sun, was using a sickle to cut down old vegetable growth.

"Do you want a hand?" he asked cheerfully.

The gardener stood up and looked at him. A shocked expression was on his face. Elliot could understand why. "Yeah," he continued. "I look just like him, don't I? That's the bugger about being twins. I'm Elliot, Kai's brother."

The man held out a hand. Elliot wasn't sure whether it was to ward him away, or feel that he was real. He solved the ambiguity by stepping forward and shaking it. "I hear you're called Sai Wing."

The gardener nodded. "I am." Just for a while, Sai Wing held on to Elliot's hand, as if reluctant to let it go.

Elliot pulled his hand away and looked around. "What do you want me to do?"

The man seemed to jerk himself awake. "Er...take fork and dig out roots of the vegetables I cut down." His English was surprisingly good.

"Sure."

Soon, the two of them were working away together, sweating freely in the morning sun.

"Dammit!" exclaimed Elliot as he sucked on his thumb. He'd nicked it with the sickle.

Sai Wing put his spade down and took hold of Elliot's hand. After examining it, he said. "You come to my place. I will fix it."

Elliot followed the gardener to a whitewashed concrete hut at the bottom of the garden. When he entered, he could see that it was not only a gardening shed but was also where the old man lived. A mattress lay on top of a concrete bench, and various garden tools were stacked along the walls. Two items surprised him. One was a shelf of books, and the other was evidence of a child. A crudely made toy sailing boat sat on a shelf. A child's drawings on paper, now yellow with age, had been stuck on the wall just above it.

Sai Wing saw Elliot looking at them. "They belong to Kai."

Elliot nodded.

The old man put some pungent-smelling cream from a glass pot onto the cut and bandaged it. Elliot took the opportunity to ask him about Kai. "Can you tell me about my brother. I hardly know him."

Sai Wing stopped what he was doing, frowned, and said, "He is dressed in bad clothes that do not fit." Then he continued to wrap Elliot's thumb.

Elliot wasn't sure he was any the wiser.

Sai Wing didn't give him the chance to pursue his line of questioning because he had a question of his own.

"Where do you come from?"

"I come from England, from a town called Hamble."

"It is a good place?"

"Very good. It is like this place; it's by the water. There are lots of boats."

The gardener smiled. "Water good for the soul." He paused. "Do you live with your family?"

Elliot was momentarily put off balance by the question, but he recovered quickly. "I used to live with my grandparents. But not anymore. They have both died."

The two of them walked back to the garden and continued their work.

They'd been working for about an hour when Kai arrived. He sauntered over and watched them.

Elliot stood up, stretched and said. "Get your top off, mate, and give us a hand."

Kai shook his head and looked at him disdainfully. "I am not a servant."

Elliot pointed to the rake. "Don't be a stuck-up prig. Grab the rake and pull the stuff I've dug up to the side."

With some ill grace, Kai did so.

The three of them managed to clear the vegetable patch by the time Auntie called them in for lunch.

Kai was still grumbling. "I should not do servant's work."

"Don't be a jerk. He's an old bloke. We should help him."

Kai grunted. "Sai Wing is bossy. He is good, but he can forget that he is a servant."

Elliot put a hand on his shoulder. "Mate, I think you're a poncy prig."

Auntie interrupted them. "Stop squabbling boys and have some lunch." She looked at Elliot's bandaged thumb. "What have you done?"

"Just a small cut. Sai Wing fixed it."

She nodded. "He is good with medical things."

With lunch finished, Elliot got up from his seat and gave Kai a tap on the arm. "Let's go somewhere quiet and have a talk. You and I need to do some more planning if we're going to have something to tell the girls this evening."

Elliot beat Kai to the phone by six inches when it rang. After a brief tug of war with the receiver, he positioned it so that each of them could hear.

"Elliot?"

It was Emma.

"Yes, I'm here," said Elliot. "How are you?"

"And I'm here too," said Kai, interrupting.

Elliot tried again. "How are you going?"

"We're fine. Kendal slept in until lunch time and has more or less recovered. What about you guys?"

It was great to hear Emma's voice again. The strength of the emotion he felt surprised him. He frowned for a moment, but couldn't find the answer. Elliot pulled himself together. "Yeah, we're well. I got back in time to teach…"

"…and I slept in until 11:30," added Kai.

Kendal broke into the conversation. "Hi guys."

"Hi," said Elliot and Kai together. Elliot continued, "Are you still feeling okay staying there at Tai-O?"

"Yes," said Emma. "It's good here. We're well looked after, and it gives us a degree of peace amidst the tension of everything."

"Tension?"

"Yes, tension. I'm going to bill Kendal for a long massage and some serious pampering when all this is over."

Mental images came unbidden to Elliot's mind of Emma's firm, neat little body, and of him massaging…

He cut the image short and cleared his throat. "Come on. Be honest: you've never had a massage or serious pampering in your life, have you?"

"No, but I live in hope."

Kai broke in. Elliot could feel his impatience. "I don't think we need to get too clever with this Lachlan fellow. It's really just a case of me visiting him with the photos and frightening him to do what we want."

"No, it's more complicated than that," said Emma. "We need

Lachlan to leave Hong Kong altogether. It would be impossible for Kendal to live knowing he was still alive somewhere here, or even in England. Somehow, we've got to get him to, er…"

"…really go," added Elliot.

"Yes."

Kai waved a hand dismissively. "I can arrange that."

Kendal cut him off. "If I'm going to take over the company…" She broke off. "Oh Emma, do you think I can do it?" Elliot could hear her sob.

"Yes I do," said Emma. "You've got vision, you've got talent, and you are aware of your own shortcomings. Just get the right team around you."

Kai interrupted. "Get on with it."

"No," said Emma. "This is vital."

Elliot could hear the two girls having a muffled conversation together.

After a while, Kendal's voice again came through. "The thing is," she said, "It's not enough to have Lachlan leave the company; nor is it enough that he leaves Hong Kong…"

"What else do you need?" prompted Elliot.

There was a pause.

Emma answered for her. "If Kendal is really to take control, she needs the company shares Lachlan has in Shiffer Investments."

"Shares?"

"Yes, Evidently, Lachlan and Kendal own seventy percent of the company's shares between them. So you can see that it makes no sense for Kendal to run the company if Lachlan has the power to torpedo her at any board meeting in the future."

And he would also continue to get thirty-five percent of the company profits," added Kendal.

"I could make sure that wouldn't happen," said Kai.

"How?" demanded Emma.

"You don't need to know."

"You'd kill him, wouldn't you?"

Kai said nothing.

"Now, listen, Kai…"

Elliot could hear the steel in Emma's voice and couldn't help but smile.

Emma continued. "There is no way I am going to associate myself with anything that's remotely violent and evil. Do you hear? I can't believe you would think for a moment that any of us could. The shame and guilt of it would plague us for life. It's just wrong."

Elliot mentally cheered her on.

"Why not?" said Kai. "It is a good solution. This Lachlan fellow has tried to buy a murder and is a bad man. He should be killed. I could easily organize it."

"No!" yelled Emma. "You have no right to be judge or executioner. How would you feel if people planned to murder you for the evil you've done?"

"Some have tried."

"No, no, no! I'm going to put the phone down right now and work out something without you if you persist with this folly. Good grief, I can't believe I need to say this: we want good to win, not evil."

Elliot had seen a little of what Emma was like when her dander was up, but to hear her now in full flight was magnificent. He could picture her as she leaned into the phone to lecture Kai. Her hair would be falling forward over her shoulders, and there would be a little frown over her button nose.

Over recent weeks, his conversations with Emma had both disturbed and delighted him, so he knew something of her qualities. He smiled. She always had wise words that were good and warming. They were something anyone would look forward to coming home to, like a Golden Retriever – except that Emma was dark...and human.

He brought his mind back to the issue in hand. "What do we know about Lachlan? What is it that we need to take into account? Does he have a family?"

"Not anymore," said Kendal. Lachlan is divorced. He has an adult son who lives with his mother in the UK."

No one spoke for a while.

Emma broke the silence. "I've got an idea," she said slowly. "But it's only half-baked. I need you and Elliot to help me by telling me if it's possible."

Kai pulled the phone toward him. "Tell me your idea."

"Well, it centers on some information we have."

"What's that?" Kai demanded.

"The combination of the safe at Shiffer Investments."

Chapter 25

E lliot allowed Kai to tug the mouthpiece his way so he could speak into the phone more clearly. "And where is this safe?"

Kendal's voice came through. "It's in Lachlan's office, to the left of the reception lounge as you enter. It's hidden behind a door beside his desk."

"And what security do you have at Shiffer Investments?"

"Security men sit at the reception desk in the entrance hall downstairs. And there's another security guard in an office by the lifts on the floor where our office is."

"Which floor?"

"The top, of course."

Elliot interrupted. "Nice view?" It was an inane comment.

He could hear Kendal sigh. "Not good enough. I wish it was a lot higher."

"What do you mean?"

"Forget it."

Elliot nodded. "Remind me: where exactly, is the building?"

"It's on the south side of Jaffe Road in Wan Chai." She told him the number. "You'll recognize it by the work fence around it. They're preparing to do some renovation work on the building."

Kai tugged at Elliot's arm. "You're not seriously thinking about getting in via the balcony, are you?"

Elliot covered the phone's mouthpiece and hissed back, "I'm seriously thinking about getting in by any way I can." He lifted the phone back to his mouth. "Does the balcony have a lock?"

"Yes."

"Can you remember what sort of lock?"

"Um, pretty standard, from memory. You know: a Yale-type thing."

"And the doors?"

"Er, French doors. Glass in a metal frame."

Ideas, ephemeral and disconnected, began to float around in his mind – all of them impossible. Elliot rubbed his forehead. "And is your company the only company on the top floor?"

"No, we share it with an insurance firm. But only ours has the balcony. Lachlan insisted on it. He said he wanted somewhere to entertain, but in reality, he only uses it to smoke his cigars."

Elliot nodded. "Right, Kai and I will have a look at it." He paused. "Give us a call tomorrow about the same time."

Emma's voice came through the phone. "Just a moment."

"What?"

"Can you get back to our apartment, Elliot?"

"Of course. Why?"

"You'll find a hand-held cassette recorder in the top drawer of my bedside cupboard. Can you get it and keep hold of it?"

Elliot raised his eyebrows. "I had no idea such a thing existed."

"It's a Sony TC-55; the latest technology. I used it for some of my prison interviews."

"Didn't the prisoners mind?"

"I hid it in a paper bag with a sandwich. I'd make a show of taking a bite from the sandwich and putting it back in the bag before the interview."

Elliot shook his head. Emma had surprised him so many times. She could easily be overlooked as that demure girl who was always in the background. But she was like an iceberg; most of her was not seen. He frowned, *No*, not an iceberg; that was wrong. She was warm, very warm.

"Why would we need the recorder?" he asked.

Emma told him.

"No!" Kai raised two hands in front of him, as if to push Elliot's idea away. "You are crazy."

"No, I think it's doable," insisted Elliot. "And there's no way we can get up there from inside the building. You saw the security."

They had: a pair of security guards sat at the front desk alongside two receptionists. Anyone using the lifts either had to show their security pass, or be registered as a visitor and be issued with a temporary pass.

Elliot craned his head back and pointed to the top of the building. "If I managed to get you up to that balcony, could you get us in?"

"You're kidding me. It's eight stories high. The scaffolding doesn't even reach the top."

Elliot shielded his eyes from the sun and looked at the bamboo latticework clinging to the side of the building. "It almost does. The vertical poles are in place."

Kai shook his head. "No, I'm not liking this idea at all."

"Humor me, Kai. If you were on that balcony, could you get us inside without anyone knowing we'd been there?"

Kai shrugged irritably. "Yes, probably, but…"

Elliot interrupted. "Probably?"

"Yes. If the lock is a Yale, then it's probably an imitation one made in China. And even if it's not, I should be able to open it. I've got a set of skeleton keys."

"And you know how to use them?"

"Of course."

Elliot shook his head, and then glanced around him. He spotted a smart restaurant at the base of a tower block across the road. Elliot pointed to it. "Let's get a drink and talk."

They crossed over to the restaurant and sat at a table by the window where Elliot could continue to study the building opposite.

A waiter came to take their order. Elliot ordered a beer for Kai and a coffee for himself.

When the drinks came, Kai paid for them, which he did with some ill grace. He lifted the bottle of beer and looked at it with disgust. "Do you know how much this cost? It's crazy."

Elliot was inspecting the scaffolding and only half listening. "People have to make a living. The rent here must be horrendous."

Kai continued to grumble. "I usually don't pay in cafes, and if I do, it's very little."

Elliot turned round and faced his brother. "I think we can get to the top on the scaffolding."

His brother shook his head. "No, no, no."

"What's the matter?" demanded Elliot.

"No way."

"Why?"

Kai thrust out his chin, as if daring Elliot to be disparaging. "I do not like heights."

"Ah." Elliot nodded. He was not surprised. He too had once been frightened of heights. But over the years, he'd learned to over-come his fear; largely because of the number of times he'd been hoisted to the top of the mast to free a jammed mainsail block. He could now climb a mast without the aid of a bosun's chair.[1] But even so, it was not something he enjoyed.

Kai shook his head. "There are some things that you should not do." He pointed to the building. "And climbing that is one of them."

Elliot suspected he was not going to get anywhere by pushing the issue further, so he changed the subject. He drummed his fingers on the table and looked at his brother. "There are definitely things you should not do, and trying to steal a brother's girlfriend is one of them." He paused. "At some stage, we need to talk about this, you know."

"What are you talking about?" Kai's affected innocence was not very convincing.

"Stop trying to take my girl away from me." He leaned back. "Is that clear enough?"

Kai inclined his head. "I do not think Kendal is anyone's girl."

"Oh, I think she is."

"Really?"

"Yes."

"You haven't even kissed her yet, have you – I mean properly: on the lips – taking your time – like Hollywood."

"I would have, if all this rubbish..." he pointed to Kai, "and you, hadn't turned up."

Kai was still for a moment, and then he began to laugh. "Sometimes I think you are so dumb that you can't possibly be my twin brother."

Elliot scowled. "What do you mean?"

"There's so much you don't see, even when it's right in front of your face."

"What?"

Kai drained the last of his beer and rose to his feet. He paused a moment and looked at him. An expression, somewhere between pity and laughter, danced across his face. Then he shook his head, turned, and walked to the door.

Elliot scrambled to his feet and hurried after him. "Wait. I want to talk to you."

Emma and Kendal had to wait for twenty minutes before the Chinese woman in the phone booth finished her call. From what Emma could overhear, the woman was complaining to some friend or relative about the wayward activities of her daughter.

She gave the lady what she hoped was an encouraging smile, and squeezed past her, impatient to call Elliot.

Auntie answered the phone. "How are you dear?"

"We're fine, Auntie. Except that Mrs. Lund is feeding us too much."

Auntie chuckled. "I suspect she is very glad you are there. Her

210

son has left home, so she has no one except her husband to fuss over." She paused. "She lost her only other child, a daughter, when she was young."

"Oh, that's sad."

"She's just grateful she didn't also lose her son to heroin, so let her spoil you. Now, wait a moment, and I'll get the boys. They're outside."

A few seconds later, Elliot came on the phone. "Are you okay?" he asked straight away.

"Yes, we're both fine."

"Hmm."

She could hear a touch of uncertainty in his voice. "Why? Is anything the matter?"

"Um, probably not."

"What's got you concerned?"

Elliot began hesitantly. "Well, I, um, got your cassette recorder...,"

"And?"

"I think someone's been into your room since you left."

Alarm flooded through her. "What makes you think that?"

"You and your fastidious habits."

"My what?"

"Your slippers are always side by side near the chair, and the top of your dresser is scarily neat." She could hear him draw a breath. "Things had been moved out of place, just a little, but moved." He paused. "Emma, if anyone was snooping around, is there anything important they could have seen, that they shouldn't?"

She shook her head. "No, I don't think so. I've got my finished report with me, and I've got rid of all the rough notes I've made." She paused, as a troubling thought came to her. "Elliot!"

"What?"

"My last conversation on the cassette recorder – I didn't erase it. I've just been relying on the next conversation to do that."

"So someone could have listened to what you said?"

"Yes."

"What's on it?"

"Um…, notes I made for myself on the way back from Lan Tau on the ferry. I was sitting next to an army colonel, so I mostly spoke into it in Cantonese, just little reminders." She drew a deep breath. "I actually couldn't say much at that point. I was…" she trailed off.

"Yeah, you were pretty rattled. I remember. It was the first time I saw your tidy room."

Emma also remembered – all too well. She'd been in her bra and panties, wet through. "But there wouldn't have been any technical information on the tape. I was pretty careful. Just a few words, reminders only."

She could hear rustling on the other end, and Kai's voice came through. "Hi. I'm here too now. Is anything the matter?"

Emma swallowed. "I hope not. Elliot will explain." She wanted to change the subject. "Is everything in place? Do you still want me to call Lachlan?"

She could hear a muffled conversation going on between the boys.

Elliot's voice, so similar to Kai's, but distinguishable because of the lack of American intonation, came back. "Yes please. Kai's not too sure, but I think it's our only chance. Give him a call, then call me back when you've done it. Umm…"

"Umm what?"

"Good luck."

"Thanks."

Emma put the phone down and picked it straight back up again, knowing full well that if she delayed, she would probably not have the courage to ever do so. As she did, she turned to Kendal. "What's the number?"

Kendal told her.

A few moments later, a receptionist put her through to Lachlan Shiffer.

"Lachlan Shiffer, speaking."

Emma listened to his voice. It was deep and husky, probably due to smoking. Rather surprisingly, his voice didn't sound like someone who was the devil incarnate. She had to remind herself that the man to whom she was speaking had contracted a killing, and was the cause of all their angst. She tried to conjure a picture of him from his voice, and failed.

Emma put on a strained, wavering voice. "Oh, hello Mr. Shiffer. My name is Annette Guthrie. I've recently been widowed and inherited a significant sum of money. I was wondering if I could talk with you about how best to invest it."

"Absolutely. That's what we do." Shiffer paused. "How much were you considering investing?"

"Quite a lot."

"What: over a million?"

"Significantly more than a million. The trouble is, I don't travel very well, so I was wondering if you would come to me."

"Where do you live?"

"In Repulse Bay."

"Certainly, Mrs. Guthrie. I'm very happy to come to you. Give me an address and let's make a time."

Kai swept the mop over the floor of the landing in a desultory manner for the umpteenth time. *Come on, you bastard.* He was sweating in his gray overalls.

Ostensibly, he was mopping the landing two floors below Emma and Elliot's unit. Elliot had been told by his own cleaner that the occupants of a unit on this floor had gone to the UK on holiday. The information was volunteered during a conversation about whether or not she would still be paid if she didn't clean Elliot's unit for a week.

Kai listened to the hum and clunk of the elevator as it made its way up and down the building.

Finally, the elevator whined to a halt on his floor and signaled its arrival with a 'ding.'

Kai applied himself to the task of mopping with fresh vigor.

A large man with a florid complexion stepped out of the lift. Kai summed him up in a second. He was tall, had poor muscle tone and a fat belly. That was good. He would not be a physical threat.

"Sir," he said. "Be careful. The floor is wet. Here, let me help you across it."

"I don't need any help," said the man crossly, and stepped over toward the door of the unit.

Kai nonetheless took him solicitously by the elbow.

When the man knocked on the door, the door swung open. It had been left unlocked. He expressed surprise and began to push his way in. "Mrs. Guthrie. Lachlan Shiffer here," he yelled.

Kai removed a lead-weighted cosh from his pocket and brought it down on Lachlan's head. With some satisfaction, he watched him crumple to the floor.

He dragged him into the unit and pushed the door shut.

It took longer than expected for Lachlan Shiffer to wake up. Kai was not unduly worried. He glanced at his handiwork. Shiffer was strapped into a dining chair. His wrists had been taped to its arms by silver duct tape. It was good tape. The manufacturers had made it flame resistant, which had proved useful in the past. More tape held Lachlan to the chair back, and yet more was wrapped around his mouth.

The man did not present a pretty sight. The fact that he was missing his trousers probably didn't help.

Shiffer began to moan through his nose.

Kai waited for the man to fully realized his predicament. It didn't take long. Shiffer's eyes opened wide with fear, then he began to writhe and jerk in his seat, trying to get free of the tape. It was like watching a turtle attempting to escape its shell – a useless exercise. The man stopped only when Kai stood in front of him.

"Mr. Shiffer, this is your first face-to-face meeting with 14K. You made the mistake of challenging our demands during your last phone call." Kai waved a remonstrating finger at him. "That was bad." He pointed to the heavy-duty secateurs that lay on the table. A ball of string and white towel lay next to it.

"That's what I'll use to cut off one of your fingers. It'll come off your left hand, as we may still want you to be able to write." Kai affected a disinterested shrug. "We'll do that to one of your fingers each time we meet." He smiled. "We find that it helps keep people's attention."

Shiffer's eyes rolled back in his head in terror.

Kai knew that his words were vile and shocking, and that to some extent, he was bluffing. The success of what he wanted to achieve in the next few minutes relied on his skill in reading Shiffer's reaction, and applying the right mental pressure.

Kai leaned forward and patted Shiffer on the cheek. "If you really please me in this interview, who knows, you might even leave here with all your fingers. Is that what you want?"

Shiffer nodded his head, hesitantly.

Kai leaned forward inquiringly. "I'm sorry. You haven't been clear with your reply."

Shiffer nodded vigorously.

"Ah, that's better." He reached behind him and picked up the pile of photos he'd left on the table. He shuffled through them, taking in, yet again, their content. They were shocking. The brutal way the chains bit into Kendal's body and her look of terror had haunted him for days. And the man responsible for it all was now in a chair in front of him.

Seething anger again rose up within him.

Kai tapped the photos together, and stood in front of Shiffer. One by one, he held up the images before him. Then he reached over, took one end of the tape across Shiffer's mouth and ripped it away. The tape left a red welt.

The man yelped as it came off, but he didn't scream. That was good.

Kai stared at his captive, assessing whether he had any more fight left in him.

After a full minute, he decided he didn't.

Kai put a hand in his pocket and nodded slowly. "I want you to tell me in your own words what it is that you contracted us to do, just so that we are clear."

Shiffer turned his head away.

The man still had a little bit of fight. Kai picked up the secateurs. "Tell me," he smiled.

The man's eyes opened wide in terror. "No! Er...the contract was to kill er, Kendal Shiffer."

"And how much are you offering?"

"A quarter of a million Hong Kong dollars."

"And did my organization force you to put his contract out, or was it entirely your idea?"

A sullen look came over Shiffer's face. He lowered his head. "It was my idea," he mumbled.

"I didn't hear you," snapped Kai.

"It was my idea," he shouted.

"Yes it was. And now I have come to collect. You have seen the photos. Are you now fully satisfied that your niece is dead?"

"Yes," he said weakly.

"You don't wish to see the photos again?"

Shiffer shook his head then turned away.

"Ah, well: in that case, we can talk about payment." He took Shiffer by the chin and turned him back to face him.

"Do you have the quarter million dollars ready at hand, as you were instructed to?"

"Yes."

"And it is is in a safe place?"

"Yes. It's in a safe in my office. I am..." he paused, then continued. "I am now the only one who knows the combination."

Kai nodded. "Good. Listen carefully. I will come to your office first thing in the morning." He smiled. "Who knows, we might want to invest it with you. Maybe I'll dig around a bit. Find out how good you are. What do you think?"

Shiffer said nothing.

Kai continued. "Please don't be tempted to have the police waiting for me. You are not just dealing with me. You're dealing with an organization that will not tolerate failure to comply." He smiled. "Did I tell you that the removal of a finger was just stage one?"

Kai again took Lachlan by the chin and forced the man to look directly at him. Then he reached down, grabbed Lachlan by the testicles, and squeezed.

Lachlan screamed.

"Now let me tell you about stage two. That's when we cut things off, put them in your mouth, and tape it shut. Do you know how long it takes before people can bring themselves to chew and swallow?"

Shiffer arched his head back in terror.

Kai shook his head. "And you really don't want to know about stage three. It is lethal... eventually."

Chapter 26

E lliot sat on the bus next to his brother, nursing a rucksack on his knee. It was 10pm and dark, so there was little to see out the windows.

He glanced at Kai. His twin had been in a dour mood ever since returning to Auntie's from Repulse Bay. Elliot had been unable to work out why, because Kai's meeting with Lachlan Shiffer had evidently been successful.

He decided to risk a question. "What's the matter, mate? You've been in a foul mood all evening. I need you to be on top of your game tonight."

Kai turned and regarded him with bleak eyes. "It is nothing."

"No, it's not nothing. What is it?"

Kai turned away. "It is nothing important. It's just that I…hate myself, sometimes – often, actually."

Elliot raised his eyebrows. This was not the sort of conversation he was expecting. "Er, has anything particular prompted this feeling tonight?"

Kai sighed. "Maybe it was the things I said to Kendal's uncle – they make me hate myself more than usual."

"What did you say?"

Kai shook his head. "I will not tell you."

"You didn't hurt him did you? Emma will have your hide if you did."

Kai snorted a laugh. "Ah, your little kitten. She can scratch."

"Seriously. She won't forgive you."

Kai grunted. "There can be no forgiveness for someone like me, anyway." He waved his hand. "No, I didn't hurt him."

Something of his brother's torment reached his heart, but he was at a loss as to what to say. Eventually, he cleared his throat. "I've, er…been talking to Auntie about some of these things."

"What things?"

"About forgiveness and hope."

"Pah. She is an old fool."

Elliot shook his head. "No, I don't think she is. And neither do you if you're honest." He paused. "Do you want to know what I think?"

Kai didn't answer.

Elliot continued. "I think she's found something that looks a lot like truth." He sighed. "And whatever she's found, it's made her a darn sight happier than you."

The bus ground its way up the winding road to the high spine of Hong Kong Island, and then dropped down past the lights of Happy Valley racecourse into the city of Wan Chai.

They got off the bus and began to walk west down Jaffe Road. Five minutes later, they approached the building that housed Shiffer Investments. Elliot looked at it in dismay. The lights of the city were so bright that they showed up a good deal of the scaffolding. They would be visible to any sharp-eyed person as they climbed.

He swung the rucksack to the ground and took out two builder's safety helmets. Elliot held one out to Kai. "Put this on. We've got to look the part."

It was as well they did. As they were heaving a section of fencing aside in order to squeeze through the gap, a voice hailed them from the pavement in Chinese.

A policeman, in his brown uniform, short sleeves and baggy shorts, came to the fence.

Kai gave him a friendly wave and pulled a clipboard out of the rucksack. He walked over to the policeman and showed it to him, jabbering away in Chinese as he did.

Elliot held his breath.

He knew Kai would be explaining that the building contractors required the scaffolding to be inspected for the soundness of its construction before the platforms were laid and work began. Elliot had drawn a diagram of the scaffolding and numbered its main crossbeams. He'd typed a label on the top: 'Scaffolding Safety Assessment.'

A few minutes later, Kai returned, and the policeman continued his beat.

"Is no problem," said Kai. His brother then gave the nearest bamboo upright a push and looked up. "But getting up there is a problem."

Elliot fished out a coil of nylon rope from his rucksack. "I'll tie you to me so that it will be impossible for you to fall more than a few feet. Come here."

With a great deal of mumbling and complaining, Kai did so.

Elliot made a rope harness for Kai using a figure-of-eight knot, and then made a similar one for himself. "The trick is to go slow and take it easy. Just climb one level at a time, and then wait 'till I climb the next one." He decided to put a little of Kai's hubris and competitiveness to work. "You're probably fitter than me, so I don't want you rushing me; okay?"

Kai nodded.

"And one more thing."

"What?"

"Don't look down."

The two of them began to climb.

Except for the occasional curse, Kai climbed well. He froze just once when his shirt snagged on a tensioning stick protruding from one of the scaffolding knots. But Elliot was able to talk him through it, and Kai was soon climbing again.

As the scaffolding around the building was still in the process of being erected, no ladders or planks had yet been laid. Elliot had never been this close to bamboo scaffolding before and was intrigued by how it was put together. The bamboo poles were lashed together with coir rope. Just occasionally, a stick had been used to tension a knot. He wondered idly how they worked out when a knot should be given extra tensioning. Hopefully they'd got their math right.

Elliot chatted to Kai as he climbed to help ease his brother's nerves and bring a sense of normalcy to what they were doing.

But he knew that what they were attempting was far from normal.

The two of them worked their way up to the seventh floor without incident. When Elliot risked looking down, he could see the dizzying sight of tiny cars and buses tooting and revving their way along the streets below. It was surreal.

"Now what are you going to do?" said Kai. He was standing on the crossbeam next to him and was looking above to the top story. The challenge was plain to see. They were standing on the very last crossbeam. The others going to the top had yet to be laid.

"I'll shin up one of the poles and pull you up."

Kai shook his head. "I don't like it. You're not strong enough."

"Cheeky blighter. If you're worried, you can give me a hand by at least trying to climb the pole."

"I could pull you down if I fell."

"No you won't. I'll tether myself at the top."

Without further ado, he began to climb.

Kai reached for Elliot's forearm, gripped it tight, and heaved himself over the balustrade. He landed inelegantly on top of his brother. For a moment, he wanted to laugh hysterically. But fortunately, the immediate need to catch his breath took precedence.

Elliot disentangled himself and began untying the rope that bound them together. There was now no need to rush as they were not visible to anyone watching from the ground.

Kai went to the rucksack and removed two pairs of washing up gloves, size small, so they were tight fitting. Then he took out the wallet that held the skeleton keys. He was competent in using them, but not well practiced, so it took a while before he felt the door onto the balcony unlock.

Elliot, wisely, did not try to rush him. He stood to one side and shone a pencil light onto the lock while he worked.

"We are in," Kai said. "You got your gloves on?"

"Yes."

"Remember," he whispered, "there's a security guard on the other side of that door."

Elliot nodded.

Kai took charge of the pencil light and led the way to the foyer area. The layout was very similar to the diagram he'd drawn from Kendal's description. He breathed in relief. *No surprises yet.*

Lachlan's office was where he expected it to be. The door into it had a frosted glass panel in the top half. Lachlan's name was stenciled on the glass in gold lettering. Kai reached into his pocket and removed a small bottle of oil. He inverted the cap so it produced a spout and oiled the hinges of the door. Kai then oiled the door handle. After wiping away the excess, he gave the door a gentle push.

It opened without a sound.

Kai flashed the torch around the office and saw the door that hid the safe. He whispered to Elliot, "Give me the combination number."

Elliot fished a piece of paper out of his pocket.

Kai took it and began to oil the hinges on the door behind the desk.

The door opened to reveal a safe. It stood about four feet high and was bolted into the concrete wall. Kai glanced at the piece of paper he'd been given, squatted down, and began to turn the wheel of the combination lock.

When the final number had been dialed, he took hold of the handle and pulled. The heavy door gave a grunching sound and a squeak. Kai froze.

For three minutes, he listened for any indication that the security guard had heard the sound.

Kai heard nothing.

Then, very slowly, a fraction of an inch each time, he began to ease open the door of the safe. When he was satisfied he could reach inside, he shone the torch into its interior.

There were four shelves. Three of them held bundles of paper and folders. The bottom one held a black, box-shaped briefcase.

Disturbingly, a black pistol lay on top of it.

He picked the pistol up and turned it over in his hands. It was a Walther PPK, the same gun that Hitler had used to shoot himself. Who had told him that? Ah, yes, he remembered: a Burmese gunrunner. He'd gone through the guns in his catalog once when they'd done some business.

After checking the safety catch, Kai slipped the gun into his pocket, being careful to conceal it from his brother who was rummaging through Lachlan's desk drawers behind him.

He pulled the briefcase out and opened it. Neat piles of money stared back at him. Kai breathed a sigh of relief and beckoned Elliot over so he could bring the rucksack. His brother put some stationary that he'd collected from the drawers into the rucksack and passed the bag to him.

Ten minutes later, they were back on the balcony in the balmy night air.

Elliot looked at Kai as he tied the rope harness around him. "Okay: it's the same as going up – except for one difference."

"What's that?"

"You have to look down."

Chapter 27

Kai levered himself from the wall he was leaning on and folded his newspaper. "Good morning, Mr. Shiffer. You are early for work."

Lachlan Shiffer jumped back and held up an arm defensively.

Kai continued. "Lovely morning, isn't it?"

In reality, it wasn't. The streets were already hot and busy at 8am. Kai forced a smile. "Let's get all this over with in the next ten minutes, and then you can get on with your life."

Lachlan Shiffer recovered from the shock of being accosted outside his own building and nodded dumbly.

Kai picked up a folder that leaned against the wall by his feet and stepped aside to let Lachlan Shiffer pass. "Shall we go?"

The two of them entered the foyer and approached the reception desk.

The receptionist smiled. "Hello, Mr. Shiffer." She turned to Kai. "May I have your name, sir?"

"Mr. Guthrie. I'm here to see Mr. Shiffer."

"Certainly sir. Here's a visitor's pass. Please hand it back here when you leave."

The lift took them to the top floor.

They stepped out onto a landing that had a small glass-fronted office leading off it. It must be where the security man sat. There was no one in it at the moment, so it was probably only staffed at night. Alternatively, the man could be in Shiffer's office with a gun drawn, waiting for Kai to enter. Kai knew it was unlikely. Lachlan Shiffer had everything to lose if his story became known to the police.

They passed into the offices of Shiffer Investments.

Shiffer blundered past a receptionist talking on a phone behind a counter and pushed open the door of his office.

It opened without a squeak.

Once inside, Shiffer rounded on Kai. "Once this is over, I never want to see you again." Shiffer's confidence had grown enough for him to show a bit of fight.

Kai sighed. He would have to prick his bubble.

"You may remember that I was thinking of investing this money with you." Kai sat on the edge of the desk and pointed a finger at Shiffer. "But it would be a bad idea, wouldn't it?"

Shiffer stood behind the desk with one hand on the wall, as if bracing himself.

Kai continued. "I've been checking up on you." He waved a remonstrating finger. "And I have learned that you are very bad at investing."

"I am not!"

"Oh, but you are."

Lachlan Shiffer lifted his chin. "Markets can be unreliable. No one can always get it right."

Kai stood up and faced Shiffer. "But for you; making bad decisions is normal – yes? He ticked off his fingers as he spoke. "Do you remember the Thompson Group? Their investments grew by just two percent before they took their money away. This happened when the market was booming at sixty percent."

Shiffer's mouth dropped open in shock.

Kai pressed on. "And, Mrs. Cheesman: you pretty much lost her all her inheritance. Then there was The Hung Fook Institution.

That was bad, very bad." He shook his head. "You should not be in business, should you?"

Shiffer said nothing.

"Should you!" Kai shouted.

Lachlan lowered his eyes and mumbled, "I suppose not."

Kai now knew that Lachlan Shiffer was suitably cowed and would not do anything silly. He nodded slowly. "So I will take my money and go."

Shiffer still did not move.

"Now!" shouted Kai.

The man jerked himself into action and opened the door behind him.

Kai moved to the other side of the desk to give Lachlan Shiffer the illusion of privacy as he squatted in front of the safe.

The safe's heavy door swung open with a familiar squeak.

Shiffer froze.

"Is anything the matter?" Kai asked. "There had better not be. Your life depends on it."

"No. No." said Shiffer. He stood up and laid the black briefcase on the desk. A sheen of sweat was visible on his brow. "Take it and go."

"Open it," demanded Kai.

Shiffer did so. As the lid lifted, Shiffer's legs gave way, and he sprawled across the chair. "I don't believe it. I don't...I've been robbed," he sobbed.

Kai held up his hand to silence the man. Then he turned the briefcase around and looked inside it. After a moment of silence, he said, "Oh dear."

He looked up at Shiffer and could see that a damp patch had appeared below his crotch. The man was wetting himself.

Kai kept his voice neutral. He didn't want Shiffer to begin screaming. He pointed to the empty briefcase. "This changes everything."

A dangerous silence hung in the room.

"Do you wish to continue living?"

There was a whimper.

"Do you?" snapped Kai.

"Y...yes."

Kai pointed at him. Shiffer shrank back. "If you are to live, 14K must profit. Do you agree?"

Shiffer's eyes were wide in terror. He nodded.

"So three things are going to happen." Kai opened the folder he'd been carrying with him and laid it down in front of Shiffer. "First, you will sell all your shares in Shiffer Investments to us through this shell company." He picked up a pen from the desk and held it out. "Sign the transfer papers."

Shiffer stared at the folder in front of him. Kai had already filled in most of the form under Kendal's direction. The only change he made was to halve the amount Kendal said Lachlan should be paid for his shares. Shiffer would still get a lot of money, but he would not profit overly from the sale.

"This amount is ridiculous," protested Shiffer.

"It is the price of murder," said Kai savagely.

Shiffer signed the papers, and then threw the pen on the desk. "These signatures need a witness."

"Oh, don't worry about that. I'll think we'll find one."

Lachlan glowered at Kai. "Now will you go?"

"Oh no, that's just stage one. Now, stage two." He smiled. "It can either be my stage two – you remember it, don't you?"

Shiffer shuddered. "Yes."

"Or it can be your stage two."

"What's that?"

"You sign your resignation letter from Shiffer Investments." He shrugged. "You're lousy at investment anyway." Kai turned the pages over in the folder until he reached the right page. It was a resignation letter that Elliot had typed up on Emma's typewriter from notes taken during his phone call with Kendal.

"Where did you get this notepaper?"

Kai handed him the pen again. "You still don't understand, do you? We can get anything. Sign."

He did, and laid the pen down. "Now go."

"Oh, no. We have one more stage: stage three. Again, it can be yours or mine. Which would you like?"

Shiffer lowered his head. "Not yours."

Kai nodded approvingly. "Wise choice."

"What do I have to do?"

"Quite simple: you are never to set foot in Hong Kong again, nor in the UK." Kai smiled. "Did you know that we have a branch there? They are young and in the process of establishing themselves. Do you know what that means?"

"No."

"It means that they need to be particularly violent." Kai banged a forefinger down on the desk. "So don't go to the UK. You have 48 hours to flee Hong Kong…or you will experience my stage three."

Shiffer looked at him bleakly.

Kai put his hand in his pocket and produced Emma's hand-held cassette recorder. "Just to encourage you on your way, this is a recording of you giving us instructions to kill your niece." He pressed the play button.

Shiffer's face turned pale as the words from their last conversation together were played.

Kai switched off the recording and put the cassette back into his pocket. "Just imagine what the police would make of this, particularly if we also gave them the photographs of your niece's murder." He shrugged. "If the courts don't send you to prison for buying a murder, they will sentence you for attempting it." Kai smiled. "We'd quite like to introduce stage three to you in prison. It's a place where we are particularly active."

Lachlan Shiffer put his head in his hands and groaned.

Chapter 28

Waiting for two days before returning to Hong Kong Island from Lan Tau was one of the hardest things Emma had ever done. She had bouts of glee where she wanted to hug anyone within reach, then moments of anxiety over whether things really were over. Above all, she wanted to see Elliot again – and, she told herself, Auntie and Kai.

She and Kendal caught the bus from Tai-O to the ferry terminal on the west of the Island. They were now on the upper deck of a ferry watching Victoria Harbor come into view.

"What are you going to do when you get back?" Emma asked.

Kendal appeared to be lost in thought.

Emma repeated her question. "Kendal; what's the first thing you're going to do when you get back?"

"Ah, sorry." Kendal paused for a moment, and then said, "I'm going to meet with the owners of the building we lease, and offer to buy it from them."

"Oh." Emma was thinking of entirely different things. She was looking forward to Elliot teaching her to swim again, and... *no, don't go there*. Emma distracted herself by forcing herself to continue Kendal's agenda.

"Now you have sole control of Shiffer Investments, you'll be able to do what you've always wanted. Once you get ownership of the building, will you knock it down straight away?"

"No. First I need to find those who want to invest in the building project. Then I'll knock it down."

"How long will that take?"

Kendal grinned. "I want to begin within a month."

Emma could see both hunger and excitement in her eyes. "Wow." She lapsed into silence and allowed herself to bathe in the joyous feeling of being free of the tension and terror of the previous week. Elliot had confirmed in a phone call that morning that Lachlan had gone. He'd put a phone call through to Shiffer Investments himself to check that it was true.

She shook her head. The plan had worked, and what made it particularly sweet was that everyone had a hand in its success. She'd come up with the idea. Kendal had supplied the legal and financial information. And Kai, well, his role had been particularly crucial. They'd all had to rely on his ability to intimidate. It was not a thought that sat comfortably with Emma. She sighed. Finding the right moral path through life was not always an easy thing to navigate.

And finally, there was Elliot. He'd done much of the administration: finding forms and registering a company. And if that wasn't enough, he'd hauled Kai to the top of an eight story building – climbing at night up partly erected scaffolding.

She gazed out the open window of the ferry at the iconic view of Hong Kong Harbor. The city seemed to pulsate with energy and celebrate its diversity. Humble wooden bumboats shared the harbor with luxurious cruise liners, and towering skyscrapers stood next to scruffy refugee camps. It was a place where East and West held hands and agreed to work together.

The engines of their ferry rumbled in reverse to slow it down as it nosed its way alongside the wharf. People were crowded behind the barricades waiting their turn to get on the vessel. Emma had learned to love Hong Kong's ferries. They carried humanity in all its rich and varied forms. When viewed from a distance, the wooden vessels looked like green and white, double-storied wedding cakes.

Moments later, they were jostling their way along the exit ramp…and then she saw them. Elliot and Kai were leaning on the barricades.

She wanted to drop Elliot's kit bag and run, but Kendal was holding the other handle, so she controlled herself – until it came to the last five yards. Then she dropped the bag and ran to Elliot.

He swept her up in his arms and twirled her round.

It felt good to be in his arms. It was thrilling, it was safe, and it felt so right. She choked back a sob.

He held her by the waist and allowed one hand to move a few inches up and down, as if to check she was really there. "You feel so…er, it's so good to have you back," he said.

Kendal came up behind, hauling the kit bag on her own.

Kai came forward and took the bag from her, pausing a moment to squeeze her arm.

Elliot disengaged himself from Emma and pushed past Kai. Then, without ceremony, he put an arm around Kendal and kissed her full on the lips.

Emma blinked, unsure for a moment of what she was seeing. She felt as if the earth might give way.

From the corner of her eyes, she saw Kai roll his eyes.

Emma remonstrated with herself for allowing herself to forget that Kendal was Elliot's girlfriend. But there had been a moment, a brief moment, one that she would cherish forever.

They walked past the taxi ranks across to a line of shops. Auntie was waiting for them in one of the food stalls. She lifted one of her sticks in salute as she saw them.

Emma rushed over to her and gave her a hug. Kendal was not far behind. Questions and laughter tripped over each other.

By the time their bowls of *geng* soup arrived, most of the questions had been answered and the laughter had subsided.

Auntie looked at Kendal and patted her on the hand. "My dear, I need to take you to visit a friend of mine."

Kendal looked at her quizzically.

Auntie continued. "He's a very senior policeman, a man I trust and who is sympathetic to the work we do in the Walled City."

"Why do you want to see him?" asked Kai.

"I called him the day Kendal was rescued from the Walled City, to tell him the truth about what had happened so the police wouldn't waste their time and resources looking for her."

"What?" exclaimed Kai. "You told them everything?"

"I told him the truth about my involvement."

"What was that?" Kendal asked.

"Just that I'd found you in a distressed state outside the Walled City. You told me you'd been kidnapped and held for a few days before you were released. You couldn't remember anything much because you had been sedated by drugs. You'd not been physically hurt by the ordeal, but you had been terrified by it. The only thing you wanted to do was to go into hiding in order to come to terms with everything that had happened. You didn't tell me where you were going, but promised that you would see the police when you returned." Auntie smiled. "We need to honor that promise now."

Kai nodded approvingly. "You are sneaky."

Auntie pointed at him. "It is just as well for you that I am, young man."

"I'll go with you," said Elliot.

Auntie shot a glance at Emma and then turned to Elliot. "No Elliot, you and Kai take Emma back to Tai Tam. Kendal and I will join you later and we'll have dinner together."

Auntie presided over dinner much like a queen. Earlier, she'd taken Kendal down to the bottom of the garden to see Sai Wing and get some more of his medicinal tablets. Auntie now sat at the head of the table with every appearance of contentment, casting her eyes over everyone present.

Emma smiled. "Counting all your chicks in, Auntie?"

"Yes, I am." The old woman looked at her. "You and I should talk sometime soon Emma."

"Of course. Umm…about anything in particular?"

For a moment, Auntie didn't answer. Then she patted Emma's hand and said, "Perhaps."

It wasn't an entirely helpful answer.

Before she could ask for clarification, Auntie turned to Kendal.

"Kendal is an unusual name. Where did it come from?"

Kendal smiled. "Dad was born in Kendal. It's a pretty market town in the English Lake District – famous for its mint cake. Evidently, he enjoyed an idyllic childhood there, so he named me after it."

"That's nice. Have you been back to visit the place?"

"Yes. Once, three years ago."

"Are you ever tempted to go back and live in the UK?"

Kendal shook her head. "No. My heart belongs to Hong Kong." She paused. "I love the pace of life and the opportunity here."

Auntie nodded. She turned to Elliot. "And what about you? Where does your heart belong?"

Emma found herself holding her breath.

Blithely indifferent to the double entendre Emma was wrestling with, Elliot replied. "My place is a tiny village on the south coast of England. Not much happens there, it's quite remote. The only people able to find it are the tax department."

Emma caught herself laughing a bit too loudly.

Auntie smiled and leaned back in her chair. "I have some news," she said.

Everyone turned toward her.

"I had a private chat with my policeman friend about Lachlan Shiffer. He suspects, by the way, that there is a connection between your abduction and his sudden departure from Hong Kong. Evidently, Mr. Shiffer boarded a flight to the Philippines. He's also left instructions for his unit to be sold and has resigned from his role as CEO of Shiffer Investments." She paused. "My police friend asked if I could shed any light on it all."

"And did you?" asked Kai.

"No." She shrugged. "I am just a crippled old woman."

Emma smiled.

It was now getting late, and no one had talked about who was staying where. Emma asked the question.

Kai said he was heading back to Kowloon.

Auntie laid a hand over Kendal's arm. "Your home is here for as long as you like."

"Then I'd very much like to stay," said Kendal. "And I'd like to talk with you about an idea that Emma gave me."

"Certainly, dear."

Emma glanced at Elliot. "And what will you do?"

He looked at her in surprise. "I'm going home to our place of course."

His answer warmed her heart.

Everyone began to disperse. Elliot helped Auntie carry some dishes to the kitchen while Kai walked to the front door with Kendal.

Emma followed behind them carrying some more dishes. As she stepped into the hallway, she saw Kai slip an arm around Kendal's waist.

Emma stepped back into the shadows, unseen. However, she was able to hear their conversation.

"You kidnapped me." Kendal's voice.

Kai answered. "You captured me."

There was a pause. "You don't know me." Kendal again.

Kai laughed bitterly. "I don't know me."

And then the two of them went out into the night.

Elliot pushed open the door of the apartment and switched on the lights. He did a quick scan to check all was well inside then stood back, and with exaggerated gallantry, ushered Emma through.

Matching his manners, she curtsied and stepped into the doorway. "I thought for a moment you were going to carry me across the threshold," she said. Then she seemed to realize what she'd uttered, because she suddenly became flustered. "I mean…just to welcome me back. Not…"

Elliot's response was to scoop her up in his arms.

"Put me down," she squealed. Emma thumped his chest with her fist, but her protest was not very convincing. Then she laughed.

Elliot wondered briefly if he should carry her to his bedroom, but it was just a fleeting thought. Instead, he carried her to the couch and plopped her down. He stayed leaning over her once he'd done so and smiled. "I do declare, Miss Templeton, you are blushing."

Emma pushed him away, got to her feet, and stalked to the door of her bed-sit. "I'm going to have a very long shower, and then you, Elliot Gleeson, can make me a jasmine tea." It was probably not quite the dignified exit she'd hoped for, but it was, nonetheless, a pretty fair attempt.

Elliot grinned and went back to the landing to retrieve the kit bag.

Half an hour later they were both sitting on the balcony in the darkness, looking across the moon-silvered water. In the distance, he could see golden specks of light that marked the position of the boats fishing west of Lamma Island. The peace of the scene was balm to his soul after the anxiety of the previous week.

He nursed his mug of tea and cast a covert look at Emma. Her legs were tucked up onto the chair, and she was holding her cup against her chest with two hands.

Neither of them said anything for a long time.

"It's good to be back," he said eventually.

"Yes."

Elliot wished she would say a bit more. He wanted to talk. Elliot cleared his throat. "I've been talking with Auntie about your religious stuff."

Emma looked at him over the rim of her tea cup. "And...?"

"She gave me this." He picked up a paperback book that he'd put beside his chair. "It's called, 'Good News for Modern Man.'"

"That's the New Testament in modern English."

He smiled. "Yeah, with cartoons."

"How are you finding it?"

"It's, er...good news – very, actually."

"Hmm."

They lapsed into silence again.

Elliot tried again. "I'm trying to come to terms with the fact that I'm the sole signatory of a company – a company!" He grinned. "I've never owned a company before."

Emma gave him a wry smile. "Don't get too ahead of yourself. It's just a shell company. You'll be transferring it over to Kendal in the next few days."

"Yeah, but right now, I own thirty-five percent of Shiffer Investments." He grinned. "That makes me a very rich man. So be nice to me."

Emma rolled her eyes, then lapsed into silence again.

"What's on your mind?" he asked.

"Lots of things."

"Good or bad?"

"Some…" she paused, "exquisite." She rushed on. "And some troubling."

"Anything particularly troubling you?"

"My work here in Hong Kong is finished. And the report I've compiled over the last few weeks is…er, pretty explosive."

"The triad stuff?"

"Yes. I have to assume that if someone broke into here to snoop around, they were looking for my report." She shrugged. "They didn't take the cassette recorder, so it wasn't a standard robbery."

"Are you frightened they'll come back now you're back."

She nodded. "Yes. Somehow, I've got to keep it safe until I organize a flight back to the UK."

Elliot frowned. Facing the fact that Emma would soon be leaving was not pleasant. He couldn't imagine not seeing her face or hearing her voice again. He swallowed. "And when do you fly back?"

"I'll phone my boss in London in a moment to tee it up. We're eight hours ahead, so it'll be early morning there."

"Would you feel safer if you spent tomorrow with me?"

"Yes."

"That would mean sailing with me in the afternoon."

She nodded. "Great. Um…"

"Um, what?"

"Will you give me another swimming lesson in the morning?"

Memories of their last time together flooded back – tight, cool flesh, lightly textured – utterly feminine. He nodded slowly. "I'd enjoy that." He paused. "And one more thing."

"What?"

"If you give me your report, I'll hide it so no one finds it."

Emma shook her head. "You don't really expect me to give you a folder containing things of national security, do you?" She pointed at him. "I know you; you'll just stuff it in the pocket of your smock top or stick it in a locker on a boat somewhere."

"Can you think of a better place to hide it?"

She chewed her lip. "Not really."

"Then give it to me tomorrow."

"But where will we put it when we go swimming?"

He smiled. "I'll slice open the kick board we bought you to teach swimming, and stick your report inside."

"You're joking." She furrowed her brow. "Can you really do that?"

"Yeah. I've got epoxy and a sharp knife in my ditty bag."

"Ditty bag?"

"My canvas work bag."[1]

She nodded. "I suppose I can wrap the report in plastic and tape it, but it would be good if the kick-board was also watertight. Is that possible?"

"Yes."

Emma smiled. "You're pretty amazing, sometimes, Elliot Gleeson – even though you steal my breakfast."

He laughed.

She began chewing her lip again. "And when do you fly back to the UK?"

"In about four days, I've just about finished what I have to do. They've allowed me a bit of time to go sight-seeing before I leave."

Emma looked at her watch. It was 9:45pm. Although it was dark, plenty of people were still about; some were even on the beach. It had been magical sitting on the balcony with Elliot, but she could no longer postpone her phone call to London.

"Do you fancy a walk?" she said.

Elliot lifted his feet from off the balcony railings and sat up. "Sure. Where do you want to go?"

"I need to call my boss to organize my flight home, but I need to do it from a phone that…" she trailed off.

"…that wouldn't be tapped," finished Elliot.

"I have to assume it's possible."

"Sure. Where do you want to go?"

"They should have a phone at the Repulse Bay Hotel. I can put through a reverse charge call from there."

"Okay. Let's go."

They walked along the beach to the hotel. Both carried their sandals as they padded along the sand, allowing the waves to wash in over their ankles. She was wearing a lightweight sarong. Elliot had been prevailed upon to wear his smarter shorts because they were going to a hotel. But he had to wear his smock top in order to hide her report that was tucked into his waistband. It was a pity, she thought. He had a lovely, well-toned torso.

The crests of the waves rolling into the beach were highlighted by the streetlights along the foreshore. It gave them a mystical, ghostly appearance.

Neither of them said anything much until they got to the hotel. After dusting the sand from their feet and putting on their sandals, they entered the old colonial building. Emma spoke with a receptionist behind the counter and was granted permission to use the phone in the lobby for a reverse charge call.

Moments later, she was speaking to John Egerton at his MI5 office in London.

"Ah, Miss Templeton. How safe is this phone?"

"I'm in a hotel lobby."

"What do you need?"

"I've finished," her voice cracked slightly. "I'm ready to come back."

"You've really finished?"

"Yes, I've done all I can."

"Are the findings significant?"

"Yes."

"Do they include names?"

"Only a few, but there are some surprises." She paused, wondering how much she should say. "There's need for a big clean up here."

Nothing was said for a moment.

"Then we'll bring you home. I want you to book a flight home in five days, but you will actually be coming home the day before under another name."

"Oh." Emma was not at all confident that it was legally or practically possible to leave Hong Kong anonymously. "Do you want me to send the report to you via a locked bag in the diplomatic mail?"

"Definitely not. You must operate as you have. Don't report to anyone in Hong Kong. We don't know whom to trust. Bring the report with you in person."

Emma's heart sank. She would dearly love to be rid of the thing.

Egerton interrupted her thinking. "Is the report safe?"

She massaged her forehead. Her report was currently sitting against the well-muscled belly of a sailing instructor who had a distinctly casual attitude to life. "Yes," she said.

"Good. Don't let it out of your sight."

Emma wasn't sure how much to say. Eventually she blurted out, "Someone may have been snooping around in my apartment."

"What could they find if they were?"

"They didn't find the report. I had it with me."

"Good." He paused. "Do you feel safe?"

Emma looked at Elliot lounging against the wall beside her, pretending not to listen. "I, er…have a friend who is protecting me."

Elliot turned to her with a raised eyebrow.

"He's keeping a close eye on me, and I think he's competent."

She looked at Elliot and spoke into the phone loud enough for him to hear. "He's even able to accompany me home – provided you fly us both back first class. He's used to luxury."

She shot Elliot an inquiring look.

He nodded enthusiastically.

"First class?"

"Yes."

Egerton sighed. "What names will I book you under?"

Emma swallowed. "Mr. and Mrs. E. Gleeson. That should throw anyone off the scent." She looked at Elliot for some sort of reaction.

There was none.

John Egerton came straight back. "But your passport will show your true name."

"I could be a feminist who's chosen to retain her old name."

Egerton chuckled. "You are taking to this sleuthing business far too well."

Chapter 29

It wasn't strictly true that Elliot needed to teach sailing all afternoon. All he needed to do was to hear a couple of instructors re-sit an oral exam, something which would only take forty minutes. What Elliot really had in mind was to spend most of the afternoon alone with Emma on board *Soleil*. She had shown a natural aptitude for sailing, and he was looking forward to developing that skill further – at least, that was what he told himself.

In the event, there was very little wind, so Elliot allowed *Soleil* to ghost along in the light airs until they were just off Lamma Island. The water was a beautiful aqua blue and so clear that they could just see the ocean floor. He dropped the anchor just off a sandy cove, and sat in the cockpit eating a picnic lunch.

Once they'd finished, they decided to go swimming.

Elliot rigged the boarding ladder and watched Emma step down it into the water. Her dark complexion meant that she had developed a tan over the last few weeks. Elliot watched her move, agile and easy. *Why hadn't he noticed that before?*

He dived off the side and joined her in the water.

Emma's swimming had progressed to a point where she could dog-paddle for a while without the aid of the kick board, but it was still tiring for her. When she was exhausted, she clung to Elliot's back, holding on as if he was giving her a piggyback.

The water was colder than he expected, causing his skin to have goose bumps. But when Emma held onto his back and wrapped her legs around him, a wave of warmth washed through him that had nothing to do with water temperature. He could feel her skin, firm and cool. It was delicious.

Elliot watched her lithe body as he followed her back on board. It was, he told himself, her innocence that he found so disturbing. She had no idea about the effect her body had on him when they were playing about in the water. He frowned. *Or did she?*

As he climbed on board, he noticed that the wind had become stronger. The shrouds were now humming in the breeze, murmuring, telling Elliot that *Soleil* was impatient to be doing what she was designed to do.

He started the engine and edged the boat forward so Emma could pull in the anchor. Elliot watched her heave in the anchor line, determination written all over her face. She was, as usual, eager to do things right.

He smiled.

It wasn't long before *Soleil* was bowling along with the wind. Emma was on the helm and loving it. He glanced astern at their creaming wake. As he did, he noticed a speedboat curving through the water on a course that would intercept them.

He shielded his eyes from the sun and stared at it.

Emma was blissfully unaware. Her hair had dried and was fluttering over her shoulders. She looked magnificent.

As the speedboat came closer, he could see it contained three people. It swept up behind them and surged back over its own wake to come to a near stop.

Elliot eased the sheets until the sails began to flap and *Soleil* slowed down.

One man climbed over the foredeck of the speedboat and attached a line to *Soleil's* stern cleat. Elliot recognized him instantly. It was Kai.

An older man sat next to the driver's seat, someone he didn't recognize. The third man aimed a pistol at him.

"What the hell…" he exclaimed.

"Step back. We come on your boat," the old man barked. He had a curious high-pitched voice.

Emma had her mouth open in shock. "Kai," she said. "What on earth are you doing? What is this?"

Kai did not answer.

The old man snapped, "Shut up."

Elliot glanced at his brother. Kai met his gaze for only a second then turned away to help the old man climb aboard *Soleil*.

Kai's expression told him everything.

Emma tugged at his arm. "Elliot, tell him. Say something. Do something." She turned to the old man. "Who are you?"

Elliot was fairly sure he already knew.

Kai answered for him. "He is Mr. K, my father," he shot a glance at Elliot. "And your father."

Elliot stared at him. He expected to feel something, a connection of some sort. But he felt nothing. It was strange. This was his father, for goodness sake. But all he saw was a stranger – a stranger with a nasty, antagonistic expression. It was bizarre.

The old man looked at him and nodded. "So you come back. Will you stay Hong Kong?" His English was poor.

The man with the gun stepped aboard and stood on the stern hatch behind the cockpit, aiming his gun at Elliot's chest. Elliot looked at him and saw the dispassionate eyes of a killer. He reached over and pulled Emma behind him. His first priority, his only priority, was to protect her.

"No!" he roared. "You will not harm anyone on this boat."

Mr. K pursed his lips. "We do what we want." He indicated the man behind him holding the gun. "Ah Keung – very good shot. He like killing."

An awkward silence followed.

Kai took station on the stern quarter, steadying himself with one hand against the backstay.

Mr. K pointed to Emma. "You speak Cantonese. I know."

Emma lifted her chin. "I speak some."

"I think you speak very good. You trick my brothers in prison and learn things. This I know." He paused. "Who you work for?"

"I work for a department under the Home Secretary."

Mr. K turned to Kai, and the two of them spoke to each other in Chinese. Mr. K eventually nodded and turned back.

Emma continued to speak. "I have finished my work and I will go back to England in a few days. My report has been sent." She shrugged. "So if you had planned to stop anything by coming here, you are too late."

Elliot held an arm out to prevent her from coming from behind him. He was both amazed and appalled at her courage.

Mr. K again leaned back to speak to Kai, presumably to make sure he understood Emma rightly. The old man turned back.

"Maybe you have. Maybe no. You die anyway so you don't tell boss man. He shrugged. "Or you die to show boss man we are strong."

Elliot's head spun. This couldn't be happening. Before he could think, he blurted out, "She will not die. She is under my protection, and I am your son."

The old man looked at him disdainfully. "Will you join 14K and be loyal?"

Elliot shook his head. "No. I hate what you do."

"Then you not my son." The old man tapped his chest. "I am Dragon Head. People must be loyal, or die."

Emma broke in. "You listened to me speaking on my cassette recorder, didn't you?"

"Yes." The old man pointed to her. "You are tricky. So you die."

"No!" screamed Elliot. He pushed Emma behind him again as she'd stepped out to challenge Mr. K. "You cannot kill her."

"Why?"

"Because…because she is my fiancée. I plan to marry her."

Emma stared at him with her mouth open. "Your what?"

Elliot cleared his throat. "I plan to marry you." He pushed her back behind him again.

"Elliot," she shouted, "you don't have to…"

Mr. K interrupted. "Shut up," he barked. He pointed to Emma. "Kill her." Then Mr. K. pointed to Elliot. "And kill him too."

Elliot was standing in front of the binnacle. He had one hand behind him and was gradually turning the ship's wheel. The wind was now quite fresh and coming from behind them. This meant that even though *Soleil's* sails had been let as loose as possible, they were still catching enough wind for *Soleil* to continue to move through the water at a goodly pace.

If he could just turn the boat a little further.

Further.

Suddenly, the wind that at one moment had been blowing on one side of the mainsail now blew on the other. Four-hundred square yards of sail instantly flung the heavy boom from one side of the boat to other.

Elliot watched in anguish as Ah Keung ducked underneath it to stop himself from being knocked overboard.

Soleil heeled slightly to the other side, and continued to push through the water.

Mr. K screamed again. "Shoot them."

Two shots rang out.

Somewhere nearby, a seagull screamed.

Ah Keung collapsed and fell against the safety rail. The gun that was in his hand toppled free and dropped into the sea. Then, with a small sigh, the man crumpled sideways along the side deck.

Soleil bucked and nodded as if nothing had happened.

Mr. K swung round and stared at Kai with a frown of disbelief. "What you do?" he screamed.

Kai was holding a gun. His face was pale. He answered in a flat, dispassionate voice, "You do not kill my brother or the woman who will be his wife."

The old man stamped his feet. "You will obey. You will be honorable." He pointed to Emma and Elliot. "Kill them now. I order you."

Kai swung the pistol round so that it pointed to his father. "You speak of honor." He shook his head. "You have never been honorable. And you have never done any good thing the gods would like."

Kai spat out words of contempt. "I am ashamed of you. You have never been someone I am proud of – and you never will be."

Two further shots rang out.

Mr. K was hurled back so that he lay dead across the body of Ah Keung.

Kai looked at his father, as if struggling to come to terms with what he'd done. He glanced at the gun in his hand and threw it into the sea. Then he sank down on deck and put his head in his hands.

Elliot climbed out of the cockpit, squatted down, and put an arm around him.

An animal-like wail escaped his brother. "What...?" Kai's chest heaved as he fought to control his emotions.

Elliot squeezed his brother's shoulders. "Take it steady, mate. I've got you."

"I...I've killed my father," Kai sobbed.

"You saved Emma – someone who is..." He cleared his throat, then continued hoarsely. "...very special to me." He squeezed Kai's shoulders again. "I'll never be able to thank you enough."

"How...how did you know I was not going to kill Emma...or kill you?" Kai shook his head. "I am not a good man."

Elliot grunted. "I knew you wouldn't let anything bad happen to us when you first turned up. You gave me a look, remember?"

"You knew?"

"Yes."

Emma interrupted them. She pointed to the bodies lying crumpled against the guard rail, and backed away in horror. "What are we going to do with...?" She couldn't finish the sentence.

Kai pushed Elliot's arm away and got to his feet. He said to Elliot, "Pull the speedboat alongside."

Elliot helped Kai lift both corpses into the boat. As he did, he noticed two large pieces of concrete breeze-block on the floor of the boat. Both had a piece of chain threaded through them and a shackle. The means by which Mr. K had planned to dispose of Emma and himself was abundantly clear. He shivered.

Emma remained in the cockpit hugging her knees. She looked to be in shock.

Elliot pulled a bucket from a cockpit locker and began sluicing the blood off the side deck. He needed to do something to distract himself from seeing Kai chain the two pieces of breeze block around the waists of Ah Keung and Mr. K.

Elliot did not look up when he heard two splashes. But he did look up in time to see Kai strip the blood-soaked floor covering off the bottom of the speedboat and throw it in the water after them. Without a word, he handed Kai the bucket to wash the streak of blood off the side of the boat.

When that was done, Kai climbed back on board *Soleil* and sat down in the cockpit. He moved mechanically, as if he was a robot.

Emma lifted her head and looked at Elliot. "Did you really say you wanted to marry me, or was that...?"

Elliot nodded slowly. "I meant every last word of it."

"What...?" she couldn't finish her question.

Elliot put a hand on her shoulder. "The idea of spending my life without you is, well..." he tried to find the right words, "...too horrible to bear," he finished lamely.

She furrowed her brow. "But I saw you kiss Kendal."

Elliot nodded. "Yeah, I did. I was conducting a, a sort of, experiment."

"An experiment!"

He nodded. "And I wanted to piss my brother off."

"Oh."

Emma turned to Kai. He again had his head in his hands. "Kai, I'm so sorry," she said. "Whatever else he was, Mr. K was your father."

Kai looked up, his face stricken. "There is now no hope for me."

Emma closed her eyes, trying to come to terms with everything that had happened. Part of her wanted to run away screaming from the killing she had witnessed. It had been so sudden and brutal. And the bodies had been tipped, without ceremony, into the sea like unwanted fish offal.

Another part of her was trying to fathom the fact that Elliot had proposed marriage to her. She desperately wanted to get Elliot on his own so she could question him closely about it, because at the moment she couldn't believe it. But what if it were true! She shook her head. What if she could finally feel joy, and luxuriate in Elliot's love. How wonderful that would be. At last, she'd be free to show him her love. Her heart cried out for him – followed closely by her body.

But the most pressing thing that claimed her attention at the moment was Kai. She could see that he was stricken with anguish.

Kai had covered his face with his hands and was sobbing.

She moved along the cockpit seat so she could put an arm around him.

His shoulders heaved with emotion.

"There is no hope," he said. "I have killed my father. I have betrayed everything I know, and every oath that I have made. The gods will damn me to hell."

Emma shook her head. "No, no, Kai. That is not true. You saved Elliot and myself from evil." She squeezed his shoulders. "I thank you for that, and I honor you for doing so."

Kai laughed bitterly. "No, you don't understand. There is no salvation for me. There cannot be. You know nothing of my life." He tried to pull away from Emma. "I have raped, cheated, killed, tortured, and bullied." He looked at her. "Did you hear that? He stabbed the cockpit bench with his finger as he said again, "I have raped, cheated, killed, tortured, and bullied. What god can forgive that?"

Emma did not allow herself to be shaken. She nodded. "Yes, they are very bad things." She looked at him. "Only the one true God of heaven and earth is big enough to solve that problem." She squeezed his arm. "He came and died on a cross to pay the price for all the bad things we've done." She paused. "God is waiting to forgive – if you ask."

Kai snorted with scorn. "He will not forgive me."

"All of us need forgiveness, Kai."

"I have killed my father. That is great dishonor." He shook his head. "I do not even have a surname…and there is nothing that I have ever done in my life that says I deserve one."

"You have done something heroic and good today, Kai. You have saved…" she swallowed, "…your brother from being killed. I will always be grateful."

Kai looked at her for a moment. "Is it true that you work for the British government and have come to find out about triads?"

"Yes. We want to know how to protect people – to stop the tears."

He nodded slowly. "You are a good person."

She said nothing.

"I…" Kai paused. "I will never betray my 14K brothers."

Emma furrowed her brows. Kai had just killed his father, the Dragon Head. But somehow, in Kai's mind, he was able to make a distinction between loyalty to his father and loyalty to 14K.

"I won't ask you to," she said.

"But I will tell you the names of the top policemen we pay, if it will help bring…" he trailed off.

"…less suffering?"

"Yes." He paused. "Maybe your God would like that, yes?"

"Yes."

He nodded to himself. "They are greedy men, these policemen."

Kai began to mention a few names.

"Hang on," said Emma. "I'll get something to write with."

Elliot pushed himself away from the binnacle and reached for the companionway. "I'll find you something."

A few seconds later, he handed up a marine chart and a pencil. "Here: use the back of this."

Moments later, she was jotting down names, payments, and dates. It was extraordinary information. Two of the names came as no surprise. Some of the others shocked her.

When Kai had finished, he flopped back in his seat. "So you think that the gods would approve of what I have done?"

"I think the one true God of heaven and earth, the God that your ancient emperors honored each year, would feel you have acted honorably."

Kai dropped his head. Then he reached for the pendant hanging around his neck. He lifted it from around his neck and handed it to Emma. "Here, take it."

"Why?"

"You understand it."

Emma opened the clasp on the ivory locket and stared at the dragon stone inside it. "Are you sure?"

"Yes. You, of all people, know that I can no longer wear it."

She nodded. "That is true; you can't. This dragon stone no longer defines you."

Emma reached around her own neck and undid her necklace. It had a small silver cross attached to it. She took Kai's hand, placed the necklace in it, and folded his fingers over the top.

"This is to remind you that no-one is ever beyond God's forgiveness."

Kai opened his hand and stared at it. "I don't think that can be possible." Then, with a deep sigh, he got to his feet.

Elliot was standing by the wheel. He turned and faced Kai. For a while, the two brothers said nothing. Elliot leaned forward and laid a hand on Kai's shoulder. Kai reached up and put his hand on top of it. Nothing was said. After a moment, Kai turned and climbed over the taffrail into the speedboat.

Seconds later, he was speeding back to Hong Kong Island.

Emma stood and watched him go with a feeling of sadness.

Elliot pulled in the sheets so that *Soleil* was correctly trimmed and could sail properly. *Soleil* responded and began to surge through the water with a new sense of purpose. He then stepped behind Emma and folded his arms around her.

She turned within them and faced him, allowing his arms to imprison her fists against her chest.

"How are you going?" he asked.

She tried to laugh, but sobbed instead.

"In the last half hour, I've been threatened with murder, had a marriage proposal, watched 2 men die, and I've comforted a triad member who has killed his father."

She wiggled her arms free and put her hands behind Elliot's

neck, interlacing her fingers. "Do you mind if we do this marriage proposal thing over again, sometime?"

Elliot leaned against the ship's wheel and pulled her to himself. "How about every day of our lives?"

She could feel his hands running down the side of her torso until they rested on the curve of her hips. His fingers splayed out above her bottom. The passion that had built up over the weeks and been so hard to repress, would not be denied any more. She pushed herself against him and lifted her head.

Elliot bent over until his lips lingered above hers, as if searching. Then he brought his lips down on hers in a hungry, searching kiss. She could feel his passion. But a moment later, his kiss softened into one that was tender, full, and generous.

Initially, she was quite stiff, unpracticed in the art of kissing. Then she melted and allowed her mouth to explore his with growing passion and hunger. It was sublime, and it lasted a lifetime – or so it seemed. She moaned, giddy and overwhelmed, then reached for him again with fresh passion, her body shameless in what it insisted on doing.

Soleil ran downwind with her helm unattended. If she objected to the lack of attention being paid to her, she gave no hint of it.

Chapter 30

K ai caught Kendal at her offices at Shiffer Investments an hour before they closed for the night. After a brief chat, she accompanied him to a bank. Once their business there was complete, they walked back to her offices.

By the time they finished their business, it was late. The office staff had left, and they were alone.

Kai scratched at the gold lettering on the door as Kendal sat at her desk, finishing up the paperwork. Lachlan's name was still on the door, but Kai was satisfied that he'd done enough to deface it. He leaned against the wall. "Elliot asked Emma to marry him this afternoon."

Kendal lifted her head. "Wow." She paused. "So you've seen them today?"

Kai swallowed. "Yes."

Kendal smiled, but there was a hint of sadness in her eyes. "I am not really surprised."

"You did not want to marry Elliot?"

For a while, she said nothing. Then she sighed. "Perhaps I would have liked the chance to explore the possibility." She shrugged. "But I am like you; we have both been made in Hong Kong, and our hearts are trapped here." She tapped the papers on her desk together and put them in a drawer. "I think we've done everything that's necessary. I can get the rest done for you later."

He nodded. "Thank you."

Kendal got up from her desk and stood in front of him. The half-light of the dimmed offices burnished her hair with gold.

He reached forward and bunched it in his hand.

Kendal did not move.

Kai murmured, "I have had many women. I even thought I loved some of them. But none have affected me like you." He paused. "We would make great lovers."

Kendal lifted her chin. "I am not sure. Would you be tender, or would you be selfish and cruel, like a gang member?"

He continued to squeeze her hair and run his fingers through it. "I do not know," he murmured.

She laid a hand against his chest. "I feel your passion, Kai – really, I do. And it doesn't go entirely unanswered. You have..." she paused.

"I have what?" he asked.

"You have power, and I find that exciting." She took him by the shirt collar and shook it gently. "And you are handsome." She shrugged her shoulders. "But..."

He nodded. "I am triad and have been ruined by all I have done."

"Yes."

Hong Kong's evening traffic tooted, revved, and growled its way along the busy streets outside.

Kendal lifted her face to him. "It could never work out between us. You know that."

He moved his hand behind her neck. "I could rape you now, you know."

She took his hand, put it on her chest, and covered it with her own. He could feel her fullness. "Yes, you could." The look in her eyes was one of deep sorrow.

He shook his head. "You have ruined me, Kendal Shiffer."

She took his hand from her chest. "You kidnapped me."

"Yes. I did." Kai paused, then stepped away from her toward the door.

"Will you remember me?" he asked.

"Yes."

He nodded, and left.

Kai walked down the side street that ran off Garden Road. To his right stood the imposing bulk of St. John's Cathedral. Its stately colonial architecture seemed to whisper the peace and stability of another era, but it was probably just an illusion.

He walked round the building until he came to the front porch at the cathedral's western end. The porch had a Gothic arch on each of its three sides, and a black and white tiled floor. Everything looked clean and neat. If the recent *lap sap cheung* campaign to rid Hong Kong of litter was working anywhere, it was working here.[1]

He entered the porch and looked at the large wooden doors in front of him. They were shut.

Kai sighed. It was fitting that they be closed. He was, and had to be, shut out from the presence of God.

He walked to a corner of the porch and slid down the wall to the floor.

The doors were unyielding and impenetrable. They stood between him and God.

But Emma's words still rang in his ears. He took out her necklace and looked at the cross. He'd come to St. John's Cathedral to be as close to God as he could, not really believing he could be forgiven. Could it be true?

He hoped it was. Kai put the necklace around his neck. Then he reached over to the plastic shopping bag he'd been carrying and took out a tourniquet, syringe, a small plastic bag of white powder, a teaspoon and a cigarette lighter.

Chapter 31

E lliot chased Emma through the door to their apartment trying to grab the towel from around her waist. Emma squealed and scooted behind the sofa. He gave up the chase as the phone rang. As he picked it up, he grinned. It was highly doubtful that Emma's swimming had improved much at all as a result of their outing, even though they had both spent a lot of time in the water. She was, he discovered, delightfully tactile, wanting to feel him close. And it was not possible to be as tactile decently when lying on the sand.

"Hello, Elliot Gleeson speaking."

"Ah, hello dear."

He smiled; it was Auntie. "Yes, Auntie."

"Can you and Emma come over to my house? I'm afraid I have some bad news."

Elliot frowned. "Sure. We'll be there in half an hour." He paused. "Are you okay?"

But Auntie had put the phone down.

A taxi took them along Tai Tam Road with its beautiful views. However, the cheerfulness of the sun on the water and boats floating at their moorings belied the sense of foreboding in his gut.

When they arrived, they walked down the hallway and found

Auntie sitting at the dining table. The room was dark, and she was alone. She had her head in her hands, and it was obvious that she'd been crying.

Emma immediately rushed forward and put an arm around her shoulder.

Elliot stood in front of her, grim. "What's the matter, Auntie?"

The old woman held a hand out to him. He stepped forward, and she hugged him to herself. "Oh Elliot, I'm so sorry. Your brother is dead."

Elliot's head spun. "What? No!" He groped for a chair and sat down. "What's happened?"

"He died last night. The police called me this morning, and I've just got back from identifying his body." She began sobbing again.

Elliot shook his head. "How did he die?"

Auntie curbed her weeping with a shuddering sigh. "The police say it was the result of a heroin overdose – a tragic but all too common event in Hong Kong." She sniffed. "They said that as the case appeared straightforward, his body would be released within a day or so."

Emma frowned. "Heroin?"

"Y-yes. Evidently it was a significant overdose, four times the average amount. The police were not very sympathetic and wondered how on earth Kai thought he could survive such a dose."

"Has Kai ever used drugs?" he asked.

"No. He was too familiar with the damage it did to go down that path."

"Then, this is not an accidental overdose."

Emma pulled a chair round and sat next to Auntie so she could hold her hand. "Where was he found?" she asked."

Auntie wiped her eyes. "Well, that's the surprising part. He was found in the porch of St. John's Cathedral, in the city."

Emma nodded. "I…I think I know why he was there. He was trying to get close to God in his own way…before he committed suicide."

"But why would he want to commit suicide?"

Elliot knew he would need to have this conversation and had

been postponing it. He leaned forward and put a hand on Auntie's arm. "Auntie, how close are you to your father?"

She looked at him quizzically. "Not at all. He has never been a father to me, or indeed a husband to my mother." She paused. "I'm afraid he's not a good man."

Elliot pursed his lips. "Auntie, Kai shot your father dead yesterday on a boat that Emma and I were sailing. He shot him because he was about to kill Emma and myself." Elliot went on to recount all that had happened the previous day.

Auntie showed no emotion at all when she learned of the death of her father. However, she was a great deal less sanguine when she learned of the appalling danger Elliot and Emma had faced.

It didn't take long for the full significance of what had happened to be understood. The old woman nodded slowly. "Kai couldn't bear the dishonor of killing his father." She sniffed. "I understand now why he committed suicide."

"You've always known it was suicide, haven't you Auntie?" said Emma.

"Yes dear, I have. The police were able to call me because he had my name and telephone number in his top pocket." She smiled weakly. "He has known my telephone number very well for many years."

Auntie reached for her walking sticks and stood up. "There is something I now need to do. I need to tell Sai Wing." She sniffed. "He had a big hand in bringing Kai up when he lived here."

Elliot also got to his feet. "I'll come with you if you like."

"No dear. I'd like to do this on my own."

No one had any heart for lunch, and the afternoon was spent largely in silence. The only exception came when Elliot told Auntie that he'd proposed to Emma. The old woman had held his hand and then reached out for Emma's hand. "I have seen this for a while, my dears. I am delighted."

Emma spluttered. "For a while?"

"Yes dear."

Auntie's comment succeeded in stunning Emma into silence.

However, the news only brought a brief respite. The enormity of Kai's death again dropped its dark cloak over them.

Elliot spent much of the time trying to make sense of his own grief. He'd only just found his twin brother. To have him whipped away now was cruel. And yet Kai was, in many ways, so alien. But he was his twin. There was a sense in which he knew him and understood him in very profound way – instinctive, almost.

As he pondered these things, he remembered Kendal. He went to find Auntie. She was on the veranda. "Auntie, has Kendal been told?"

"Yes, dear. I called her just a while ago."

"How did she take it?"

"She cried."

He nodded.

Later that evening, Elliot and Emma joined Auntie for dinner. It was a light meal, as no one felt much like eating. As they were finishing, the cook came in and whispered into Auntie's ear, then left. A few minutes later, Auntie looked at Elliot and said, "The cook has told me that Sai Wing has not come up to eat his tea as he usually does. As he has not had any lunch, I'm a little concerned. "Elliot, would you be kind enough to take his meal down to him? Although I doubt he'll eat it."

"Of course."

Elliot collected a plate of food from the kitchen and walked to the garden shed where Sai Wing lived. He could hear the man weeping even as he tapped on the rough wooden door.

It was a while before the door opened. When Sai Wing opened it, Elliot could see he was holding one of Kai's childhood drawings in his hand. The old man looked at Elliot with an expression of shock.

"Yeah, it's me – Elliot," he said gently. "Sorry to upset you. I know I look a lot like Kai." He shrugged. "Can't help it." He tried to smile, but it didn't really work. Elliot held out the plate instead. "Auntie says you need to eat."

Sai Wing took the plate, laid it on a bench, and stood with his head bowed. He looked so forlorn that Elliot stepped forward, put his arms around him and gave him a hug.

Sai Wing immediately started to weep and hugged him back fiercely.

Eventually, the old man's weeping subsided, and he was able to let Elliot go. Sai Wing bowed his thanks as Elliot left. "Thank you," he said simply.

When he returned to the house, Emma and Auntie were sitting out on the veranda watching the day gradually surrender to twilight. He sat down with them deep in thought; thinking about the man he'd met for only a few minutes – his father. The man had been cruel and loathsome, and that was the only memory Elliot would ever have of him. Kai, of course, had known him all his life, but from the exchange that he heard between them on the boat, Kai's opinion of his father had been no better than his own.

"What are you thinking about?" asked Auntie.

Elliot passed a hand over his face. "I was just thinking about the man who was my father. It's not a nice heritage. I can't help but wonder what that might mean for the sort of person I might become."

Emma looked at him with apparent disbelief. "Elliot, you can't seriously…"

He acknowledged her faith in him with a smile and turned back to Auntie. "Why would Kai complain about not having a surname, Auntie? Surely he has one."

"Not all Chinese have a surname, dear. To have one is a privilege. Families without a surname are not considered to be civilized." She smiled sadly. "Honor was important for Kai."

"But did Kai…did we," he corrected, "have a surname? I'd like to know who I am, even though I can have no pride in it."

For a long moment, Auntie said nothing. Then she said, "Pass me my walking sticks, Elliot. I want to get something to show you."

Auntie returned a few minutes later with a metal tin tucked under an arm. She sat down with a grunt and opened the tin.

"Elliot, I'm going to tell you a story – a sad story," she paused.

"But it is your story." She pulled a number of envelopes from the tin box. They looked old, having yellowed with age.

"Your mother died when you were born, and it was my job to clear up all her belongings. In the process of doing that, I found this tin box buried deep at the bottom of her camphor-wood chest. It was a tin full of letters."

"Oh? Who from?"

"They are love letters written to your mother."

"What? From my father?"

Auntie didn't answer his question. She continued with her story. "My father, Mr. K, always wondered why he didn't sire any more children after I was born, despite the scores of women he'd seduced or coerced. So three years before you were born, he asked a doctor, one in the Walled City who had been trained in China, why. The doctor discovered that my Father was no longer producing any sperm, but he was too frightened to tell him. He simply said that everything was okay."

Auntie sighed. "My father then seduced a very young English girl and made her his concubine. Sadly, he used to abuse her so much that the doctor often had to attend her − the same doctor who my father had gone to see. Well, one thing led to another, and the doctor and your mother became lovers, and as a result, you and Kai were born."

Elliot was incredulous.

Emma looked at Auntie in puzzlement. "So, who is Elliot's real father?"

Auntie raised her hands. "Let me finish." She laid a hand on Elliot's arm. "Tragically, your mother died when you were born, and the very same doctor was attending her at the time. He was so grief-stricken at the death of the woman he loved and felt so guilty that he couldn't save her, that he gave up being a doctor." She shrugged. "He worked at various odd jobs for many years doing menial work, until I managed to find him."

Elliot swallowed. "So, who is my father?"

"He is the man I asked to help raise Kai." She paused. "Your father is Sai Wing. You know him as the gardener."

Elliot blinked. "Sai Wing?"

"Yes."

Nothing was said for a while.

Emma broke the silence. "And does Sai Wing have a surname?"

"Yes dear, he does. It is Kua." She turned to Elliot. "Your father's full name, Elliot, is Kua Sai Wing. He is related to one of the most noble medical families in China."

Elliot put his head in his hands and tried to find his way through the storm of emotions he was feeling. There was sadness, wonder, and, very significantly, relief. The extraordinary revelation also helped him understand why Sai Wing had behaved as he had toward him.

Eventually, he nodded to himself and got to his feet.

Emma put a hand out. It didn't quite touch him. "Where are you going?"

He bent over and kissed her on the forehead. "I'm going to see my father."

Elliot knocked on the door of the garden shed.

Sai Wing opened the door. "Hello."

"Hi," said Elliot. It was a woefully inadequate salutation.

"Come in." Sai Wing stepped back, holding the door open.

Elliot stepped inside.

Sai Wing stood before him erect and dignified. Only his eyes betrayed emotion. They were full of tears.

Elliot cleared his throat. "Sai Wing. Last time, I came here as a friend."

"Yes."

"This time, I come as a son."

Chapter 32

Emma gazed at the fishing boat rocking gently at the wharf. She doubted that it had ever looked as it did now in its hard-working history. It was the same boat that Kai and Elliot had hired to take them to Lan Tau Island, although she'd be forgiven for not recognizing it. Even the young boatman had changed. He was now dressed in a crisp white shirt and clean shorts.

Every bit of clutter had been removed from her decks, and there had obviously been some attempt at cleaning her. White flags and lanterns hung from the mast and rigging. Some were also flying from bamboo poles. The flags lifted and fell, as if they were trying to come alive.

Emma reached across and took Elliot's hand. They were part of a small knot of people standing by the wharf just below Auntie's house at the water's edge. They had walked there from the house following the hearse. Only Auntie rode in the vehicle with Kai's coffin.

The hearse came to a halt, and for a while, there was almost an eerie silence. It was as if the steep hills surrounding the bay were holding their breath. Auntie had asked that no fire-crackers be set off, or cymbals bashed to ward off the evil spirits. She had simply said that there wouldn't be any evil spirits.

Emma felt Elliot stiffen. She looked up at him.

He was staring at two large Chinese men standing in the car park area next to a flatbed truck.

"What's the matter?" she asked.

"I recognize those two men. They were Kai's bodyguards, but I've forgotten their names." He frowned. "I hope there won't be trouble. Perhaps I'd better go over and find out. The difficulty is, I don't think they speak much English."

Emma's heart began to pound. "I'll come with you," she said. "Perhaps I can interpret for you."

As they walked over to them, Elliot said, "Ask them their names."

Emma stopped before the two men, bowed, and asked them who they were.

They told her.

"They're called Ah Tsoi and Ah Ming," she whispered. Then she spoke to the men again in Cantonese. "Why have you come here?"

Ah Ming pointed to the hearse. "He is Goko, my big brother."

She waited for him to say more.

Ah Tsoi took over the conversation. "Kai should not be buried in the sea. It is not right. It is not the Chinese way."

A frisson of alarm ran down Emma's spine. Things were now in danger of getting out of hand. She smiled at them. "Things are special for Kai because he was a special man." She pointed over to Auntie who was getting out of the front seat of the hearse. "Mamma-san has asked that Kai be buried in the sea, away from the evil spirits. She wants to be able to look at the place he was buried every day and pray for him."

The two men talked briefly with each other and finally nodded. Ah Tsoi lifted his chin with a touch of arrogance. "It is okay," he said.

Relief flooded through her. "Thank you," she said.

Elliot murmured. "What's happening?"

"It's okay." She paused. Elliot was still frowning. Things could very easily not be okay if Elliot's anger at the 14K coming to his brother's funeral became apparent. She leaned toward him. "If you whisper to me what you want to say to them, I'll translate."

He nodded. "Ask them what they want."

Emma bowed and said in Cantonese. "If you have come for Kai's funeral, you are welcome."

Ah Tsoi and Ah Ming nodded, their faces expressionless.

Elliot tugged at her arm and said. "Tell them that I hate what they do and what they represent."

Emma nodded, and spoke to the men. "Elliot wishes to thank you for guarding Kai and for being his friend. He honors the loyalty you have shown."

Elliot whispered again. "Tell them that they can come on the boat, but they are to stay out of the way."

Emma hissed back. "Elliot, the coffin has been weighted so that it will sink. It's very heavy. Why not ask Kai's two friends to help carry it onto the boat?"

He grunted. "I suppose so."

She turned back to the men. "We would be honored if you would both help carry Kai's coffin onto the boat, then stand guard over it, so that it does not move."

The men nodded.

Emma stepped aside and indicated that they should walk to the hearse where a Chinese undertaker was waiting to remove the coffin.

Ah Tsoi and Ah Ming spoke briefly with the undertaker, and then took station either side of the coffin. They picked up either end of a webbing strap that went underneath the coffin and eased the coffin out of the hearse. Elliot and Sai Wing then stepped in and helped them.

The four of them edged along the wharf and shuffled onto the boat. The coffin was heavy enough to cause the boat to lean alarmingly as Ah Tsoi and Ah Ming stepped on board. Neither of the men appeared to worry, and soon the coffin was lying across the front deck. Ah Tsoi and Ah Ming took station at either end. Both wore a demeanor that discouraged debate.

Auntie stood alongside Kendal, watching.

Emma walked over to them.

Kendal was dressed in black – very un-Chinese. It was a simple dress, but Kendal could not help but look beautiful. Emma shook her head. How had Elliot allowed himself to fall in love with her and not Kendal? It was ridiculous. But somehow, he had.

Elliot helped Auntie onto the boat, and she and Kendal filed on board behind her. Kendal dabbed a handkerchief to her eyes. She glanced at Emma and smiled sadly. "Love makes a woman look beautiful. Grief makes her ugly."

The boat-shaped coffin was double-ended and had a curved lid. It was painted black and had some red Chinese characters painted on the sides. It was hard to think that Kai was inside it.

The boat spluttered to life with a belch of black smoke, and they were soon chugging out to the entrance of Tai Tam Bay. It seemed only a moment before the engine was cut, and the stubby-nosed fishing boat drifted to a standstill.

Auntie took charge. A seat had been placed for her on the foredeck. Everyone else was standing. "I am going to speak, and then invite any of you to do the same." She stood up, collected her sticks, and hobbled to the coffin. She turned and spoke.

"Kai was a son to me. He was the son I never had. Throughout his life, good and evil battled for his soul. It was painful for a mother to watch, for there is only so much that a mother can say." She sniffed. "But I believe that he found hope, even if he didn't find peace." She pointed to the coffin. "Kai is wearing a necklace, a silver chain with a cross. It was round his neck when he died. He was looking for a God who wants to be found by those with soft hearts. Kai tried to find that God – hungry for the hope of forgiveness." She looked around at them all. "Death is the final test of the truth you live by. I want you to find the hope Kai was looking for."

Auntie looked at Elliot. "You are Kai's brother, Elliot. Please say something."

Emma saw Elliot start with surprise, and then pull himself

together. After a moment's hesitation, he stepped forward and placed both of his hands on the coffin. He spoke, but it was not to those listening. Elliot spoke to Kai.

"Kai, I'm glad I discovered you and that we were able to meet. It's…" he paused, "sort of good to know I've got a brother – particularly a twin. I can't help but wonder what we might have got up to if we'd stuck together in life, but we didn't." He shook his head. "I knew you so well, although in many ways I didn't know you at all. But this I do know: your actions saved Emma's life and my life, and I shall always be grateful to you for that. My prayer is that I will do justice to the life you bought for us both." He stood up. "I am proud to be your brother."

When he'd finished, Emma took his hand and gave it a squeeze. Then she stepped forward and read from her pocket Bible. It was the passage from chapter one of Peter's first epistle. It spoke about having a living hope through the resurrection of Christ.

No one else elected to say anything. Sai Wing did, however, kneel down beside the coffin, put his arms around it and weep.

Eventually, the old man got to his feet.

With a nod from Auntie, Sai Wing and Elliot lifted one end of the coffin and slid it over the side.

Afterward, everyone except Ah Tsoi and Ah Ming returned to Auntie's house. Elliot was feeling odd, as if disconnected from reality. They were all sitting on cane chairs under the veranda. He decided to take charge of his discordant thinking and ask Auntie a question that had been troubling him.

"Auntie, will you be able to continue living here now that your father is dead?" He paused. "This whole…thing probably won't be reported to the police, so it could all end up pretty untidy, and any resolution could take a long time."

Auntie patted him on the hand. "Don't you worry dear. I've just had an interesting conversation with Kendal and learned some things I didn't know."

"Oh?"

"Yes. She learned from Kai that my father wanted to sell the house when his Number One Wife died." She shrugged. "I would have had no home. But evidently, Kai bought it from him so I could stay. Kendal told me that Kai made a will and left the house to me."

"But how will you live day by day?"

"Again, Kai has made provision. He owned another property in Kowloon. He's asked Kendal to sell it and invest the proceeds so that I can have an income."

"Wow!"

She nodded. "He has blessed me in every way."

Sai Wing was not with them on the veranda, having returned to his hut at the bottom of the garden. Elliot went in search of him.

Sai Wing opened the door to him, and stepped back to allow him to come in.

Elliot walked inside, unsure of what he was going to say. He picked up Kai's toy sailing boat from the shelf and turned it over in his hands, then put it back again. "How are you doing?" he asked.

Sai Wing's fingers held on to the edge of the table. It was the only thing that betrayed his true emotions. "I am well. It was a good funeral."

Elliot nodded. "Sai Wing, you are the only father I now have. I am very pleased to have found you."

The old man considered his words for a while and then nodded. "You will live as a man of honor?"

"I will…" he paused, "Father."

Sai Wing lowered his head. Elliot could see him fighting his emotions. Then, without a word, Sai Wing blundered forward and embraced him.

Elliot hugged him back, feeling the passion of a father's heart, and responding as a son.

Sai Wing choked back a sob. "You will have grandchildren. You will send pictures, yes?"

"I will."

Sai Wing nodded, then let him go. Elliot kept hold of him by the arm. "Will you look after Mamma-san for me?"

"Yes."

"Thank you." He paused. "There is a special dinner at her house tonight. My fiancée Emma will be there, as well as our friend, Kendal. It would be an honor if you would join us."

"Mamma-San has already invited me. Yes, I will come." He smiled. "I wish to speak more to your woman, Emma."

Emma gave a deep sigh. There was a sense that everything was done. Elliot had retrieved her report from a locker somewhere on board *Soleil*, and she had added the information Kai had given her. She was in no doubt that it made for an explosive addendum. Emma resolved to sleep with the report under her pillow tonight – their final night in Hong Kong.

Kai's funeral earlier in the day had left her feeling drained. Now she was relishing being with Elliot on the balcony of their unit at Repulse Bay. It was late, but she did not feel she was ready for bed.

Elliot stepped behind her and enveloped her in his arms. She leaned back into him. "You know I never said, 'yes' don't you."

He nuzzled her neck. "Liar. You may not have used words, but you said yes, alright."

She giggled and pulled his arms tighter around her, ensuring they pushed up against her breasts. "Will you change your surname now you know who your father really is?"

"What surname would you like it be, Mrs. Kua or Mrs. Gleeson?"

She turned in his arms. "If I know you, you will want to acknowledge those who raised you."

Elliot nodded. "You're right. I do. Are you okay with that?"

"Very." She leaned her head against him.

Somewhere in the darkness, a barking deer yapped its hoarse cry.

"It's hard to believe that we're flying out tomorrow," she said.

"Hmm, as Mr. and Mrs. Gleeson." Elliot kissed the top of her head. "Sounds good, doesn't it?"

Chapter 33

E mma stood in front of the cottage and shook her head. "It is ridiculously pretty, Elliot." She turned to him. "And all this is yours?"

"Yes. It's almost exactly all I own."

"It's beautiful."

"It may look good on the outside, but there's nothing on the inside." He grinned. "Bit like me."

Emma dug him in the ribs. "You've got plenty inside you, Elliot Gleeson. Never doubt it."

He nuzzled her neck. "You've been responsible for putting a lot of that there, girl."

"Hmm." She arched her neck and luxuriated in his love.

Emma gazed at the old brickwork and stone and wondered what stories the cottage could tell and the stories that it would tell. "Let's go inside."

Elliot shook his head. "No. Leave your luggage on the doorstep. I want to show you the river. It's only a hundred yards away."

"Ah, the famous river where you learned to sail."

"Yes."

She let Elliot lead her down the cobbled street to a pub. Emma could read the sign above the door; 'The Bugle.' To her left, she could see the foreshore of the river. Boats were floating contentedly at their moorings. It presented an idyllic scene.

She breathed in the air. It smelled of brine and seaweed. Above the estuary, wheeling birds sought out their roosts. Others were still working the shallows, looking for worms and shrimps.

Elliot looked at her. "Are you sure you would be happy living here? It's a long way from London."

"Hmm. I decided many days ago, Elliot Gleeson, that I would live here with you." She glanced up the cobbled road. "I know how much you love the place, and now I can see why."

He looked at her incredulously. "You decided days ago?"

She looked at him coyly. "Yes. I've resigned from MI5." She shrugged. "They've asked me if I can do the occasional bit of contract work for them, and I'm still thinking about that."

He put an arm around her. "Only if it's safe." He paused. "So what will you do?"

"I put a few feelers out while I was still in Oxford, and one of them has yielded a result."

"What's that?"

She grinned. "I've been asked to help redevelop the history department at Southampton University. My special focus will be colonial-oriental history."

"Wow! Just your thing."

"Yes."

He grinned. "Well that means we have to get married here. Let's see the minister at St. Andrew's Priory tomorrow so we can have our marriage banns read."

She reached up and pulled his head down for a kiss. "I'd like that very much."

"Now then, lad. Don't you go kissing girls. They have a nasty habit of keeping a man's feet on dry land."

Emma spun round to see who had spoken. She saw an elderly couple walking down the street toward them. It was the man who had spoken. He wore an untidy beard and was carrying a coiled rope over his shoulders.

Elliot smiled and said loud enough for them to hear. "Emma, meet my very good friends Nettie and Horace." He gave an exaggerated sigh. "And please don't judge all the folks round hear on the basis of meeting Horace. Most of them are nice."

The woman smiled at her, then turned to Elliot. "Kissing a girl in public, Elliot. This has got to be serious. Who...?"

Her husband interrupted her. "Now lad, come out to *Windsong* with me and help me sort out my ground tackle. I've got myself into a bugger's muddle with it."

Elliot shook his head. "No Horace, I have other plans tonight."

Horace turned to his wife in apparent shock. "Blast that boy. Nettie, did you hear what he just said to me?"

The woman smiled and tugged his arm. "Come on Horace. Come away home with me. Don't you go saddling yourself on young love. And while you're about it, try and conjure a bit of the same love for me."

Horace looked at her askance. "What are you saying, woman? I told you I loved you when I married you. If there'd been any change, I would have told you."

Nettie rolled her eyes, took him by the arm and towed him away.

Twenty minutes later, Elliot and Emma were standing in front of the cottage again. Elliot had the door keys in his hand, but Emma restrained him. "Elliot, before you show me your home..."

"Our home," he corrected.

She smiled. "...our home, I want to give you something – something that also needs to find its right home."

He raised an eyebrow.

Emma reached out and placed Kai's ivory locket in his hand. "Kai's dragon stone doesn't belong to me. It is your story, not mine."

Elliot weighed the locket in his hands. "It doesn't really belong to me either. And nor does my dragon stone. The man who gave it was not my proper father, so it has no claim on me."

"So, what will you do with them?"

"Yet the stones are part of my story, I suppose." After a moment of appearing lost in thought, he nodded. "I know what I'll do with them. I'll hide them in a secret place behind the mantle-piece. In a very real sense, that's where the story began."

Emma furrowed her brow.

Elliot walked up the steps to the door. "Come in, I'll show you."

A month later, a letter dropped through the letter slot in the kitchen door onto the mat. Elliot picked it up. It was from Kendal Shiffer. He began to read.

Dear Elliot,

Kai opened a bank account at the Hong Kong and Shanghai Bank. However, he did so using your name and your identity. He deposited the two-hundred thousand that you took from Lachlan.

Kai came to see me in my office the afternoon he died to invest all the money in his account in my new building project. I added the five dollars you gave me when you first met me – I hope you remember.

I'm pleased to say that the value of the building has appreciated significantly in the last three months, even though it is not yet built. The current market value of your investment with us is one million, three-hundred thousand dollars, or thereabouts.

Let me know if you want to cash your investment in. I have plenty of people now wanting to buy in to the project.

I've also been to the library and researched the place you spoke about so often with such affection – Hamble. It looks as if it is well overdue to have a state-of-the-art marina, perhaps with a sailing school attached. If you wish to talk to me about this, let me know.

Give my love to Emma. She's a lucky girl.
Have a nice life.
Kendal

Notes

Chapter 2

1. OICCU is the Oxford Inter-Collegiate Christian Union. It is the second oldest university Christian Union in the world.

Chapter 3

1. "Wog," is a highly derogatory term for a foreigner.
2. The "hard" is an area of hard standing above a slipway. It is often used as a park for boat trailers.

Chapter 25

1. A bosun's chair is a seat (usually just a piece of wood, like a child's swing) that someone can sit on in order to be hoisted up the mast. It is hauled up by one of the ropes used to hoist the sails.

Chapter 28

1. A ditty bag is used by sailors to hold the tools and materials needed to carry out small maintenance jobs on a boat. It typically contains a knife, a sail-maker's sewing palm, twine and spare shackles.

Chapter 30

1. *Lap sap cheung*, literally translates 'rubbish insect.' It is the nearest that Cantonese can get to the English word 'litterbug.'

Note from the author

Thank you for reading *The Dragon Stone*. I hope you enjoyed it. Please consider leaving a review on Amazon for the benefit of other readers.

A lot of what you read was based on my personal experience of living in Hong Kong with my twin brother during the summer of 1972. It was there that I encountered the darkness of the Walled City—and experienced being snatched and apparently beaten up, so the Triads could see what my brother would do.

The "Stone Collection" has grown to include:

The Celtic Stone
The Pharaoh's Stone
The Peacock Stone
The Fire Stone
The Martyr's Stone
The Syrian Stone
The Atlantis Stone
The Viking Stone
The Scorpion Stone

Keep up to date on new releases, by signing up to my mailing list at www.author-nick.com. New subscribers will receive a free novelette, *The Mystic Stone*.

About the Author

Nick Hawkes has lived in several countries of the world, and collected many an adventure. Along the way, he has earned degrees in both science and theology—and has written books on both. Since then, he has turned his hand to novels, writing romantic thrillers that feed the heart, mind, and soul.

His nine full-length novels are known as, 'The Stone Collection.'

His first novel, *The Celtic Stone,* won the Australian Caleb Award in 2014.

Also by Nick Hawkes

The Atlantis Stone

Benjamin is part Aborigine, but nightmares from the past cause him to disown his heritage. Unfortunately, he feels no more at home in the Western world and so struggles to know his identity. Benjamin seeks to hide from both worlds in his workshop where he ekes out a living as a wood-turner. However, an attempt on his life propels him into a mysterious affair surrounding the fabled "mahogany ship" sighted by early white settlers near Warrnambool in Australia.

Felicity, a historian, is seeking to rebuild her life in the nearby town of Port Fairy after a messy divorce. The discovery of the "Atlantis stone" whilst scuba diving results in her joining Benjamin in an adventure that takes them overseas to the ancient city of Cagliari in Sardinia.

An anthropologist dying of cancer and an ex-SAS soldier with post-traumatic stress, join Benjamin and Felicity in an adventure that centres on a medieval treaty, a hunger for gold… and, of course, the Atlantis stone.

More details at www.author-nick.com

(See next page for more)

Also by Nick Hawkes

The Fire Stone

Sebastian, a young farm hand living in the Australian mallee, is being watched by Val, a fugitive hiding in the forests on the banks of the River Murray. Val has an official document that confirms his death fourteen years ago. There is no official document that confirms his particular skill: assassin.

Pip divides her life between her musical studies at the Adelaide Conservatorium and her work as a barista. Her ordered life is shattered when bullets fired through the window of her home reduce her cello to matchwood. The violence appears all the more bewildering given that she lives with her father David an Anglican cleric and retired missionary.

A web of violence draws all four of them together.

Everything in Sebastian's life begins to change when he is given the gift of a Koroit opal—*The Fire Stone*. It begins a journey in which he is challenged by David's wisdom and confronted by Pip's love.

The four of them seek to escape the violence that pursues them by sailing across the Pacific to the islands of Vanuatu. There, in the village community of Lamap, the final drama is played out...

...before *The Fire Stone* makes an unexpected return.

More details at www.author-nick.com

Made in United States
Troutdale, OR
09/17/2023

12975760R00181